Spring on Rendezvous Lane

Spring on Rendezvous Lane

Angela Britnell

Where heroes are like chocolate – irresistible!

Published 2022 by Choc Lit Limited
Penrose House, Crawley Drive, Camberley, Surrey GU15 2AB, UK
www.choc-lit.com

A CIP catalogue record for this book is available
from the British Library

ISBN 978-1-78189-516-0

Printed ⟨ A.

*To Edgar Lee Britnell, my beautiful
new grandson, whose arrival was
a bright light in a challenging year.*

Acknowledgements

I enjoyed picking the brains of my talented daughter-in-law Brita when I needed help with the "Spice Street Sage" food blogger side of Taran's character because she has built a successful business with her awesome blog "Food with Feeling" and could tell me everything I needed to know!

Thanks, as always, to the Tasting Panel readers who said "yes" to the manuscript and made publication possible: Dimita Evangelou, Shona Nicolson, Lucie Wheatcroft, Amy Nordon, Donna Morgan, Carole Rowsell, Deborah Warren, Gill Leivers, Sharon Walsh and Alma Hough.

Chapter One

Sandy grasped onto the last invitation she needed to deliver and knocked on Beth Parson's door. As far as the loosely named Hospitality Committee was concerned, every resident of Rendezvous Lane counted when it came to community events and that included the temporary occupant of number five. Sandy was determined that dear old Beth wouldn't be able to call them out for being unfriendly to her grandson while she was away, although as far as she knew Taran Rossi hadn't spoken to anyone since he moved in next to her. On the rare occasions when her old friend mentioned her daughter Naomi who had lived all around the world, an unmistakeable sadness sneaked into her voice. Beth had never even talked about having a grandson until she notified the homeowners' association that he would be living in her house and taking care of it while she recuperated from heart surgery with her son in Maine. In this largely un-gentrified neighbourhood of East Nashville they still believed in knowing and helping out their neighbours.

All of a sudden the door jerked open and she barely avoided falling off the step. 'Oh!'

'I'm terribly sorry. I didn't mean to startle you.'

Sandy tingled all over and she put it down to the combination of the unexpected British accent and the man's deep golden eyes sweeping over her. 'I've brought your invitation.' She couldn't blame him for looking puzzled. 'It's for our Spring into Spring block party. March twentieth, that's next Saturday – the Spring Equinox. Really it's just a good excuse to get together.' Her babbling explanation sent his dark eyebrows shooting up to meet the thick tawny hair flopping over his forehead. Sandy was proving an epic fail on the not making-a-fool-of-herself front.

'It's very kind of you but—'

'Your grandmother always joins in with everything.' Despite the wide difference in their ages she missed Beth's company. 'She brings a tray of cupcakes to share at all our get-togethers.'

'I don't bake.'

The fleeting trace of a smile inched across his face. It was a face made to be captured in charcoal with its sharp planes and moody, interesting shadows. The dark gold stubble blurring his square jaw and exotic skin colouring reminiscent of rich maple syrup hinted at a more varied heritage than that of his grandmother. Beth had Tennessee's thick red clay soil running through her veins.

'Then just bring a bottle. It's being there that's the important thing.' Her challenge made him chuckle and the warm rumbling laugh took her by surprise.

'Why?'

A trickle of irritation scratched at her previous good temper. 'Look it's only a neighbourhood barbecue. Don't turn it into a big deal. Come or not. Doesn't matter to me.' Sandy strode off before he could ask any more stupid questions.

In Taran Rossi's case being blessed with an abundance of good looks clearly didn't come with an agreeable personality. She'd done her job and could leave him alone now with a clear conscience.

All Sandy knew was that no one here would miss him at the party.

Taran studied the woman's retreating figure; her brisk pace indicated a natural efficiency mixed with a touch of annoyance. The dappled sunlight caught her short strawberry blonde hair and he guessed the soft waves would run through his fingers like silk. When she first spoke her wide blue eyes had glowed with warmth but that faded when he wielded his

2

non-existent charm on her. He hadn't even possessed enough manners to ask her name. He couldn't use his nomadic existence as an excuse because one constant remained the same the world over, well-mannered people exchanged names and offered whatever gesture of welcome was typical for the area. Of course she hadn't offered her name either but Taran laid the blame for that on his gruffness.

He wouldn't be in this awkward situation now if he hadn't mentioned to his mother in one of their rare phone calls that he planned on taking a break from travelling.

'Why don't you come and stay with us in Cornwall? It's truly beautiful here. We've got a spare bedroom and you might surprise yourself and want to put down roots here too.'

He'd struggled to find a polite way to turn down an offer he was sure she only made from a sense of duty. After a lifetime of travel around the globe, his parents visited Cornwall three years ago to see the remote part of England where his great-grandparents had met, and had fallen in love with the place.

'If you don't want to do that I've another idea. You could help me out by going to Nashville. Your grandmother had heart surgery recently and she's been banished to recuperate with my tedious brother in Maine. She's fretting about her house standing empty.'

Taran hadn't had a better alternative at the time and combined with a rare sense of guilt where his family was concerned he'd agreed to his mother's bizarre request. Now he was condemned to spending at least three months here and possibly longer depending how his grandmother's recovery progressed.

He returned to the kitchen and tossed the unwanted invitation into the recycling bin. Being stuck in this tiny house wasn't working for him but luckily the garages in Rendezvous Lane were at the back so he could escape out to the car without being seen. The chance to drive his grandmother's big-assed pale blue Cadillac DeVille was one of the few perks of his new residence. The forty-year-old gas guzzling relic with its immaculate paintwork and gleaming chrome trim still turned heads although its ability to start was unpredictable. Thankfully today it behaved first time.

When he did some research on the area around Rendezvous Lane he discovered it was developed as affordable housing for working people after the Second World War. That explained why the small, narrow wood-framed houses were all built in a similar cottage style and close together. Over the last twenty years property prices in East Nashville had crept up but that prosperity hadn't reached as far as Rendezvous Lane yet. Despite that most of the homes struck him as well cared for with their fresh paint and neat gardens now full of the signs of spring. He'd spotted a few local businesses when he was out on his regular early morning runs but none of the trendy bars and shops spreading like wildfire a few miles away. Something told him the people around here would be happy to keep it that way.

Taran's mobile buzzed and Leona's name flashed onto the screen. He swiped right to reject the call. He and Leona had been a couple for a few months in Australia last year but when he moved on that had been it where he was concerned. He tried to choose his female companions with care and always warned them that he didn't do long-term relationships. Taran discovered far too late that Leona believed she could change him. His father's job with a big oil corporation meant that he'd lived in ten different countries before he turned eighteen and his unusual childhood defined his outlook on life. In his view there was too much world out there to be confined to one spot and the same applied to people.

He turned left back onto Rendezvous Lane and slammed on the brakes as a flash of red caught his attention. Fear clutched at Taran's throat as he skidded to a halt close to a small boy, frozen with fear in the middle of the road. He fumbled to undo his seat belt and managed to clamber from the car as a woman raced out from the house next to his grandmother's.

'You could've killed my son!' The same bright blue eyes that dismissed him earlier now blazed with fury. 'I suppose you were on your stupid phone?' She clung onto the boy. 'It's all right, Chip.'

'He ran out in front of me. I'm terribly sorry.' Beads of cold sweat prickled the surface of his skin and Taran became aware that they weren't alone. Several people had drifted out from their homes to see what the fuss was about. He forced a smile. 'Sorry, kid. I didn't mean to frighten you.' The timid child buried his face in his mother's stomach and tightened his grip on her legs.

'My neighbour was babysitting him so I could concentrate on some work I'm behind on but he slipped out of the yard while her back was turned.'

'Are you sure he's okay?' To get back in the car and drive off struck him as callous but what else could he do?

'He'll be fine.'

'If you're sure there's nothing I can do I'll get going.'

'I've thought of something.' Two vivid pink splotches bloomed on her round cheeks. 'You can come to the party on Saturday.'

'Oh right. Okay. I'll see you there Mrs—'

'Sandy Warner. Ms.' She swept the little boy up into her arms and marched away.

That told him.

Chapter Two

Sandy rested her hands on the kitchen counter in an effort to stop them shaking.

'Mommy, you said I could have a cookie.'

'After we talk.' She turned around and the sulky expression that settled around her son's mouth reminded her so much of Andy. After nearly six years, Chip's resemblance to the father who died before he was born could still catch her out. 'Let's sit down.' Sandy steered him towards the kitchen table.

'I thought I heard the ice cream van and I took some money from my piggy bank. I ran out but it wasn't there.'

The urge to scream at her precious son came and went. It didn't matter how lengthy an explanation she gave now, and for a not quite six-year-old there was a limit, until Chip had his own children he wouldn't understand the terror he'd put her through today. The sight of him standing motionless in the road with Taran Rossi's car on a direct path towards hitting him would haunt her sleep for years to come. There would always be the "what if" questions. If Taran hadn't braked in time the outcome could've been horrifyingly different but if she'd finished work and come downstairs a minute earlier he wouldn't have been outside alone. Those were the same kind of questions she'd asked after Andy's tragic death.

'What was the last thing I said when I left you with Mrs Betty?' She'd found her poor neighbour in hysterics after the near miss.

'You told me not to go outside unless she was with me,' he whispered. 'But—'

'But nothing.' Sandy almost said that order was negated if the house was on fire or he was hurt but didn't want to ramp up her little boy's imagination any higher.

'I'm sorry, Mommy.' Chip's hiccupping sobs broke her heart.

'I know you are. Why don't you eat your cookie and watch *Sesame Street* while I get dinner ready?'

'*Paw Patrol.*'

'Okay.' Sandy didn't have the strength for another battle.

Chip bounced off the chair and raced towards the stairs shouting something about getting all his *Paw Patrol* figures from his bedroom. She turned on the TV and set down his cookie and juice. Back in the kitchen she considered doing something with the package of ground beef she'd defrosted for their dinner but couldn't resist pulling her sketchpad from the drawer. Sandy longed to capture Taran Rossi's dark gold eyes and the long silky lashes brushing his almost Slavic cheekbones before they eluded her.

Her hand flew across the paper and within minutes a clear likeness emerged and with a few more deft smudges it exploded into life.

You can come to the party on Saturday.

What on earth made her say that? Sandy's index finger traced over Taran's profile and lingered on his wide full mouth where she'd nailed his brief flicker of amusement. She'd learned an important lesson from her train wreck of a love life before she met Andy, Chip's father and gravitated towards him with a huge sense of relief. Women often dismissed men like Andy for being "too nice" but he'd fitted her desire for a more ordinary life. But their expectations had clashed and when she unexpectedly fell pregnant it put a strain on their relationship. Andy's tragic death put a brutal end to their efforts to make a life together work. She couldn't afford to have any sort of interest in Taran Rossi because her efforts to be the best possible mother to Chip and keep her bank account in the black every month took every scrap of energy she possessed. A personal life was one of many luxuries she couldn't afford.

With only a faint sliver of regret she scrunched up the drawing of Taran and tossed it in the bin.

The overload of cayenne, paprika and hot sauce set his mouth on fire in the best possible way. He was savouring his first experience of the famous Nashville hot chicken. Taran discovered his passion for street food as a five-year-old boy when he tasted arancini, delicious Italian fried rice balls, in the back alleys of Palermo. From there he went on to explore everything from Philipino kwek to Australian meat pies and Russian chebureki. Nothing fazed him. He didn't care what part of the animal or corner of the world his food came from and particularly these days the spicier the better. The only reasons he didn't resemble a hippopotamus were good genetics and the ten-mile runs he tortured himself with at least four times a week – rain or shine, jet-lagged or hung-over.

After checking on Twitter, a trick he employed worldwide, he'd tracked down a food truck called Smokin' Hot that was scheduled to be parked along Riverfront Park. Perfect for his late lunch. Usually he would've taken artistic pictures of his lunch, chatted to the food truck owner and fired off multiple tweets and Instagram posts but his "Spice Street Sage" alter ego was taking a brief hiatus. He'd scheduled his social media presence far enough ahead no one should miss him for a while. Today he was content to find a spot to swig a cold bottle of the local Yazoo beer and stretch out on the warm grass.

The mild, sunny Sunday weather had brought the locals out in force allowing joggers, cyclists and strollers to enjoy the paved trail along by the Cumberland River. Water always drew people whether it was a seemingly endless ocean or in this case a wide, brown, murky river. The amount of barge traffic surprised him and he'd already spotted one loaded with black, shiny coal and another with pyramids of yellow sand. Taran strolled past a line of trees covered in beautiful, cloudlike white blossoms and picked a spot close to the water, away from the families out for a picnic and groups of Frisbee players vying for space on the broad expanse of grass.

Spring was his favourite season in this kind of climate because the weather became conducive to spending more time outdoors. He brushed off an ant determined to crawl up his leg and idly watched a kingfisher dive and swoop into the river before coming back up triumphant and clutching lunch in its beak.

Taran's jangled nerves had settled enough to consider the morning's events more objectively. His shaking and cold sweats following the near accident with Chip were completely understandable and the fact it hadn't been his fault was no consolation. Sandy was a different kettle of fish. He wasn't immune to the pull of an attractive woman but two things were deal-breakers where he was concerned and Sandy fitted both criteria. It might sound harsh to other people but after he made an unforgiveable mistake in his mid-twenties, Taran's policy now was to avoid dating women with young children. He would never again inflict the ramifications of his here-today-gone-tomorrow attitude on a defenceless child who might get attached to him. The other out and out no-no was the whole suburban lifestyle. Taran could never picture himself living in a cookie-cutter house, mowing the lawn on Saturdays, attending parent-teacher meetings at school and … enduring Spring into Spring barbecues. Saturday would be nothing more than his payback to Sandy and end his venture into community life on Rendezvous Lane.

Chapter Three

Sandy dumped another bag of ice over the beer cans stacked in a large white cooler outside of her kitchen door. Because her house was one of those that backed up to the patch of scrubby common ground the locals optimistically called Rendezvous Park it had become the central organising spot for the community events. Rusty Naylor took charge of buying the meat and ruled over a couple of large grills with his twin brother Jake's help and a donation box on the food table covered their expenses. The rest of the food was pot luck and no one ever left an event hungry unless it was by choice.

She shaded her eyes from the early evening sun and located Chip playing tag with the other children. It was a struggle for her to adjust to a more settled lifestyle after she lost Andy but they'd planned this together when they first discovered she was pregnant and she'd felt compelled to follow through. Now six years later she knew it'd been the right choice. Occasionally she would watch a travel programme and get nostalgic for her free-wheeling days but then she would discover a bag of home-grown green beans on her doorstep or sit outside on the porch after Chip went to bed and be greeted by everyone who walked by. They would stop and ask how her little boy was doing, admire her flower garden or rant about the property developers moving in their direction.

'Mommy, Mr Rusty told me a lie.' Chip's eyes flashed with indignation.

'What did he say, sweetheart?'

'I asked for another hot dog but he said I'd eaten two already and would burst.' He huffed. 'I've eaten three before and I didn't bursted did I?'

Sandy bit her tongue to stop from laughing. 'No but he probably saw you eating one of Mrs B's brownies. I spotted a plate of Mr Pete's famous loaded nachos too so I bet you've sneaked a few of them.'

'Maybe.'

From across the grass Jake caught her attention over Chip's head and they shared a smile. They'd hit it off as soon as she moved into Rendezvous Lane and had been on a few casual dates. Sandy's intuition picked up that the divorced entertainment lawyer was angling for a closer relationship but she wasn't ready for that and sometimes doubted she ever would be. *That's not what your body said when Taran Rossi checked you out.* She spotted the man in question heading towards her and brandishing a bottle in one hand.

'Why don't you help me indoors for a minute?' She steered Chip away as Edith Beasley grabbed Taran's arm and nabbed him for a chat. 'We can share a can of Coke if you help me restock the soda cooler.'

In the safe confines of her kitchen she didn't make her usual fuss when Chip tossed the soda cans haphazardly into the cooler. Sandy kept one eye on Taran's tall, muscular figure and smiled at his stiff posture. She grabbed a couple of red plastic cups and started to pour their drinks.

'You've got more than me,' Chip protested. 'That's not fair.'

She wasn't in the mood to argue and slopped some of her drink into her son's cup. 'There you go. Take it outside where it won't matter if you spill it and I'll join you when I've put the drinks back in place.' Sandy shooed him out of the door and prepared to heft the heavy cooler.

'I'll get that.' Taran materialised out of nowhere, set a wine bottle down on the table and wrested the cooler from her hands.

'I can manage.'

'I'm sure you can but it's not a big deal.' He swung the disputed object out of her reach.

It is to me, she thought.

*

Taran watched the clear conflict between being polite and sending him away with a flea in his ear play out over Sandy's expressive face. 'Do you want this put outside?'

'Uh yes please. By the door if you don't mind.'

He set it down to one side of the steps. 'Chip's enjoying himself.'

'Yeah.'

He wondered if the absence of the boy's father put the wistful edge in her voice. Taran got the impression, rightly or wrongly, that she was raising Chip alone.

'Did Edith give you the rundown on everyone?'

'She mainly talked about my grandmother.' He didn't usually think much about his lack of family involvement but Edith's obvious disapproval when he'd admitted he hadn't visited his Granny Beth since he was a boy had bothered him. 'She did throw in a few pertinent comments on other people.' Sandy's colour deepened and he should reassure her that she hadn't been one of those discussed but didn't.

'I expect she bragged about the Tangled Yarns group she started. It's a mixture of readers and knitters because there weren't enough people to form two separate groups. They meet once a month.'

'Are you in the group?'

'I sure am. I'm not a knitter but I love reading when I have the time and this way they don't have as many chances to talk about me.'

Sandy's throaty laughter kicked his hankering for her up another notch. Behind the light-hearted comment he sensed there were things in her past she preferred to keep private. Perhaps they had something in common after all.

'I'm going to see if there's any food left.'

'Oh I left the wine I brought on your kitchen table.'

'Pop back in and grab it, then come and join us over there.' Sandy pointed across the grass.

'I'll be there in a minute.' Taran dived back inside and collected his wine then seized the chance for a quick look around. Despite an identical layout, this room bore little resemblance to his grandmother's traditional dark wood and country decor that hadn't been touched in decades. Sandy's cabinets were hand-painted with sky blue frames and sunshine yellow doors. Four mismatched chairs with colourful patchwork cushions were spaced around an old oak table. Along with the collection of bright pottery chickens tucked into any available space it said Sandy was a woman of bold tastes who wasn't afraid to express them. Her bright red refrigerator was covered with the expected child's paintings but off to one side she'd pinned up a crumpled drawing that definitely wasn't Chip's work.

Sandy had captured him in charcoal. She was clearly a talented artist and Taran's hawklike profile was unmistakeable. The wrinkles in the paper hinted that she tried to throw the picture away but couldn't. What did that say? Taran remembered what he was supposed to be doing and hurried back outside. He skirted around the edges of the large noisy group before spying Sandy next to one of the smoking barbecue grills. A smile suddenly lit up her face and he wondered who had put it there. The clean-cut man with his jeans, college sweatshirt and short dark hair peeking down under a Tennessee Titans baseball cap would've stood out as an American anywhere in the world.

'Taran, come and meet my friend Jake.' Sandy beckoned him over. 'This is Jake Naylor. He lives over on the other side of Beth from me.'

He felt the man's assessing gaze.

'Where are you from, Taran? We haven't seen you around here before. I don't think many folks here knew Beth even had a grandson.'

Taran dredged up a tight smile and tried to work out a polite reply.

Chapter Four

'Uh, why don't you serve us a hamburger first before they're all gone?' Sandy was bewildered by Jake's curt attitude.

'Sure.' He grabbed a couple of paper plates and slid two hamburgers onto them. 'There you go.'

'What do you like on yours, Taran?' Sandy added ketchup, lettuce and dill pickle slices to hers.

'Crow?' He cracked a wry smile. 'I'm sure Jake would be happy for me to eat some.'

She treated her old friend to one of what Chip called her Cross Mommy stares and a flash of heat coloured Jake's face.

'Of course not. Sorry.'

'No problem.' Taran shrugged off the insincere apology.

Sandy watched him layer Pepper Jack cheese, pickled jalapenos and queso sauce on his burger. 'Goodness, you like a lot of spice.'

'Yes, the spicier the better.' He held Sandy's gaze long enough to make her blush then turned back to Jake. 'I didn't get around to answering your question. I'm from everywhere and nowhere special. Give me a specific year and I'll narrow it down.'

'So you've moved around a bit. Big deal.'

'That's not what I meant. Different doesn't make it better or worse.'

Jake looked sullen.

'I expect Beth's told you that my mother grew up here but she dropped out of high school and ran off to backpack around Europe with her boyfriend. She promptly dumped him when she met my father Jakub in Genoa. He's half Italian and half Polish and worked in the oil business until he retired three years ago. He worked all over the world so I lived in ten different countries before I turned eighteen which makes me what they call these days a—'

'TCK. Third Culture Kid.' She relished Taran's surprise. 'The simple definition is having parents from two different cultures but being raised in another, or multiple others in most cases. President Obama is the most famous one. American mother. Kenyan father. Grew up primarily in Indonesia and Hawaii.'

'You're one too?' Taran said.

'Yep. Military brat. American father and German mother.'

'Interesting. I wouldn't want to live any other way now but I'm guessing you don't feel the same or you wouldn't have settled here. We'll have to swap stories sometime.'

Sandy wished she'd kept her mouth shut. It hadn't stretched the truth too far when she moved to Nashville to hint that she was recently widowed and too grief-stricken to answer painful questions about the past. She'd no intention of correcting his assumptions about her either. Let him believe what he wanted to.

'Mommy, I'm going to the potty.' Chip tugged at her hand. 'I'll come right back out.'

'I'll take you. Sorry, guys.' Sandy tried to smile. 'Duty calls.'

'I don't need you to come with me.'

She ignored Chip's protest but when they reached the house she let him race off to the bathroom alone. It hadn't been easy to construct a so-called normal life with little or no experience of such a lifestyle and Taran Rossi wasn't going to pull it apart. She'd seen the hurt in Jake's cool grey eyes. They were supposed to be good friends but it'd taken a casual question from a stranger to reveal something she'd kept from him and everyone else here. Other people tended to put a lot of store by where a person came from and she'd spent a huge portion of her life trying not to appear the odd one out. The muddled accent she'd acquired from her parents and her extensive travels wasn't hard to explain away by telling a little white lie that she'd moved from California. To most people around here the majority of non-southerners sounded similar.

Third Culture Kids tended to go one of two ways when they grew up and she and Taran were polar opposites in how they emerged from their nomadic childhoods. Every time Chip took it for granted that the Rendezvous Lane Easter Egg Hunt was followed by the Memorial Day Picnic and then the Fourth of July Parade, she quietly celebrated. It made her feel warm inside to put together his Halloween costume when every house would be decorated and the children would collect enough candy to go into a sugar coma. After that there was the community Thanksgiving dinner then Rusty Naylor would dig out his Santa costume again ready for the Christmas party. This was what she and Andy had wanted for their son. Taran was clearly the other sort of Third Culture Kid who had constant itchy feet and a restless urge to be on the move again, never calling anywhere home. If she needed any other reason to avoid getting involved with him there it was.

Taran sensed that both he and Jake wanted to chase after Sandy but suspected their motives were very different. As soon as he'd asked whether she was a fellow Third Culture Kid the shutters hadn't simply come down, Sandy locked and bolted them. He itched to reassure her that everyone had their skeletons. If she preferred to keep hers locked away that was more than fine by him because his own pile of bones would keep the neighbourhood dogs happy for months. He heard so many different accents in his travels that it hadn't struck him as odd when Sandy didn't sound particularly southern. On the other hand it was clear that Jake couldn't believe Sandy held back something this significant. At a guess he'd say that was the tip of the iceberg where her secrets were concerned. It was time to make a strategic retreat so he wolfed down the burger and tossed away his plate.

'Word of warning, pal. Stay away from Sandy.' Jake glowered at him.

Before he could decide the best way to reply a burly man in denim overalls ambled over from the other grill to join them.

'All right, Jakey boy?' The man grinned at Taran. 'I was too busy slinging burgers to say howdy before. I'm Rusty Naylor, twin brother to this troublemaker.' He cuffed Jake's head in a playful swipe. 'He's a lightweight. Give him a couple of beers and he thinks he can put the world to rights.'

Twins?

'Yeah I know we're not exactly Tweedledee and Tweedledum.' Rusty patted his round belly. 'He's the brains I'm the brawn.'

He sensed a warning lingering in the man's casual manner. Mess with one brother and the other will have his back. 'It's good to meet you both and I'm sure I'll be seeing you again while I'm here.' The spring party had proved to be far more interesting than he'd expected. Maybe these next few months wouldn't be as tedious as he'd bargained on after all.

Chapter Five

'Hurry up, Chip,' Sandy yelled up the stairs. She'd persuaded him to eat a boiled egg and half a slice of toast for breakfast in between explaining how bees made honey and avoiding his question about where they'd be going on holiday this summer. The answer would've been nowhere, unless she won the lottery. Her own breakfast was a pot of yogurt snatched between fixing their packed lunches. If she was late for work again it would stretch her boss's incredible tolerance to the limit.

'I can't find my Superman top.'

The wobble in his voice heralded a possible meltdown which was the absolute last thing she needed on a Monday morning. It would make things worse if she ordered him to choose another shirt. 'I'm coming.' When she walked into Chip's bedroom Sandy could've cried. Piles of clothes were strewn all over the floor, carelessly abandoned during the search for the missing top. Yesterday afternoon she spent several hours sorting through his wardrobe and she'd packed up several bags for the thrift shop before organising the rest. 'It's all right, sweetheart.' Sandy hugged him. 'Go down and put on your shoes. I'll find your top.'

'But it's not there,' he wailed.

'I'll find it. I promise.' She normally avoided those two words like the plague. Sandy shooed him away and took a few calming breaths. They had five minutes max before it became mathematically impossible to drop Chip off at school and make it to her office on time. She waded in and methodically tossed clothes out of the way. All of a sudden she noticed a sliver of faded blue material poking out from under Chip's bed. She grabbed it and raced downstairs with her prize. 'There you go.' She waved the shirt in the air. 'Didn't Mommy promise she'd find it?' Chip's amazed smile made her frenzied struggle worthwhile. 'Arms up.' She tugged the shirt over his head and smoothed down his hair. Before he could come up with any other reasons to delay them she hoisted on his backpack and handed Chip his lunchbox. Sandy slipped on her short black wool jacket that had done work duty for three years now. Like her it was showing its age. 'Right let's go.'

She always parked outside on the street because it wasn't worth the effort of putting her car away in the garage – nobody in their right minds would steal the battered twenty-year-old Toyota Camry with over 150,000 miles on the clock. Rusty had been kind enough to find it for her at a decent price shortly after they moved into Rendezvous Lane and she'd desperately needed transport. When Chip started kindergarten last August she sent him on the school bus for the first couple of weeks but he couldn't cope with the combination of the crowded hot bus and the noise of the other children. They might try again when Chip moved up to first grade but for now she juggled her work schedule to fit around school hours.

'Are you buckled up?' she asked as she hopped in, swivelling around to check. Sandy turned the key in the ignition but all she heard was an ominous grinding sound. She tried again and added a whispered prayer this time. That didn't work either. Third time lucky? Nope.

'Having car problems?'

She wound down the window and found herself at eye level with Taran Rossi's broad chest.

'Sorry. I probably smell a bit. I've been for a run.'

Sandy laughed off his apology. 'Trust me your sweat is the least of my worries.'

'Do you want me to take a look at the engine?'

'Are you any good at mechanics?'

'Uh not really but it's what men are supposed to say.' Taran's sheepish grin made her smile.

'It's not a problem. I can walk Chip to school. If we hurry it's only about fifteen minutes and then I'll find a way to get to work.'

'I could give you both a lift.'

'That's kind but I'm sure you have better things to do.'

'Mommy, if I'm late Ms Vestal will put my name on the board,' Chip pleaded.

'Are you sure you don't mind?' Sandy balanced her own reluctance against her son's anxiety over being singled out in class.

'No, otherwise I wouldn't have offered.'

She conceded defeat. 'In that case thank you.'

Taran couldn't help being amused by her grudging acceptance. 'We'll have to keep our fingers crossed that Beth's old car starts. It can be a bit temperamental. I'll go in for my keys then drive around to pick you both up. You can get Chip's booster seat out of here ready for me.'

'Sure.'

Five minutes later they were on the way with Sandy sitting in silence next to him while Chip chattered away in the back seat.

'What do you enjoy best at school?' he asked.

'Lunch and recess.'

The prompt response made Sandy burst out laughing and he joined in.

'Why is that funny?' Chip frowned at them.

'It's all right. We're not laughing *at* you,' Taran said. 'Those two things used to be my favourites too.'

'Until you got old?'

'Chip, that's a very rude thing to say.' Sandy's face turned bright red. 'You need to apologise right now.'

'It's okay, he's right.' He winked at the little boy in the rear-view mirror. 'Unless they're lucky most grown-ups don't get any recess where they work. I bet your mom doesn't.'

'I wish I did! Most days I don't even get a lunch break.'

'That's sad, Mommy.'

'It's okay.'

He guessed she probably grabbed something at her desk to finish earlier and pick her son up from school. Taran decided a long time ago he wasn't cut out for the self-sacrifice needed to be a good parent. He'd experienced enough of the opposite not to want that for any child of his. His parents were too caught up in their own lives and they'd considered expensive schools and a rotating list of nannies an adequate substitute for time and attention.

'You need to turn right at the next light for Chip's school,' Sandy interrupted. 'If you can pull over somewhere and drop us off I'll run him inside.'

'No problem.'

'I like your car, Mr … w … ussy.' Chip grinned at him.

'His name is Rossi, sweetheart,' Sandy corrected her son.

'I'm good with Taran if that's easier?' The offer made her frown. He didn't want to undermine her opinion of what was considered good manners here in the south. Those sorts of things were a minefield all over the world. 'How about Mr T – would that work?'

'Perfect. Look, there's a space.' Sandy pointed to a small gap between two badly parked SUVs and then giggled. 'Oops, I guess this monster won't fit.'

'Don't worry. I'll drop you both off near the gate then drive around to pick you up again.'

'Are we going home again in Mr T's car after school?' Chip sounded excited.

'It's fine with me if your Mommy's good with that?'

'Thank you.' Sandy's tight smile said she hated to rely on anyone. 'Rusty's great with cars so hopefully he can pop over to take a look at it later and it'll be an easy fix.'

'Have a good day at school, Chip.' Taran let them out and

did as he promised. 'So where are we going?' This opportunity to find out where she worked would fit another piece in the Sandy puzzle. After finding the drawing she'd done he had her pegged as creative, maybe a professional artist or something connected to the lively Nashville music scene. 'What's the name of the business?' He pulled out his phone to look it up.

'Williamson Homes. They're a mobile home company. I do debt collection work for them.' A defiant tone slipped into her voice. 'The pay is decent and I can work flexible hours around Chip's schedule.'

'That's important.'

'It sure is. Nothing else matters right now.' Her firm stare dared him to pity her and Taran drove without another word.

Chapter Six

Sandy opened the crumpled brown paper bag and pulled out her squashed peanut butter and jelly sandwich. Lunch at her desk. No recess. Remembering Chip's horror brought back her smile after a long gruelling morning. If she had her way it would be a long time before Chip realised the reality of their pay-cheque to pay-cheque life. She worked every hour she could while he was at school then did data entry processing at home for a health care company in the evenings. The money she made from selling charcoal drawings at local craft fairs was a tiny added bonus. Despite all of her efforts she breathed a sigh at the end of every month if her bank account wasn't in the red.

She shrugged off her jacket and draped it on the back of the chair then whipped out the small mirror from her top drawer. Her face was still flushed thanks to Taran Rossi. The tight fitting running clothes he'd worn this morning had made it impossible to ignore his spectacular body and gleaming dark mahogany skin. She was a healthy thirty-six-year-old woman who missed sex. Nothing abnormal about that. Maybe if she took up an energetic sport that might work off some of her frustration. Kick-boxing instead of sex? Sandy wasn't certain that would do the trick.

'Hey girl how's it going?' Lashonda perched on the edge of the desk. 'What do you think of these?'

She studied her friend's extravagant long nails. 'Are those real flowers?'

'Yeah they're embedded in gel nails.'

'How do you do any work with those?'

'Carefully.' Lashonda's teeth gleamed in her ebony face. 'Why were you smiling when I came over?' She pointed to the remains of Sandy's sandwich. 'Don't try to tell me lunch excited you. Spill the dirt. Did old man Perkins finally ask you out?'

Her friend was incorrigible but if it wasn't for her, Sandy couldn't have endured working this job for three long years. They'd met the first week on the training course for new recruits and bonded because they were roughly the same age and both single mothers struggling to keep it all together. Lashonda gave birth to her twin sons before she turned seventeen and raised them alone after their father did a vanishing act. Because of their mother's gritty determination the boys excelled in high school and were now studying at the University of Tennessee at Chattanooga on full scholarships.

'Don't be silly. For a start, Harry's not that much older than us and we both know it's you he's got his eye on.' Their boss was far too professional to cross the line with an employee but she hadn't missed the lingering looks he gave her friend. 'When are you going to put him out of his misery and promise you won't sue him for sexual harassment if he asks you on a date?' She touched Lashonda's hand. 'Your boys are out of the house and doing good so why not?'

'I'll think about it.'

They were both as bad as each other about the idea of starting another relationship. Scared.

'You still haven't told me what's up? It's gotta be either money or a man.'

'Nothing to do with money *ever* makes me smile and it's not really a man either.'

'Well honey he either is a man or he isn't.' Lashonda's dark eyes shone.

'He is but—'

'I knew it.'

She shushed her friend's raucous laughter and whispered a brief, highly edited version of her run-ins with Taran Rossi.

'Well I might just happen to be outside at three o'clock today when this hunky man picks you up.' Lashonda grinned. 'Don't worry, I'm joking. Anyway how about you take your own advice? It sounds as though Chip likes the guy.'

'But what if he gets attached to him? It wouldn't be fair. From the little he's let slip I'm pretty sure Taran isn't planning to hang around Nashville when his grandmother gets back.'

'Chip wouldn't have to know he's anything more than a friend. I've managed a few discreet no-strings relationships over the years to … keep my hand in.'

They both collapsed in giggles more suited to a couple of teenage girls. Po-faced Marcia who sat at the next desk threw a disgusted glance in their direction.

'I'm not saying it's easy with an observant little boy around but it's not impossible either. Think about it.' Lashonda plopped back on her feet and straightened her tight black skirt down over her generous curves. 'Hey, girl I'll give it a go if you will.'

'Off with you.' Sandy struggled to smile.

Mr T. Taran could kick himself. He shouldn't have encouraged Chip with that casual nickname because it verged into dangerous territory. If Sandy was a different sort of woman he might consider suggesting they enjoy a brief fling with well-defined boundaries but the last time he tried that in Australia it was a miserable failure. One problem he couldn't get around these days was the fact he was getting older and the women who appealed to him were too. They tended to want more than he was prepared to offer and the only viable alternatives seemed to be dating younger women or taking a break from all of them for a while. Neither option tempted him.

He pulled up his detailed work plan for the year on his laptop and stared at the screen. After university he became a freewheeling traveller who paid for his addiction to new sights and new places by becoming a digital nomad, needing only a decent internet connection to make a decent living designing websites. The unpredictability of his lifestyle horrified his parents. That had struck Taran as ironic because they hauled him all over the globe as a child, almost guaranteeing he wouldn't be happy to end up in the regular corporate world. About a decade ago he started to select his travel locations by following his nose for spicy street food. At first he simply shared his best food finds on Instagram but soon took his growing following with him to start "Spice Street Sage", a food and travel blog. After a few years it made more money for him than designing websites ever would so he gave that up and concentrated on building his digital brand. But success came at a price. Influencer and affiliate marketing were his buzzwords and the more contracts he signed with various companies the more constrained his life became.

The urge to chuck it all in hit him last year along with a dose of malaria he picked up in India. Although he recovered in the standard couple of weeks, the type of disease he suffered often reoccurred and he'd already suffered one flare-up. That prompted him to take the plunge and schedule a six-month sabbatical from March until September. He had outsourced a few guest posts to other bloggers, people with less name recognition who were keen to piggyback on his success and he'd also put together a retrospective of his most popular posts – that sounded better than repeating old material. He was back to pounding out his regular ten-mile runs now but his hope was that the break would put his mind in a better place too.

It never suited him to be cooped up indoors for long so Taran wandered over to the kitchen window and peered out on the back garden. His grandmother had sharp words for him when they spoke on the phone after he arrived.

'I don't expect to come home and find the grass up to my knees. My crape myrtle and butterfly bushes need pruning. Make sure to dig out all the crabgrass from the flower beds. They say don't plant anything in Middle Tennessee until after the fifteenth of April because of the danger of frost but I always wait an extra week to be on the safe side then put in a few flat trays of petunias, salvia, marigolds and coneflowers. With a bit of luck, I might be back by then.'

He'd never gardened in his life but how hard could it be? Taran wasn't averse to hard work and would use YouTube videos as a last resort. When he was growing up his father's well-paid jobs meant they lived either in opulent city apartments or large country houses that came with a raft of cooks, housekeepers and gardeners to take care of them. The set-up was normal among the bubble of ex-pat kids who attended the British or American international schools and moved in the same social circles as the Rossi family. It was only when he wandered outside the narrow confines of his safe life that he discovered not everyone lived that way.

Surely he was capable of running a lawnmower over the square of straggly grass in the back and even smaller one in the front and digging up a few weeds?

Ten minutes later he swore at the old mower and gave it a hard kick.

'Need a hand?' Rusty Naylor leaned in over the back fence.

'That would be great but don't you have work to go to?'

'Nah I'm on second shift this week. Don't go in until four this afternoon.'

'In that case thanks very much.'

'Beth's a stubborn woman. I cut the grass for her these days and I warned her when I put that ancient machine up for the winter it wouldn't last another cutting season. She insisted it would see her out.' Rusty eased off his frayed baseball cap, scratched his bald head and settled the cap back in place. 'The damn thing's gotta be nigh on thirty years old. We can try drainin' the fuel tank and puttin' in fresh gas, change the oil and replace the spark plug. Apart from that the best place for it is the scrap heap.'

'I'd be happy to buy her a new one but—'

'Your granny would throw a hissy fit. I get it.' Rusty grinned. 'Mine was the same way. Didn't matter that I was three times her size by the time I was thirteen. I'll fetch what we need from my workshop and we'll give it a go. You can have a large mug of black coffee with three sugars ready when I get back.'

'Will do.' He knew Rusty was offering to help for his grandmother's sake and nothing else. Beth was the centre of the community according to several people he'd spoken to at the spring party. She'd helped many others when they needed it and now it was her turn. What must it be like to stay in the same place for thirty plus years and know everyone who lived within shouting distance of your house? He couldn't wrap his head around the idea. The longest he had lived anywhere was Aberdeen, Scotland for three years back in the early 90s when his father's job contract got extended. This settled life appeared to suit Sandy although they had similar upbringings so what sent one person in the direction he'd chosen and another in a completely different one? For some reason it seemed crucial to answer that question.

Time to make coffee for Rusty and do battle with a lawnmower.

Chapter Seven

Sandy thought about last month's high electric bill and tugged on an old thick blue jumper before turning down the heat. With Chip tucked up in bed it was time to settle on the sofa with a mug of coffee. She needed the caffeine boost to stay awake for the three hours of data entry work she ought to do. At least instead of fretting how to afford a new car she'd only had to pay out a hundred and fifty dollars for the new battery that Rusty installed. The word "only" was a misnomer because her monthly budget was calculated down to the last dollar and that unexpected expense meant giving up a few more hours of precious sleep to crank out tedious healthcare spreadsheets.

She should open her laptop and knuckle down to work but pulled out her sketch pad and pencils instead. An hour later when she forced herself to stop, half a dozen sketches of Taran lay strewn across the sofa. She'd thought long and hard about Lashonda's suggestion before rejecting it. Sandy didn't do casual relationships these days. Unfortunately that supposedly straightforward decision only worked until she climbed into Taran's car again that afternoon. His midnight blue open-necked shirt had offered a fleeting glimpse of sun-darkened skin, a recent shave showed off his prominent jaw line and a gleam reflected off his freshly showered tousled hair. Sandy had struggled to convince herself that any good-looking man would have the same effect but knew a lie when she heard one. If that statement were true she would've responded to Jake's overtures long ago. Jake made sense. Taran didn't. Making good choices hadn't always been her forte but when she'd tired of her freewheeling lifestyle that was where Andy had come in.

They bumped into each other in a dusty back street in

Naples. Literally. He wasn't looking where he was going and sent her sprawling to the ground. By the time he apologised and bought her a large pistachio gelato, Sandy had concluded that the soft-spoken Englishman could be the key to her future. Her unplanned pregnancy shook their relationship but they tried to take it as a sign they were meant to be together and started to make plans. Andy's family in Surrey were far from thrilled when he announced his plan to marry an unknown woman and move to the United States to raise their child. They'd decided on America despite the fact neither of them had ever lived there because thanks to her late father it was the originating country on her passport and Sandy considered it as much "home" as anywhere. Andy's computer software skills should get him a good job and when the time was right she would go to art school. After his tragic death she stuck to their plan, apart from art school which now seemed an unattainable dream. The plan had given her much needed direction when her life felt like walking on quicksand.

Sandy brushed away a tear. Grief and guilt often grabbed her by the throat when she least expected it but this wasn't getting her anywhere and moping wouldn't pay the bills. Two hours later her shoulders and neck ached from hunching over her laptop and the rows of numbers were swimming in front of her tired eyes. A quiet tap on the front door made her jump. Often Edith would happen to "run out of milk" for her late night cocoa when she had a juicy story to pass on.

'Oh hi ... Are you all right?'

Taran, grey faced and sweating, swayed in front of her and she stuck out her hand to steady him. She managed to help him into the house and over onto the sofa. He lay there looking terrible but while Sandy tried to decide whether he was sick enough to call for an ambulance his eyes fluttered open and she breathed a small sigh of relief.

*

Taran struggled to focus but a jackhammer beat a relentless rhythm in his head. Nothing made sense. He was stretched out on a bright scarlet sofa that bore no resemblance to his grandmother's floral furniture. Instead of Beth's framed prints of the Great Smoky Mountains the bright yellow walls were decorated with colourful framed weavings and strange metal sculptures.

'Oh thank God you're awake. I was just about to call 911.'

Sandy's face, wrinkled with worry, swam into view as a wave of nausea coursed through him. Taran struggled to sit up and grabbed the plastic bucket she offered, immediately losing all the food he'd eaten that day. 'I'm sorry.'

'It's okay. I'll get you cleaned up.' She whisked the bucket away and returned with it empty and rinsed out and a bowl of water. 'Remember I've got a five-year-old.' Sandy gently wiped a cool wet cloth over his face. The familiar violent shivers started and she grabbed a soft cream blanket off the chair and tucked it in around him. 'Do you want a drink of water?'

'Yes please.'

She thoughtfully held the glass because his hands were shaking.

'Have you eaten something that disagreed with you?'

'No.' Taran guessed she was too tactful to ask if he was drunk or on drugs. 'I picked up a dose of malaria last year in India and it's the variety that often recurs. This is my second relapse. I would've taken myself to the emergency room but I wasn't fit to drive.'

'Really? You surprise me.'

He managed a wan smile. 'I thought about ringing you for help but I knew you couldn't leave Chip to check on me and I didn't know who else to ask.'

'I'm glad you had the sense to come. We'd better get you to hospital.'

'But—'

'I assume you need medicine, right?' Sandy asked.

'Yes.'

'Betty Carter is a night owl. She won't mind popping over to sit with Chip.'

He was too weak to object and rested his eyes while she made a phone call.

'You're freezing.' She touched his face. 'I'll find you something to wear over that T-shirt.'

Sandy disappeared upstairs and Taran couldn't imagine where she planned to find something to fit him. A few minutes later she returned, clutching a dark blue sweatshirt with an Oxford University crest. Her wistful expression silenced any question he might have asked about its previous owner. Taran lifted up his arms and she dragged the sweatshirt over his head. The shivering and chills were easing and from experience he knew the high fever would ramp up next.

'Cooee, it's only me.'

An older woman pushed open the door, took one look at him and shook her head.

'Oh my Lord you'd better hurry up and get that poor boy seen to.'

His eyes stung with unexpected emotion as he recalled multiple occasions when he'd been cared for by strangers. Two that stuck in his mind were the elderly German woman who strapped up his ankle when he twisted it hiking in the Black Forest and the fisherman in a remote village along the Nile River who stitched up a cut on his arm because they were several days' journey from a proper doctor.

'Can you stand up?' Sandy asked.

'I think so.' He struggled to his feet and she steadied his arm while he regained his balance.

'It's lucky Rusty put me in a new battery this morning because I couldn't drive your gran's tank.'

In the car she handed him the plastic bucket to hold in

case the nausea returned and drove to the nearest hospital. As he'd expected they insisted on admitting him for the night to replenish the fluids he'd lost and monitor him while they started the strong drugs necessary to knock out the infection.

'You go along home to Chip. I'll be fine.' Taran didn't want to take advantage of her kindness.

'Are you sure? I'll tell the hospital to ring if you need anything. I can come back in the morning.'

'That's honestly not necessary. You need to go to work. I'll call a taxi. Once they bring the fever down and the Primaquine treatment kicks in I'll be good. The last time I relapsed I got on a flight to Singapore the next day.' He held back from telling her that was an absolute nightmare and the longest eight hours of his life. He practically crawled off the plane and collapsed into his hotel bed where he didn't move for at least twenty-four hours.

'Well you'd better not do anything that stupid here.' She sounded fierce. 'Promise me you'll go straight home when they release you and we'll check on you after I pick up Chip from school.'

'Yes ma'am.' The pitiful attempt at a southern accent sapped his strength but eased the strain in her eyes. Taran lay back and closed his eyes as the sleeping drug he'd been given began to kick in. As he faded out of consciousness he had the fleeting sensation of Sandy's lips against his burning cheek as she kissed him goodbye.

Chapter Eight

'You should've seen him,' Sandy whispered. 'I thought he was going to die right there in my doorway.' She was haunted by the sight of Taran, ashen under his dark olive skin, his lean face beaded with sweat and his large body shaking with uncontrollable chills.

'But he didn't ... and I'm sure he'll appreciate it when Florence Nightingale stops by to check his pulse later.' Lashonda nudged her elbow.

'Of course, I'd still care a bunch if the same thing happened to anyone but I barely know the man. I shouldn't be affected this much.'

'Yeah, I know what you mean.'

She followed her friend's gaze across the room to where Harry was engrossed in conversation with one of the other managers. 'We're a sad pair.'

'Maybe we've simply gone through enough to know nothing's straightforward.'

'You're right there.' After leaving Taran at the hospital, Sandy only managed a fitful few hours of sleep, fretting about him every time she startled awake.

'Changing the subject for a minute, are you coming to the barbecue on Saturday?'

Once a quarter the company hosted an event supposed to foster camaraderie among the workforce. Sandy mostly avoided going because she preferred not to stir up unwanted questions about her private life.

'You could invite Taran?'

'He'd probably prefer another malaria relapse. He's not much for those sort of gatherings. Are you planning to go?'

Lashonda shrugged. 'We could go together and—'

'Stalk Harry?' According to the rumour mill their boss

wasn't married, and he always came alone to work events. Those things could mean anything or nothing. 'Okay. We'll come for once. Chip will enjoy playing with the other kids and it gets me out of cooking.'

'Awesome. If you change your mind and bring lover boy along I won't mind being a gooseberry.'

'That is so not happening.' Sandy checked the time. 'I'm off home.'

'Good idea. Must be time to wipe Romeo's fevered brow.'

Anything else she said would only stoke her friend's mischief so she simply walked away.

When the doorbell rang, Taran didn't shift from the sofa. Sandy had a key to let herself in and if she caught him doing anything more strenuous than laying down she'd probably string him up. His health problems had started in the garden yesterday. After a lot of swearing, Rusty fixed the mower so Taran had eaten an early dinner before starting to cut the grass. It didn't take long for the first chills to rear their ugly heads and at that point he'd retreated back inside to rest in the vain hope that would ward it off. *Oh yeah that really worked well*. It always impressed women if a man practically collapsed on their front doorstep before throwing up.

'It's only us.' Sandy hurried across the room. 'Oh, you're looking so much better.'

'Told you I'd bounce back.'

Chip grinned at him. 'Mommy said you threw up more than me when I ate three jelly doughnuts and a huge piece of chocolate cake at my friend Billy's birthday party.'

That clearly raised him in the boy's estimation.

'We brought crackers and bananas for you.' The kid held up a plastic carrier bag.

'Thanks, I really appreciate it.' He started to struggle to his feet.

'Sit back down right now.' Sandy glowered.

'Before I almost fall at your feet again? I'm sorry if I scared you.'

'If? There's no "if" about it.' She peered into his face. 'Have you been hydrating well today? Did you manage to eat anything?'

He'd become inured over the years to taking care of himself and although it was a novelty to be fussed over he mustn't get used to it. The disadvantages to his wandering lifestyle were few and far between in his opinion and occasional loneliness was a small price to pay for his independence. 'I'm good.'

'I'll put these things in the kitchen and we'll leave you in peace.'

'But Mommy you said I could have a snack and cheer up Mr T because he's sad and doesn't feel well.' Chip's complaint made him smile.

'I know but sometimes when people are sick they want to sleep a lot and not talk to anyone. I'm pretty sure that's what Mr T feels like today.'

'I like your idea much better Chip and I could do with some company for a while. Do you think we can find a good cartoon to watch while your mom fixes me a drink?' He raised an eyebrow in her direction. 'If that's okay?'

'It's fine with me.'

'Do you like *Paw Patrol*?' Chip thrust the remote control at Taran and plonked down next to him. 'It's my favourite.' He launched into a long rambling explanation about a group of dogs who rescue people and rattled off all their names and full descriptions of the dogs and their vehicles. Sandy's smile deepened as if to say he'd asked for it.

In the kitchen, Sandy laid slices of banana on a large plate, smeared peanut butter on one stack of crackers and left the rest plain. She'd spotted a chink in Taran's armour when she admitted how scared she'd been when he got sick. His surprise touched her. The idea of anyone being concerned about him obviously struck him as unbelievable and how sad was that? A jarring realisation sneaked in that at one point in her life she would've felt exactly the same way.

She poured out a small glass of milk for Chip and a large one of ice water for Taran.

'For heaven's sake girl, when there's an interestin' man around put on some lipstick and fluff up your hair. It was all right when we were sixteen to rely on our tight little bodies and perky boobs but we've got to work a whole lot harder now.'

When Lashonda spouted that piece of folklore recently she had protested and claimed that she was comfortable in her skin and not going to change for any man. Her friend rolled her eyes and told her in that case she might as well face up to being single and celibate the rest of her life.

The deep pink lipstick lurking at the bottom of Sandy's handbag ended up on her mouth but she couldn't find her comb so resorted to running her fingers through the short, soft waves. Sandy picked up the tray and pushed open the kitchen door. 'Snack time.' She noticed the threads of gold in Taran's eyes brighten as he checked her out. *Not that sick then.* 'Chip, make sure you leave the plain crackers for Mr T. He mustn't eat peanut butter yet. I hope you don't mind me helping myself from Beth's cupboard?'

'You're welcome to it.' Taran grimaced. 'I hate the stuff.'

'Seriously?'

'Yep, I never tasted it until I was about ten or eleven. The smell put me off to start with and when it stuck to the roof of my mouth it almost made me—'

'Okay I get the idea.' She didn't need Chip copying Taran's revulsion for peanut butter when it was their go-to cheap protein.

'Join us.' He picked up a cracker. 'We won't bite.'

Why did she feel out-manoeuvred?

Chapter Nine

Taran might only be functioning at half-strength, and that was a generous assumption, but he still recognised freshly applied lipstick when he saw it. He didn't have the energy at the moment to question whether Sandy's hint of interest pleased or scared him. 'How was your day?' He whispered the question to her over Chip's head and her silent shrug told him that debt collection didn't have good days only less bad ones.

A slow smile widened across her face as she gazed at Chip. The little boy had burrowed into Taran's side and fallen asleep.

'It's a long day at school and he often naps while I'm fixing dinner. I ought to take him home. We should leave you to rest.'

Sandy stroked a lock of hair away from her son's face and his eyes fluttered open. 'It's time we went home buddy.'

'Don't want to.'

'I'm fixing your favourite mac and cheese for dinner.'

'No peas. You hid peas in it last time.'

'Guilty as charged. How about green beans?'

'I suppose. If I have to.' The grudging agreement made Taran smile.

'You won't grow big and strong if you don't eat your vegetables. I bet Mr T eats his.' Sandy's look told him he'd better back her up.

'I certainly do. I like all the ordinary vegetables but I also love to ring the changes sometimes. One of my favourites is spicy sweet potato tikki with chole chaat. They're fritters served with a chickpea curry sauce and very popular in India.' They both stared at him. 'Another awesome veggie dish is

Mexican street corn. They smear plain corn on the cob with a spicy cream sauce then roll it in more spices and cotija cheese.' He couldn't blame Sandy for looking thoughtful. This was the most revealing he'd been about himself. A mistake? He wasn't sure yet.

'Sounds weird.' Chip hopped off the sofa. 'I'm hungry. Let's go Mom.'

'Will you be all right?' Sandy asked him.

'Yes. No problem and thanks for everything.'

'Don't get up. We'll see ourselves out.'

'Thanks for keeping me company, Chip.' He ruffled the little boy's hair.

'I can come and watch *Paw Patrol* with you again another day if you're bored?'

A picture of Alexei Novak's small tear-streaked face when Taran left Prague jumped into his head. 'That would be great but we'll have to leave it for a while because as soon as I'm better I've got a lot of work to do.' He couldn't meet Sandy's shrewd gaze because she'd know he was lying. This was for Chip's own good … and his.

'That's fine because we're busy too.' Sandy didn't mean to snap but she couldn't help it.

'But Mommy—'

'We only came to make sure Mr T was okay, not pester him.' She hated to cut her son off but the sooner they left the better.

'You weren't pestering me.' Taran's voice rose. 'I didn't mean that and you know it.'

'Would you mind speaking more quietly please? We don't like shouty voices do we Chip?' Her darling little boy shook his head. Despite the occasional doctor or teacher who thought they knew him better than she did, Sandy didn't believe that Chip's sensitive nature needed medicating or any special labels. Andy had been the same. Highly intelligent and the kindest man on the planet but he'd gone out of his way to avoid large crowds and excessive noise. Not everyone was programmed to be outgoing and gregarious.

'I'm sorry Chip. I promise I won't do it again,' Taran said gently. 'Your mommy and I just … misunderstood each other.'

'Okay.'

'Let's go.' She took Chip's hand. 'Call me if you need anything.' Before Taran could respond she rushed them out of the house.

All the way through dinner and bath time she steered the conversation away from their disturbing neighbour. Sandy tucked Chip in and closed the library book about elephants that they were reading a chapter of each night before bed. 'Time to go to sleep.'

'I've been thinking Mommy and I'd really like Mr T to be my daddy. He doesn't have a little boy and I need a daddy.' By his satisfied grin that logical thought process made complete sense.

She wasn't touching the "he doesn't have a little boy" part of the equation. For all she knew Taran could have a string of ex-wives, girlfriends and children strewn around the globe although instinct told her he travelled solo. After Chip was born she couldn't mention Andy's name without crying so it became easier not to speak about him at all. That changed after she was called to Chip's pre-school one day because the class had been making Father's Day cards and he got upset because he had nobody to write one to. From then on she often talked about Andy and they had photos of him all around the house.

'But you have a daddy.' Sandy pointed to Andy's picture on the bedside table. It'd been taken on a beach in Hawaii and was one of her favourites. He looked tanned and relaxed in the gaudy board shorts she'd bought him and was laughing straight into the camera because she'd been making funny faces. She could still conjure the smell of the coconut scented

40

sun cream she'd rubbed into his pale, freckled skin earlier that day.

'I want a daddy here not one in the sky,' Chip scoffed. 'Billy's daddy plays ball with him but I don't have a daddy to teach me.'

'I can teach you.'

'You're a mommy. That's no good.' Tears dripped down his face.

If he wasn't so pitiful, Sandy would laugh at what a lousy job she'd done of raising her son to believe in gender equality. She wrapped her arms around him in a tight hug. 'Shall I tell you a secret? Your daddy was hopeless at sports and couldn't throw or catch a ball to save his life. I played soccer, basketball and softball growing up, plus I can ice skate, roller skate and surf.'

'Really?'

'Yep.' Being athletic had helped her to fit in when the army moved her father again. When her new classmates found out she'd get picked first when it came to choosing teams. Recess and lunch weren't the only things she missed about her grown-up life. These days the only regular exercise she had time for came in the form of chasing after Chip. 'I'll teach you okay? I should've done before and I'm sorry.'

'Okay.'

Sandy wasn't dumb enough to believe that conversation was over. Chip was like an elephant that way and never forgot anything, often coming back to a subject when she least expected. 'If we practise every day this week you'll be a whole lot better by Saturday to play at the barbecue.'

'Really?'

'Yeah, no problem.'

Lashonda told her once that when her boys were young she forced herself to sound confident even when she was shaking inside.

'They needed to trust me. To have faith. To believe I was strong and would stand up for them against the rest of the world. After they'd gone to sleep was the only time I let myself cry.'

When Sandy had ventured to comment on how lonely that sounded, her friend grasped her shoulders and looked her straight in the eye.

'My grandmother raised six sons on her own who all turned into fine men, including my sweet daddy. One day when I was stretched to breaking point she told me off for being self-indulgent. At the time I thought she was being mean and hard but she was right. Our men aren't here. We're all our boys have.'

She breathed in Chip's clean little boy scent for a few precious moments before kissing him goodnight.

Chapter Ten

Nobody would guess it was only late March by the sweat pouring off Taran but his grandmother's back garden was a suntrap. He tossed another strand of crabgrass into the weed bucket and rocked back on his heels to ease the cramp pulling at his stomach. The side effects of his malaria drugs weren't pleasant but they were a huge improvement on the alternative. By mid-week he'd recovered enough to make a start on tackling the garden but could only work for a few minutes at a time to start with and then gradually increased the time as his strength returned. He'd been out here for an hour so far this afternoon with no real trouble but he'd give it a few more days before giving running a try.

Sandy and Chip's cheerful voices drifted across the fence between their two gardens. Before he could decide whether to keep working or sneak back indoors an American football flew into the air and spiralled down before bouncing off the top of his head. 'Ouch.'

'I sure am sorry.' Sandy peered over the fence. 'Are you all right? Should you be out here working? Aren't you still ill?'

Taran debated which question to answer first. 'I'm fine.'

'Mommy, where's my ball?'

She disappeared from view for a few seconds then Chip's bright face appeared as Sandy lifted him up.

'Your ball hit Mr T because you're getting so good at throwing.'

'Wow! Cool. Hey Mr T I need my ball back.'

'Chip! Ask nicely and say please,' Sandy said.

Taran scrambled to his feet. 'Do you want to come over and get it?' He became aware of Sandy's wide-eyed stare. He'd stripped off his shirt when he started to sweat, not expecting to be on public display.

'Mommy tells me to keep my colours on the paper and not on myself.' Chip frowned at him. 'Didn't your mommy teach you that?'

The penny dropped and his mild awkwardness had nothing on Sandy whose face glowed like an erupting volcano. 'You mean these?' He pointed to the exotic tattoos decorating his shoulders and upper body. Taran had collected them on his travels and they'd become such an integral part of him that other people's reactions frequently took him by surprise. 'They're special pictures grown-ups sometimes have.'

'They're neat. I want some when I'm big. Do you like ice pops Mr T? We've got a big box,' Chip happily rattled on.

'That's very kind but—'

'Please.' The little boy's huge blue eyes bore into him.

'You do look extremely hot ...' Sandy's face flamed. 'I mean you've been working hard and you're sweating. Plus you've been sick. It'll do you good.'

'In that case thank you, I'd love an ice pop. Do you have any lime flavoured ones? They're my favourite.'

'Yep. You can have two because I don't like the green ones.' Chip screwed up his face. 'We have to eat them outside because they're drippy.'

'Perfect. I'll come around.' When they disappeared out of sight he tugged his shirt back on and scooped up the football.

You do look extremely hot. Could she possibly make any more of a fool of herself in front of that man? Sandy laid the fault firmly on the arresting sight of his dark toned torso with its intricate designs inked into every luscious inch. Her determination to stamp on this ridiculous attraction to a man was a miserable failure so far.

'Mommy can I get the ice pops?'

'No. You sit on the steps in the shade. I'll get them.' That would give her a chance to stick her head in the freezer for a few seconds. Sandy fled inside the house and wished she had time to change out of her skimpy cut off denim shorts and sleeveless red T-shirt. She gulped down a glass of cold water and gathered a handful of ice pops.

'We can shift so there's room for you too,' Taran offered.

'I'm good.' All three of them squashed on the narrow steps together wasn't happening. She dropped down on one of her refurbished wrought iron patio chairs. Last summer she'd rescued them from a skip and the hours she'd spent rubbing them down and repainting them a cheerful bright orange had been absolutely worthwhile.

'Are you good at ball games Mr T?' Chip sucked on a lurid red ice pop.

'Pretty good.'

The next question out of her son's mouth could drop her right in it. Steering her son away from the daddy theme was crucial. 'Are you a keen gardener, Taran? Beth used to love working in her yard until she had her heart trouble.' Somewhere in the midst of her brain fog Sandy recognised she was waffling again.

'I've never done any before and I don't really know what I'm up to but I'm giving it a go.' His warm laughter rang out. 'Thank heavens for YouTube videos.'

'If you'd asked I could've told you the difference between plants and weeds.'

'I'm sure you could.' He gazed around her garden. 'How do you fit in doing all this?'

The last few years had left her sensitive to other people's perceptions of how well or otherwise they considered her to be coping. She'd flown off the handle more than once over remarks that verged on patronising.

'I'm impressed because I'm clueless about gardens and yours is awesome. Were your parents keen gardeners too?'

'No.' Sandy didn't intend to explain the ins and outs of her complicated family life. For a start, little ears were listening and Chip was too young to understand something that'd taken her thirty-six years to come to terms with. 'When I moved here this was a complete wilderness because the previous owner let things slide. I couldn't afford to pay someone else to do it so I had to learn fast. All of the gardens around here are this same long narrow shape and I really wanted to keep a decent patch of grass for Chip to play on so I've worked my flowerbeds in around it to make the most of the space. Instead of YouTube videos I had your wonderful grandmother. Beth thinks some of my plant choices are too colourful and clash but that's me and she accepts it. The garden will be at its best in another couple of months.' Sandy jumped as a chunk of melted ice plopped down the front of her T-shirt. 'Oh!'

'Silly Mommy.' Chip giggled. 'You didn't eat it fast enough.'

As she pulled the wet sticky shirt away from her skin she remembered whipping off her bra when she got home from work. There were two choices. Brazen it out or run inside to change into a clean shirt. 'Well that sure cooled me down.'

Taran's lips twitched.

'Mommy can Mr T throw the ball to me now?' Chip begged. 'I've got to be good tomorrow.'

'I'm sure he—'

'Would be delighted.' Taran grinned. 'If that's okay with your mom?'

'Of course.' She could hardly say no. 'That's kind of you.'

'What's special about tomorrow, Chip?'

His casual question made her cringe.

'We're going to a barbecue where Mommy works. You could come too. There's going to be games and food.'

'It sounds like a lot of fun but imagine if it was your birthday and the friends you invited to the party brought along other children you didn't know.'

'Oh I wouldn't mind and Mommy always makes tons of

food and I have a huge cake.' Chip flung open his arms to demonstrate and whacked Taran on the nose.

The first spurt of blood shocked them all, then her poor son burst into tears as a splash of bright red bloomed on Taran's white T-shirt.

'It's all right, Chip don't worry. It looks worse than it is.' He tipped his head back and pinched his nose.

'I'll get something to clean you up.' Sandy tugged her son's arm. 'Come and help me.' In the kitchen she took the time to calm him down first before collecting a bowl of warm water and a handful of paper towels.

'I didn't mean to hurt Mr T.'

'I know sweetheart and so does he. It was an accident.' She kissed the top of his head. 'Let's go fix him up.'

Taran had settled on one of the chairs with his legs sprawled in front of him. It left her little choice but to stand between them and ignore the heat radiating from his body as she dabbed at his face. 'Hold that in place until you're sure it's stopped bleeding.' Sandy pressed a folded paper towel into his hand. She suddenly noticed Chip staring intently at something with a terrified expression on his face.

'If your mom doesn't mind I'll get this off.' Taran tugged at the hem of his shirt and it registered that the sight of his blood-stained shirt was freaking her son out.

'Sure. Let me help you.' Sandy could almost hear Lashonda's throaty laughter in her head.

'Helping him off with his clothes? Way to go girl!'

Chip's colour was inching back and he giggled when Taran, now disturbingly shirtless again, teased that he was on track to be a world boxing champion.

'I should probably go home,' Taran said.

'It'll be safer.' She tossed the dirty water on the grass and crumpled up the used paper towels. 'Visiting my house should come with a health warning.'

'Maybe it'll be third time lucky.'

'I wouldn't bet on it.'

'Mommy.' Chip tugged on her arm. 'Can Mr T please come tomorrow?'

She couldn't work out a polite way to refuse. 'Of course he can if he's up for it.'

'Oh I'm always up for a good barbecue.'

'We'll leave at eleven. Come on Chip. It's bath time.'

'Mine too I suspect.'

Taran's parting comment forced her to glance back over her shoulder and his mischievous wink caught her off guard.

Chapter Eleven

Why could he not stay away from Sandy? And Chip? Ignoring the bra-less wet T-shirt exhibition yesterday, not the easiest thing to do, the woman had tugged on heartstrings he thought he'd cut years ago. Her shy son seemed to believe the sun shone out of Taran which couldn't be further from the truth.

He'd tried talking himself into phoning her and making an excuse to avoid today's barbecue but here he was dressed and ready to go. Jiggling a new soccer ball in his hands he locked up.

'Is that for me?' Chip barrelled towards him.

'It sure is.' The words dried in his mouth and he tried not to gawp. Sandy had stopped in the middle of loading the car and was smiling over at him. Her off the shoulder blue and white striped cotton sweater, blue leggings and high-top red sneakers made her look like a teenager. Even her hair was in playful mode and pulled back from her face with something resembling bright red oversized paper clips.

'Wow!' Chip made a grab for the ball. 'It's ace.'

'Let's save playing with it until we get to the barbecue.' Taran rested one hand on the ball. 'We don't want it rolling out in the road.' His energy level wasn't quite back to normal but he should be fine to kick a ball around with the little boy.

He'd planned on getting a rundown about what to expect at the picnic while they were driving but hadn't bargained on Chip's excited chatter and endless stream of questions.

'This is the park.' Sandy turned onto a gravel road past a baseball field. 'We've got the picnic area reserved until four o'clock this afternoon.'

The wooden picnic tables and benches were all full of people and others were sat around on folding chairs. An impromptu Frisbee game was in full swing on a wide open stretch of grass and the beach volleyball court had been commandeered by a bunch of teenagers. A bunch of little kids were racing around a man blowing huge bubbles from an oversized wand.

'Do you mind getting our chairs out of the trunk?' Sandy asked.

'Happy to.'

'We'll join my friends over there.' She pointed to a small group, sitting by a sign for a walking trail.

He could already imagine what erroneous conclusion they'd jump to about him and Sandy and the question was which one of them would that bother the most?

'But I want to play.' Chip screwed up his face.

'I know but you must say hello to Ms Lashonda and everyone first,' Sandy said firmly. 'Then we have to agree on—'

'The play rules.'

The resignation in the little boy's voice made Taran smile.

'That's right.' She twitched a smile. 'I'll race you.'

The boy took off at full speed.

'Try to keep up.' She laughed over her shoulder at him and sprinted away.

Taran wasn't an idiot. Sandy wanted to gain a few seconds and give her friends the heads-up before he joined them so he'd play along.

'It's a long story but Taran's here,' Sandy hissed in Lashonda's ear. 'I sort of got tricked into asking him.'

'You sneaky old thing.' Her friend laughed then gave a low whistle. 'Wow, is that your man? You never said he was hot, hot, hot. You'd better watch yourself there girl.'

She couldn't argue the "hot" part but picked up on her friend's veiled warning. They weren't the only ones watching

Taran wend his way through the crowd because he'd caught the eye of several of the younger women and there were a noticeable number of nudges and winks flitting around. When he arrived to join her that would set tongues wagging.

The welcome spring sunshine brought out the thick streaks of gold in his tawny hair; it was long enough to hint at non-conformity without venturing into man-bun territory. His faded jeans, un-tucked dark blue shirt and grey sweater tied casually around the shoulders worked together without giving the impression of trying too hard. She wished he didn't fit her Identikit picture of the ideal man quite so perfectly.

'Come and meet everyone.' She called him over but before Sandy had a chance to introduce him properly, Chip grabbed Taran's hand.

'This is Mr T.'

Her co-workers all stopped talking and stared.

'Pleasure to meet you all or should that be y'all if I'm trying to be southern?' Taran's swift joke made everyone laugh and his easy manner surprised her. He launched into a smooth explanation of why he was staying in the area and how he came to know Sandy.

'Can I play now?' Chip tugged her hand.

'We can kick that new ball around,' Taran said. 'If that's all right with your mom?'

'Of course it is. Have fun.' Sandy plastered on a bright smile.

'Would you mind taking care of that while I'm gone?' He tossed his sweater her way and flashed an easy smile when she snatched it from the air.

Lashonda grinned at her. 'It's the novelty of having a man around. Don't take it to heart.'

'Why not?'

'Because it takes the burden off you for a few minutes. Kick back and relax.'

Of course her old friend was right but that didn't make it any easier to be usurped by someone who would disappear as fast as he had arrived and leave her to pick up the pieces. This was why she didn't do relationships.

Sandy watched as Taran organised the bunch of kids gathering around him. He set up improvised goals with orange plastic cones someone had brought along and roped in a couple of guys from the finance department to help out. Soon an energetic if haphazard game was in full swing. She hoped he wouldn't overdo it but could hardly say anything.

'He's a good guy.' Lashonda gave her a long look. 'They're the ones you've got to watch out for.'

'Yeah. I know.' She couldn't help sighing. 'I thought the other day you were encouraging me?'

'That was before I saw him but if it's any consolation he practically had his tongue hanging out around you.'

'Don't be dumb.'

'Trust Aunty Lashonda.' She waggled her finger in Sandy's face.

They were forced to make up a story when the others asked what they were talking about. Luckily Bernie Fraser was true to form and turned the conversation back to work. Sandy laid Taran's sweater across her lap and idly stroked it while they swapped stories about the most outlandish excuses customers came up with for not making their monthly home payments.

'It's lunchtime, buddy.' Taran spotted people gathering around the food tables.

'But I want to keep playing.' Streaks of muddy sweat trickled down Chip's face.

'I know but aren't you hungry? I'm starving. I smell hamburgers cooking and it's making my mouth water. I've got the ball safe so how about we run over to your mom.'

'Okay but I'll beat you.'

He didn't need to slow his pace by much to let the boy win and would be relieved to sit down and rest for a while.

Sandy eyed her son up and down. 'We need to go to the restroom and get you cleaned up before you can eat.'

'I should do the same,' Taran said. 'I could take him to the men's room with me if you like?'

'That would be great but aren't you worn out?'

'I'm okay and I need to go clean up anyway.'

'In that case thank you. Chip thinks he's too old to go in with me but I'm not ready to risk sending him in there on his own.'

'I don't blame you. Must be tricky.'

A tinge of sadness dimmed her smile. Obviously that was only one of the myriad of tricky situations she was forced to navigate because for whatever reason Chip's father wasn't around.

'Come on buddy.' Taran held his hand out to Chip. 'We'll meet your mom over by the food. I bet we can beat her there.'

'The idea isn't to be fast but to do a good long pee and scrub your face and hands well.' As soon as the words left Sandy's mouth her face turned crimson.

'I promise we'll both obey instructions.' He stifled a grin and hurried off with the little boy. They did a thorough job in the bathroom which meant they lost the bet. 'We're ready for inspection.' They stood in front of Sandy and splayed their hands out in front of her. Taran thought it showed great restraint and maturity when he refrained from mentioning her other order. That worked until her sparkling eyes met his gaze and they both needed every ounce of self-restraint to keep from exploding.

With their plates loaded with food they sat down and Taran was happy to let everyone around him chat while he concentrated on enjoying the pulled pork sandwiches and barbecued chicken.

'Mind if I join you?' A ruddy-faced man with thinning fair hair, tortoiseshell glasses and a sheepish expression hovered in front of them.

'Of course not Harry.' Sandy pointed to a spare chair. 'Sit down.'

Lashonda, who Taran had earmarked as the vocal one of the group, didn't say a word and stared down at her plate with more interest than the hot dog and potato salad warranted.

'Taran, this is Harry Perkins. He's the poor man who tries to keep us in order,' Sandy explained. 'Harry, this is—'

'It is you isn't it? Wow!'

Did he know this man from somewhere? He was pretty good on faces but Harry's didn't ring a bell.

'You're the *Spice Street Sage* aren't you?' Harry said. 'I'm a huge fan of yours on social media. I don't have as much opportunity to travel much in real life as I'd like but I feel I've been everywhere with you.'

'Thanks I appreciate it.' Taran noticed Sandy frowning and knew he'd have some serious explaining to do later. 'Are you a food lover?'

Harry patted his soft stomach. 'Can't you tell? And the spicier the better.'

'Do you cook at home?'

'I make a pretty mean vindaloo,' Harry admitted.

Taran became aware that everyone was staring at them.

Chapter Twelve

Sandy wondered why it hadn't occurred to her to type Taran Rossi's name into her computer and see what popped up. Isn't that the first thing everyone did these days when they met someone new? Phones were being pulled out all around her now as her co-workers checked out Harry's bizarre claim.

'Mommy I'm bored. I want to go play,' Chip whined at her.

'You'll have to wait until I finish my lunch and can go with you.'

'Why?'

She almost replied 'because I said so' before reminding herself that she and Andy had sworn never to say that. 'Because there are lots of people here and you could get lost.'

'Mr T, will you play football? Please, please, please.' Chip swung on the arm of Taran's chair.

'I'll be happy to in say ten minutes. Look, I'll set an alarm.' He fiddled with his smart watch. 'When it buzzes I'll stop talking and play with you if you sit quietly now. You've got to give an old guy like me time to recover so I can run around again.'

The measured response surprised her along with her son's easy acquiescence as Chip sank down and sat cross-legged on the grass by his idol's feet.

'You've got over three million Instagram followers,' Helen Rawlings said in an awed tone, gaping at her phone.

Sandy ignored Lashonda's questioning stare. Her best friend might not believe that she hadn't known a thing about his apparently famous alter ego.

'And nearly five million follow your blog.' Mario Garcia sounded equally impressed.

'Where are you off to next? I hope you aren't taking too long a break.' Harry chuckled. 'The occasional guest posts you're having are interesting and I enjoy seeing your older posts again in the retrospective but it's not quite the same.'

She sensed Taran's hesitation and guessed he might not want his reply spread all over the internet. 'He's being a good grandson and taking care of his grandmother's house for a few months,' Sandy explained.

'Family is important.' Harry nodded. 'Maybe you could consider doing a mini "Southern Spice" tour while you're here? We've got our famous Nashville hot chicken, then there's lots of awesome barbecue all over the south and you could go down to Louisiana and trawl through all the great Cajun food.'

'Maybe.' Taran looked thoughtful. 'I've sampled the Smokin' Hot food truck already but haven't made it to Hattie B's yet. It doesn't strictly fit with my street food remit but I've been considering branching out.'

'We should all do that occasionally. Get out of our ruts.'

She noticed Harry fixing his steady gaze on Lashonda. That was a declaration if ever Sandy heard one.

'Are you a "Shut the Cluck Up!!!" man?'

Harry laughed and shook his head. 'I haven't made it past "Damn Hot!!" yet.'

'What on earth are you two talking about?' Sandy asked. Both men grinned and proceeded to indoctrinate her and any other ignorant people within earshot about the six levels of heat at Hattie B's, the famous hot chicken restaurant. Everything from mild standard Southern fried chicken to a terrifying spice level renowned for bringing grown men and women to their knees.

'Did you know the recipe came about because a woman wanted to get revenge on her fried-chicken loving philandering boyfriend?' Harry said. 'The trouble was he loved it and wanted more.' He gave Lashonda a sideways glance. 'Are you a spice queen?'

'Take me to Hattie B's on Monday evening and you'll find out.'

Her friend's raspy purr turned Harry's ruddy cheeks into flashing SOS beacons.

'Maybe the four of us could go and see what we're made of?' Taran rested his hand on Sandy's shoulder. 'If you can't get a babysitter we'll take Chip along too.'

Trust him to render obsolete the objection she was about to offer up. A sea of nudges and grins spread around their little group. Brazening it out was her only option. 'Why not? It sounds like great fun.'

Taran tried to tell himself that it wasn't a proper date but felt the same satisfaction as when he surprised a Chinese street vendor in Chengdu by wolfing down the chicken feet and pork lung in chilli oil that most westerners shied away from. Sandy was giving him a bemused look as though she couldn't believe she'd said yes.

Harry's "Southern Spice" idea was wriggling into his brain. His sponsors might consider the idea tame in comparison to his usual off-the-wall locations but it could open up a whole new audience. If he kept it casual and low-key it wouldn't be hard to shift some of the retrospective posts to make room for an occasional new one.

'It's time Mr T.' Chip pointed to his buzzing watch. 'I need my football, Mommy.'

'Are you sure you're okay with playing again?' Sandy frowned at him.

'Sure.' He took the ball from her. 'It'll work off lunch so I can make room for dessert.'

'Is food all you think about?'

'It certainly isn't.' Taran winked at her. Why couldn't he resist flirting with her all the time? 'Come on, Chip let's put your throwing practise to the test.' His knowledge of

American football was sketchy but he figured it wouldn't matter.

An hour later he was forced to admit he was officially exhausted. His idea of playing a simple game with Chip developed into an all-hands-on-deck, or rather all-kids-on-deck, melee but the little boy's pride when he caught most of the balls thrown in his direction was immeasurable. Taran caught Sandy watching among the crowd of parents cheering their kids on and her proud smile gave him a boost of energy.

'I heard someone mention home-made ice cream. Do you think there's any left?' He dangled the idea in front of Chip.

'Oh boy I hope so.' The kid grabbed his hand. 'Come on Mr T.'

Funny how that name was growing on him.

A million questions were racing around Sandy's head and she sensed Taran was waiting for her to speak first. He didn't realise that parents of small children were adept at outlasting them when it came to extracting confessions.

'I didn't purposely not tell you about the blog thing.' He looked sheepish. 'I thought I could take a break here without getting involved with people and think through my next plans.'

'You didn't bargain on "Spring into Spring" or family picnics or—'

'You.' His voice turned raspy. 'I sure didn't bargain on you.' Taran nodded at Chip in the back seat; he'd gone straight to sleep when they left the picnic. 'Or him. I planned to play the hermit for a few months while getting Beth's house and garden in shape. Worked well didn't it?'

She didn't answer but felt the rising colour in her face. That was quite a bombshell he'd dropped and she'd no idea how to respond.

'How do you do it?'

'What?'

'Adjust to so-called "normal" life? Doesn't all this settled stuff drive you crazy?'

Sandy wondered where to start her reply but more importantly where to stop. 'It wasn't easy at first. One day I want to take Chip travelling because he needs to experience the wider world but I'm determined his childhood will be very different from mine.' She didn't plan to share the more unsavoury details with him or anyone. 'How long does it take for you to get itchy feet?'

'It varies.' Taran shrugged. 'I rarely stay in any one country longer than about six months.'

His smile tightened. 'Is Chip's father another Third Culture Kid?'

'Andy is dead. He died before Chip was born and—'

'Oh God I'm sorry. I'd no idea.'

'There's no reason why you should have.' Every time she was forced to talk about Andy it stirred up a raft of conflicting emotions. His death had devastated her, not least because she felt a large measure of guilt because he wouldn't have been in the wrong place at the wrong time if it wasn't for her. The almost worse thing to live with was that she hadn't loved him as he'd deserved. 'Andy was thoroughly English. He grew up in Surrey in a very traditional British middle-class family and both his parents were teachers.' Sandy cleared her throat. 'I can't talk about him any more. Not while I'm driving.'

'Sorry. I didn't mean to upset you.' Taran rested his hand on her thigh and his touch burned through her thin leggings. 'I'd love to chat some more after Chip's in bed. Perhaps we could compare travel stories?'

'I'm not sure that's a good idea and anyway I've got work to do.'

'Fair enough.' He sounded disappointed but shifted his

hand away. 'If you want to cancel Monday night's plan feel free to say so.'

'I'll think about it.' A double date with Lashonda and Harry crossed a line that Sandy suspected would be wiser left in place.

'Of course. That's absolutely your right.'

'Why do you sound so English most of the time?'

A trace of amusement softened his grim expression. 'The international schools I attended were all British and I went to university in London. My maternal great-grandmother was from Cornwall in the far southwest of England. She met Beth's father when he was stationed there with the United States Army Air Force. They even gave me a Cornish name because Taran is the word for thunder. My parents actually moved to Cornwall a few years ago after my dad retired but I haven't had a chance to visit them there yet.'

Surely he realised how curious that particular confession sounded for a man who'd admitted to travelling the world for a living? 'I'm surprised you haven't lost the accent by now.'

'I have to a large extent.'

'We're home.' Sandy nodded back at Chip as she stopped outside her house. 'Someone won't be happy when he wakes up.'

'Home,' Taran murmured. 'I've never called anywhere that.'

She couldn't help thinking that knowing he didn't have any desire to either was the real gulf between them. One she couldn't afford to forget.

Chapter Thirteen

Taran wiped the sweat from his eyes and surveyed the results of his hard work over the last couple of days. He pulled out his phone to take a few photos to send to his grandmother. From their conversations he knew she was pining for her home and the garden in particular. She complained continually about Maine's cold weather and berated him when he boasted that this week's high temperatures had hovered pleasantly in the high sixties and low seventies. At least now he knew a crape myrtle was the woody-looking shrub in the back corner by the shed. The butterfly bush she'd mentioned was the same plant he'd seen all over Asia with its colourful long spiked blooms that had a wonderful sweet fragrance in the summer. He'd trimmed the bright sunshine yellow forsythia as his gran ordered and hopefully his rudimentary pruning efforts hadn't killed it or anything else off. An anxious knot tightened in his stomach. Would he still be around when summer came and the garden was in full bloom? Did he want to be? Sandy kept sneaking into his head and he couldn't shake off the wistful look she gave him on Saturday when he had admitted to never calling anywhere home.

Around two o'clock this morning he abandoned the idea of sleeping and worked up a few rough plans for a mini "Southern Spice" tour. He couldn't abandon his grandmother's house apart from maybe a couple of overnight trips so anything further away needed to wait until she returned. Taran's mouth watered thinking about sampling spicy chicken gumbo in New Orleans.

He and Sandy were a good pair as far as rationing out snippets of information was concerned. It intrigued him when she admitted that Chip's father was a man whose upbringing was the complete opposite of her own. Had she hooked up with Andy for that very reason? He tended to choose women who were also nomads at heart and when he broke that pattern he paid a steep price.

This new friendship with Chip was forcing Alexei back into his mind too – the lively five-year-old with his chubby face, laughing dark eyes and thick curly hair. They had spent hours kicking a soccer ball around together and going to the Prague street markets where they would buy their favourite palačinky crepes filled with strawberries and whipped cream. Those were the good times. The overwhelming pain came when he allowed himself to remember Alexei's hiccupping sobs and the jab of his little fingers digging into Taran's thighs as his mother dragged him away. Did the teenage Alexei now distrust promises adults made to him and have a cynical attitude towards love because of Taran's thoughtless behaviour? If he continued to be involved in Chip's life he must take responsibility for the consequences.

Edith is babysitting Chip. Pick me up at 7 and we'll meet L and H at Hattie B's.

Sandy's text message had popped in around lunchtime and he'd sent a thumbs-up sign in reply. He wasn't sure why she'd decided to give him this chance but spring was supposed to be the season of renewal and perhaps his life needed to move into a new season. Taran chuckled to himself. He was getting poetic in his old age.

He took a long hot shower then threw on clean chinos and a short sleeved shirt. Taran added a thin sweater that he could remove when the spicy chicken kicked in. He desperately needed a haircut. Never a fan of short hair it usually grazed his collar but had evolved over the last few months into a shaggy mess.

Taran locked up the house.

'I think we're goin' to the same place.' Edith Beasley's smile turned into a smirk as she hovered on the pavement outside his door. 'I'm taking care of Chip while you go on your date.'

He didn't bother to correct her because Sandy already warned him that the head of the Tangled Yarns group never let the truth stand in the way of a good story. 'That's kind of you.'

'Always happy to smooth the path of true love,' she trilled.

'I wouldn't say that.' Her crestfallen expression touched him. 'Not yet.' His quick wink brightened her smile again. That touch of harmless teasing could come back to haunt him but he'd take the chance.

'Sandy's redbud sure is pretty.' The older woman pointed to a tree with stunning purple blossoms. I bet you don't know it's called that because after the flowers fade they've got red heart shaped leaves. Along with the cherry trees they're the first spring colour we get. There's nowhere prettier than Tennessee in the springtime.'

He could certainly reckon up a few places to rival it but didn't waste his breath. One year he was in Japan for cherry blossom season and the amazing beauty he encountered there would stay with him forever. He'd savoured the joy – reverence was a better word for it – with which the native people greeted the season.

Taran walked alongside Edith up Sandy's short driveway and hung back while she rang the bell.

'She don't say much about what happened to her husband but that boy sure needs a father and the poor girl could do with a ... oh hello dear. Here we are.'

He hoped that Sandy hadn't overheard the other woman's pointed comments but she raised an eyebrow at him over Edith's head. Not the best start to the evening.

Sandy decided to give Taran the benefit of the doubt. There was no reason to assume that he agreed with Edith's point of view because she opened the door before he had a chance to respond. Of course he looked mouth-wateringly tempting again tonight which might've affected her decision. The dark tan chinos and cream linen shirt under a slim fitting olive green sweater complemented his colouring to an almost indecent degree.

'Chip, come and say hi.' She encouraged her shy son to abandon his hiding spot behind the sofa. 'You're going to have fun with Ms Edith.'

'But I want to go with you and Mr T.' Chip's face settled into a mutinous expression.

'I tell you what. If you've been a good boy when we get back later I'll play soccer with you tomorrow after school – if it's okay with your mom.' Taran's offer brought back her son's smile.

'That sounds a good deal to me,' Sandy said. She noticed Edith's gimlet eyes flitting between them. Asking the biggest gossip on Rendezvous Lane to babysit had been a massive mistake. 'Chip, why don't you show Mr T the drawings you did at school today while I give Ms. Edith the run down on what she needs to know before I go out?'

'Okay but don't forget to tell her about my cupcake.'

As a shameless bribe he'd been allowed to choose a cupcake from the bakery they passed on the way home from school. It took ten minutes for him to make the agonising decision before he picked the exact same one as always. Plain vanilla cake with white icing and chocolate sprinkles.

'I won't.' Sandy whisked Edith away. The older lady knew where the kitchen and living room were from previous visits but she showed her Chip's bedroom and bathroom as well. No doubt Edith would have a good poke around all of the rooms later and report back to the rest of the curious Tangled Yarns. Sandy's favourite bright primary colours and eclectic styling weren't to everyone's taste but she didn't care. The influence of Taran's travels manifested itself in his passion for spicy unusual foods whereas hers emerged in the gold Egyptian hieroglyphs she'd painted on the bathroom walls and the intricate French toile-patterned fabric Sandy framed with thin teak wood and turned into mock alcoves for her bedroom.

Taran's rumbling laughter drifted up the stairs together with her son's childish giggles.

'They're a good pair.' Edith nodded her approval.

'I ought to get back downstairs or we'll be late meeting my friends for dinner.' That made it clear she wasn't discussing the subject any further and would hopefully reinforce that they weren't going on a romantic date.

She couldn't help smiling that the kid who was so bent out of shape earlier at the idea of her leaving for a few hours forgot the last of his misgivings when Edith produced a *Cars* DVD from her bag and promised to make real popcorn with melted butter.

'Ready to have your head blown off?' Taran teased her as they walked outside.

'I've no plans to compete with you three. I don't have anything to prove.'

'You certainly don't. Are you sure you don't mind driving?'

'Not at all. It's not far and I know where we're going. I don't usually drink on weeknights anyway so you'll be free to have a beer if you want.' Sandy unlocked the car and they both climbed in.

'How about you give me the full rundown on Lashonda and Harry on the way so I don't stick my oversized feet in it? How long have they known each other?'

'Just over three years. Harry's the boss of the finance department where we both work.'

'And they've been—'

'Interested all that time?' Sandy grinned. 'Yeah. But he's

on the shy side and might never have made the first move. I couldn't let Lashonda down and not come tonight. This way puts less pressure on them.'

'What about us?'

'Us?' Her voice rose.

He regretted the words as they left his mouth. The only excuse Taran could come up with was that his common sense had taken a nosedive. The teasing closeness of her soft blonde hair and the hint of patchouli in Sandy's perfume that reminded him of India amped up her effect on him. He assumed she was forced to wear regulation business attire to work but the vivid blues and oranges of tonight's gauzy tunic and wide-legged trousers showed her true colours to the world. Whether she liked it or not her nomadic childhood had left its mark as surely as his tattoos.

'Let's go back to the condensed version of our dining companion's biographies,' Taran suggested and she gave him a brief look that he sized up as relief before rattling through Lashonda's story. The close friendship was clearly important to both women. 'What about Harry?'

'He's a kind man and a great boss. I purposely said it in that order because he really is a great guy. The grapevine says he's not married and he's never brought along a companion to any of the family get-togethers connected to work but I honestly don't know any more than that.'

'We'll find out more tonight when the hot chicken loosens his tongue.'

'Or chokes him.'

'I know CPR so it's all good.' His wisecrack made Sandy laugh. 'Are we here?' he asked as she started to slow down.

'You sound like Chip.'

'Ah but I didn't add the word yet.'

'True.' Sandy made the concession with a bright smile. 'As

it's Monday we might be lucky and find a free parking spot on the street ... There's one.' She pulled into an open space and killed the engine. 'There they are.'

Their dinner companions were standing outside Hattie B's. They'd picked their day well because the low building with its distinctive red paint and chicken logo didn't have the usual queue he'd heard could snake all the way back down the street. Sandy hugged Lashonda while he shook Harry's hand.

'Let's go in.'

Taran's mouth watered when he sniffed the spicy aroma of hot sauce, cayenne, paprika and peppers high enough on the Scoville scale to make diners weep. 'I'm ready to order.' He slipped his arm through Sandy's. 'My treat. What are you going for?'

'I'll have one plain Southern breast with French fries and coleslaw. Sorry.'

'Don't apologise. How about a drink?'

'Coke please. You have what you like.'

'I'll stick to water so I can taste the food better.' His admission made her smile. 'How about you, Lashonda?'

'The small dark meat plate. Pimiento mac and cheese and collards. Sweet tea. "Shut the Cluck Up!!!" of course.' Lashonda tossed Harry a challenging grin. 'Are you up for it?'

'Sure. Why not?'

Taran kept his fingers crossed that the other man wasn't biting off more than he could chew. Literally. It wouldn't improve his romantic prospects to go up in flames in front of the woman he was trying to impress.

They placed their orders at the counter and settled at a table by the window. He snapped a few pictures with his mind on a potential article or blog post. This was an ideal spot to start the impromptu "Southern Spice" tour.

It amused him to see Harry's confidence wobble when the bright red chicken was placed in front of him but Lashonda launched into hers with no hesitation. Taran had thought he was prepared but the cayenne, paprika and garlic in the wet sauce poured over the cooked chicken hit him first, followed by the hot sauce in the dredge and ended up with a hard kick from the habanero, ghost peppers and scorpion peppers in the marinade.

'Wow, that's something else.' Although his face burned he dived back in for more and caught Sandy's bemusement out of the corner of his eye.

'Are you okay?' Lashonda patted Harry's back when he couldn't stop coughing. If the poor man was a cartoon character, puffs of steam would be escaping from his ears and every pore in his body. She encouraged him to eat some of the plain white bread and dill pickles accompanying the chicken but it clearly didn't help.

'I give in.' Harry pushed the plate away. 'You're the spice queen. I'm a rank amateur. The "Damn Hot!!" level's got nothing on this.' When he finally caught his breath again he picked at his potato salad and gulped down glass after glass of iced tea. 'My taste buds aren't gonna function for days now.'

'Was it worth it?' Lashonda's dark eyes sparkled.

'To finally get a date with you? Yeah, absolutely.'

Taran doubted Harry's sweaty shiny face could get any redder.

'I promised my babysitter I wouldn't be too late. Would you mind if we left you to it?' Sandy gave Taran's hand a quick squeeze under the table. The last thing Edith said was for them not to rush back but he got the hint and didn't contradict her.

'We'll be okay won't we?' Lashonda beamed at Harry.

Sandy's triumphant smile told him she'd planned this from the beginning. If he could convince her they didn't need to rush home to Rendezvous Lane yet perhaps he'd finally get her alone?

Chapter Fourteen

Sandy ought to give a sensible answer. The sort of answer a responsible mother whose jam-packed days started early and rarely ended before midnight should give. But when Taran's gleaming amber eyes fixed on her, every last ounce of resolve ebbed away.

'One drink somewhere quiet. It's not much to ask.'

'Okay. One drink.' This could be the worst decision she'd made in a long time. Risking the hottest chicken at Hattie B's probably would've been safer.

'Thank you.' The shy, boyish response touched her. 'Will that place work?' Taran nodded towards a small neon-lit bar on the corner.

'I guess.'

Sandy couldn't believe how natural it felt when he held her hand to walk down the street.

'This place must've been here a while.' Taran seemed surprised when they went inside.

The lingering smell of decades-old smoke clung to the dark wood-panelled walls, rows of beer mugs belonging to regular customers hanging behind the bar and clunky old-fashioned television showing tonight's ice hockey game all made it clear that no one here cared about being hip.

'Nashville is full of flashy new restaurants and cocktail bars these days but you can still find plenty of places like this if you know where to look.' Sandy smiled. 'Or come across as the case might be.'

'What would you like to drink?'

'I'll just have another Coke please.'

'Got it.'

Sandy settled in one of the booths while Taran fetched their drinks. He slid in beside her and stretched his arm across her back to give them a little more room.

'Let's play the year game.'

'Is that a version of spin the bottle?'

'It isn't actually although we could play it that way if you like?' His eyes shone with mischief.

'Definitely not.' The thought of kissing him was enough to make her face burn and he shifted away slightly. Knowing he'd read her mind only increased her embarrassment.

He hadn't intended to flirt with Sandy but the teasing question slipped out before he could stop it. 'In that case we take turns in naming a particular year and say where we were living then and the most important thing that happened there.' He rattled off the explanation he read somewhere about kids like them who grew up marking milestones differently. 'Here's an example. I smoked my first – and last – cigarette in Bombay, India in 1996. My first kiss was in 1997 in Aberdeen, Scotland. I got into my first fight in Stavanger, Norway on the millennium eve. You get the idea?'

'Yeah.' Sandy didn't look too thrilled.

'It's a fun way to discover more about each other that's all.'

'What if we don't like what we find out?'

'I'm not doing this to catch you out. You're overcomplicating things.'

'Sorry.' Sandy nibbled her lip. 'Okay. My first kiss was in 1999 in Bremerhaven, Germany. I assume we're not saying who with?'

'Doesn't bother me one way or the other. Mine was with a buxom, Highland lass called Elspeth who was two years older and happy to initiate a naive fourteen-year-old boy into the joys of—'

'Stop right there.' Her soft laughter entranced him. 'That's verging on too much information.'

She eked out a smile. 'You don't seem to mind but I'm not a huge fan of remembering my childhood.'

He didn't correct her because he was the one who started the conversation. It would sound whiny to complain about his parents' benign neglect.

'If you're interested my father grew up in the poorest part of West Tennessee, the middle child of eight and was fostered around various family members when his parents couldn't cope with them all.' Sandy's voice was a monotone. 'He ran away and joined the army at seventeen and the first time he was stationed out of the country he met my mother in Wiesbaden, Germany. She wanted a green card to get into the States. He wanted a family of his own. They both got their wish but hers came with a high price because my dad didn't have any clue how to be a good husband or father. Soldiering suited him. The other stuff not so much.'

Taran watched her face darken and wished he'd kept his mouth shut. They'd lost the brief moment of shared humour and it was all his fault. 'Where are your parents now?'

'They're both dead.'

'I'm sorry.'

Sandy pushed away her untouched drink. 'I think it's time we went home.'

On the way to the car he didn't touch her and they made the drive in silence until she parked by her house.

'I assume you won't repeat our conversation to Chip?'

'Do you even need to ask?'

'Sorry.'

The perfunctory apology didn't fool him. 'It's your business what you choose to tell him and when but he's bound to ask one day. No one chooses their childhoods but they help shape us into the adults we are now. Add all that to the choices we make ourselves along the way and we've just got to try to make the best of it.'

'You make it sound simple.'

'Believe me, I know it's not.' He ploughed on before he could think better of it. 'Back in the summer of 2007 I fell in love with the beautiful city of Prague and the spicy red sausages called Pražská klobása. That's where I met Ingrid Novak and her son Alexei. I got deeply involved with them and stayed all through the winter.'

'What happened?'

He'd never spoken of this to anyone and suspected he'd regret it later but Sandy's quiet request left him unable to lie. 'The day Alexei called me táta, the Czech word for daddy, I packed my bag and left.' Taran grimaced at the memory. There was a whole lot more to the story and maybe one day he'd tell Sandy everything.

'Without telling them you were going?'

'No. I used my stock excuse that rootlessness is embedded in my DNA.' The atmosphere in the car closed in on him. 'Six-year-olds can't understand that.'

'Poor little boy.'

'I could use the excuse I was only twenty-four and not ready to settle down but I'm thirty-seven now and still wary of long-term commitment to anything – people or places.' His barely veiled warning made Sandy wince. 'Can you match my lousy behaviour?'

She tossed him a pitiful look. 'Andy died because of my selfishness so yeah I definitely outrank you.'

'What do you mean?'

'I'm not talking about it. I can't.' Sandy flung open the car door and jumped out.

'Don't run off.' Taran attempted to follow her but she held out a warning hand.

'Let's say goodnight here. Thank you for dinner.' Her expression softened. 'I appreciate you being truthful about what happened in Prague but it's reminded me why us being ... friends is a bad idea. I can't take the risk of Chip becoming another Alexei. I'll make up a story to explain why we don't see you as much. He'll hurt for a little while but that's better than the alternative.' Sandy's eyes shone with tears. 'You have no idea how hard I've worked to build this life. Nothing is worth spoiling it.'

'I get it.' Taran didn't blame her but that didn't make it any easier when she turned and walked away.

Chapter Fifteen

'Earth to Sandy.' Lashonda prodded her arm. 'I asked what you've got planned for the weekend and I thought you might want to hear what I'm doin'.'

'We don't have much on apart from the Easter Egg Hunt on Sunday afternoon.' Ever since the disastrous end to Monday evening she'd been in a mental fog. Her friend deserved better. 'Let me guess, you've got a date with Liam Hemsworth?'

'That pretty boy. Pah!' Lashonda grinned. 'I need a real man who knows his way around a woman.'

'In that case it must be Denzel Washington or maybe …' Sandy smiled across the room. 'A certain Harold Jefferson Perkins?' Their boss had a new swagger to his walk these days.

'Let's just say there's a table booked in our names at Husk tonight.'

'Wow, very fancy.' The popular Nashville restaurant was notoriously hard to get into. 'How did he manage that?'

'He knows people. Last night he said—'

'You saw him last night?'

Lashonda's ebony skin glistened under the strong fluorescent lights. 'Yeah, and the night before.'

'Why didn't you tell me?'

'Because you've had a face longer than the Nashville marathon all week so I didn't think you'd be interested.'

'I can still be over the moon for you. I honestly couldn't be happier. What have you been up to anyway?'

'Oh this and that.'

'Does Harry know his way around a woman?' Sandy whispered.

'Put it this way. He didn't need a road map.'

They tried to stifle their giggles.

'You're not taking things slowly then?' She was surprised that these two guarded people were moving at the speed of light now they'd finally got together.

'We've wasted enough time already. You encouraged me before so what's the problem?'

'Nothing.' Sandy struggled to be honest. 'I suppose I'm a bit jealous … I didn't mean that the way it came out.'

'I know that, you idiot.' Lashonda patted her arm. 'I thought you and Taran seemed to hit it off on Monday night?'

'We did. He's good company and yeah I fancy him but you heard him talking about his lifestyle. There's no place for Chip and I.'

'Maybe and maybe not. I know what I said before but it still seems a shame. People can change and that man sure is crazy for you. Harry saw it too.'

'Don't be ridiculous.' A rash of heat prickled her neck. They knew each other too well for her to be anything less than straightforward. 'He flirted with me that's all. It doesn't mean anything in the long run.'

'If you say so. Anyway I'm off home now to make myself irresistible.'

'You won't have to try too hard.' Sandy determined to end the conversation on an upbeat note. If anyone deserved to be spoiled and adored by a good man it was her smart, funny, sassy friend who tackled life's challenges with a bright smile and unshakable determination. 'Poor Harry struggled for three years to resist you and see what a failure that was.'

'True but I'm not gonna get complacent.' A shadow flitted over Lashonda's face. 'We both know that's when life sneaks up and bites you on the butt.' Her smile was a little less brilliant than before. 'On that note I'm off. Enjoy the weekend. I plan to.'

Sandy kept her own smile firmly in place until she was alone again.

'I must say your neighbours are all very friendly.' Taran was grateful this wasn't a video call or his grandmother would know he was lying. Beth often phoned for a chat about the house and garden and it was his task to reassure her all was well while waiting for new additions to the long list of jobs she wanted doing. 'Rusty fixed your lawnmower the other day.'

'I bet he complained about it too.' She chuckled. 'What about Sandy? I had an idea the two of you would get along well and Chip's a dear little soul.'

He needed to tiptoe around the truth. Taran told her that he went to the neighbourhood spring party but avoided any mention of playing with the little boy and steered well clear of Monday's disastrous non-date.

'I bet the Tangled Yarns are havin' a field day with y'all.' Beth's warm laughter echoed down the line. 'I'm pretty sure they'll have the two of you married off before the cherry blossoms fall from the trees.'

'They'll have their work cut out. I'm not the settling down type.'

'Neither was your mother although she and Jakub have been in Cornwall a while now.' The catch in his grandmother's voice got to him. 'I miss my little girl somethin' awful. Naomi keeps promising to visit me but that's as far as it gets. I don't suppose she ever mentions missin' Tennessee?'

'Not really.' A lame answer but better than the truth. Beth wouldn't believe how little contact he had with his parents or that it suited them all that way. 'Are you enjoying Maine any better?'

'Oh it's all right but spring is slow to come here and I sure do miss my home.'

'How much longer do the doctors want to keep an eye on you?'

'Why, are you starting to get antsy?'

Taran chuckled. 'Not yet.'

'Good because they say it'll be at least another couple of months before I'm fit to manage on my own again. You know what I think of that.' She snorted.

'I can well imagine, Granny.'

'Granny eh? You've never called me that before. Of course you were only a little tacker the last time I saw you and only saying a few words.'

If he apologised for being a lousy grandson that would open another can of worms. 'I'd better get off the phone and get on repainting your bedroom. Don't worry – I've stuck to the colour you picked out. Plain magnolia.'

'So I should hope. Now you make sure you say hi to everyone from me but especially to Sandy and Chip.'

'I will do.' Taran didn't promise when he'd follow through.

He decided to prolong his painting break by grabbing a beer and heading out to sit on the back step. Voices drifted across from Sandy's garden and he wondered whether to go back inside before they spotted him.

'Why can't we ask Mr T to come play?' Chip whined.

'Because we can't.'

'You're mean.'

'We don't speak to people that way sweetheart. You need to say sorry to Mommy '

'Sorry.'

Taran felt uncomfortable at overhearing the conversation.

All of a sudden a soccer ball soared up over the fence. It landed on top of one of his grandmother's tall rose bushes and punctured with a loud hiss. Chip started to wail and although Sandy would doubtless prefer him to ignore the situation he couldn't do that to the kid.

*

'Are you looking for this?'

'It's Mr T.' Chip bounced up and down with happiness.

Taran's smiling face appeared over the fence and he held up the deflated ball. 'I've got a bicycle repair kit we can use to try fixing this if you like?'

'We've got one too. We'll be fine.' Sandy reached up to snatch it away but his strong warm fingers tightened around hers.

'I believe the words you're searching for are "thank you".'

She put on a girlish giggle and fluttered her eyelashes in an exaggerated fashion. 'Thank you, Taran.'

'You're something else you know that?' He chuckled. 'Do you want to come around here or shall I pop over?'

'We've got ice pops,' Chip announced.

'Ah but I've got mini-Magnums. Milk chocolate ones for little boys and dark chocolate and raspberry ones for deserving mothers.'

Before she could ask how he'd guessed her weakness for the luscious ice cream bars, Sandy remembered him talking closely with Lashonda at one point on Monday night.

'Ow wow, come on Mommy.'

There was no choice but to give in. Within minutes she was sitting out on the patio next door, in one of Beth's old lawn chairs.

'There you go. Eat that and relax.'

Around you? Sandy thought that unlikely but she took the ice cream Taran held out to her and swiftly peeled off the wrapper. Chip and Taran were sitting down cross-legged on the grass and she idly listened to them work out how to salvage the ball. Taran patiently showed her little boy how to mend a puncture and for a few foolish moments she drifted off into a dream world where they were an ordinary family enjoying a pretty spring day. When everyone got tired they'd go back indoors and eat dinner together. Later after her son went to bed ... Chip's happy laughter jarred Sandy out of her fantasy. She watched him gazing at Taran with the same naked adoration as she imagined Alexei Novak once did.

'Is something wrong with the ice cream?' Taran frowned at her.

'No, why do you ask?'

'One minute you looked as though you were in heaven and next thing you screwed up your face and I was afraid it might be laced with cyanide.'

'I think I might've drifted off for a minute and had a bad dream.' She couldn't tell him what a wonderful one it'd been until she came to her senses. 'That's all.'

'Oh okay.' His smile faded and Sandy guessed he hadn't fallen for the lame half-truth. She'd made her reservations clear the last time they met and he wouldn't have forgotten. 'Let's see if we've done the trick, Chip.' They bounced the ball on the grass. 'That's hopeful. We need to leave it overnight and then put more sealant on tomorrow. I'll bring it back to you in the morning if you'll be in?'

'We'll be home. We're not doing anything fun this weekend.' Chip puffed out a sigh. 'Mommy says we don't have—'

'It's the Easter Egg Hunt on Sunday afternoon and you love that.'

'Yeah but—'

'We should go, sweetheart. Mr T has work to do.' Sandy leapt up and brushed off her shorts. 'Thanks for the ice cream.' She didn't need Chip airing his version of their tight financial situation. The automatic bill payments that went out at the beginning of the month had left less behind than usual thanks to an unwelcome increase in her car insurance and paying for last month's new car battery. It would be a challenge to make it to the first of May without increasing her overdraft at the bank. Until now she'd been too stubborn to accept the money

Andy's parents kept offering her to help raise Chip but soon she might be forced to reconsider.

'You're welcome.' He dropped his gaze to the dripping ice cream in her hand but didn't say anything more as she scrunched it up in the wrapper. 'I'll take that.'

Sandy steeled herself not to overreact as their fingers brushed together. She grabbed Chip's hand and left before her resolve to stay away from Taran Rossi weakened any further.

Chapter Sixteen

Taran shrugged on his old denim jacket and tucked the ball under his arm. Nobody answered when he rang the bell and he considered leaving the ball on Sandy's front step.

'Oh, hi.' She poked her head out around the door.

'There you go. One ball ready for action.'

'Can we play? Please?' Chip wriggled in between them. 'Mommy kicked the wall and hurt her foot.'

'That looks nasty.' He glanced down at the swollen purple bruise engulfing her right big toe.

'It was my own fault. I ...' Her voice trailed away and two blobs of heat coloured her pale cheeks.

Taran wondered if she'd taken out her frustration with him on the nearest solid object. Maybe he should admit he was equally frustrated with himself. For a moment yesterday when they were mending the ball Chip's eager smile had reminded him eerily of Alexei and for the millionth time he'd questioned what on earth he thought he was doing. 'Mommy said a bad word.' Chip giggled.

'I'm not surprised.'

'Can we play?'

'I'll be happy to later but right now I'm on my way out.' He'd planned to take a drive along the Natchez Trace and before he knew what he was doing Taran had offered to take them with him. 'The spring colours should be pretty and I've planned a couple of stops to catch some of the best views. There's a barbecue restaurant near Fall Hollow that I'm hoping to try out for lunch.'

'We couldn't possibly interrupt your day.' Sandy sounded resolute.

'Why not Mommy?'

'Yes, why not Mommy?' He parroted Chip's plea. 'It'll save you cooking dinner later.'

'You have an answer for everything don't you?'

He doubted Sandy's remark was intended as a compliment even though it came with a resigned smile. 'We can put the football in the car with us and I'm sure we'll find somewhere to have a kick around.'

'Oh I'm sure you will.' Sandy glanced between them and shook her head. 'You two are incorrigible.'

'What does that word mean Mr T?'

Taran crouched down and stage whispered in Chip's ear. 'It means we ganged up on her and she doesn't like it.'

'I heard that.' Sandy laughed.

'You were supposed to. How long will it take you to get ready?'

'I'm ready now.' Chip hopped around and bubbled with excitement.

'Your mom might not want to take you out for the day in Superman pyjamas.' He avoided mentioning Sandy's own ragged T-shirt, blue sweats and bare feet.

'We'll need at least half an hour.'

'Aw Mom.'

'Chip, if you keep complaining we won't go at all.' Sandy's threat did the trick and the little boy went quiet.

'I could wait around here for a few minutes while you get Chip dressed then he can hang out with me while you shower.'

'Am I smelling that bad?' She sniffed at her bare forearms and tilted him a teasing smile.

'Now who can't win?'

'Sorry.' Sandy grabbed Chip's hand. 'We won't be long. Make yourself … comfortable.'

He took a guess she had almost said "at home" but that was their own particular four letter word. After they disappeared upstairs he seized the chance to study her bookshelves. Because of his itinerant lifestyle he didn't hold onto possessions but several years ago he bought a flat in London as an investment. Taran paid a property company to manage it as a short-term rental and the only proviso he'd put in place was that no one could touch the locked cupboard under the stairs. That was where he stored the few special things he wanted to hold onto. Although he was a voracious reader he'd largely switched over to e-books because their convenience suited his lifestyle and only a few treasured print books were allotted space in his flat.

Sandy's books on travel, cookery, art and nature were what he might've expected but one whole shelf was allotted to jazz. The books covered all the greats from Coltrane to Marsalis and his mouth curled into a smile when he noticed that several mirrored those in his own much smaller collection.

Chip raced across the room and spun around to show off his baggy Manchester United shirt and matching shorts.

'I'm ready Mr T. My grandma in England sent them to me for Christmas because my daddy liked David Beckham who was the best footballer ever.'

'You look awesome. How about we leave your mom in peace for a while? If you give me your keys I could get Chip's seat out of your car and fix it in mine?'

'Thank you. They're hanging by the door.'

'Cheers.' Taran walked over and unhitched them and faked dropping the overloaded ring. 'Do you use these for weightlifting?' There were at least ten keys plus a collection of the loyalty cards American shops loved to foist on their customers.

'Yes and I've got the muscles to prove it.' Sandy flexed her arms.

'I'm sure you do.'

'You're cutting into my shower time.'

'We can't have that.' It was torture for his libido to think about Sandy and showers. He watched a deep blush creep up her neck. If their thoughts were running along the same lines perhaps there was still hope for him. Taran suspected that was something he shouldn't even wish for. 'Come on, Chip.' He quickly steered the little boy out of the house.

When Taran's amber eyes had darkened to the same rich shade as good molasses at the mention of her showering, Sandy's insides had turned to mush. Every time she swore to have more self-control around the man he did or said something else to rattle her all over again. It could explain why her recent drawings weren't the usual ones of famous Nashville landmarks which sold well but rather of her new neighbour – frequently shirtless and with the intricate tattoo designs that were ingrained in her head.

She hurried upstairs and took the quickest wash on record before throwing on a bright turquoise and orange patterned jumpsuit then as a nod to today's cooler weather she added a thin turquoise cardigan. Because she needed plenty of wiggle room for her sore toe, Sandy dragged on an old pair of tan sandals. She refused to ask why she finished off with a quick spray of lemony cologne and a slick of tangerine lip gloss.

Sandy hurried out of the house and almost crashed into Taran, standing on her doorstep dangling her keys in his fingers.

'Looking for these?'

'Oh right, thank you.' She snatched them away and fumbled with the door before joining them in the car.

'Mommy I've got a map to help Mr T find where we're going.' Chip waved a piece of paper around. 'He drawed it for me.'

'Drew.' Her automatic correction made Taran smile. 'That's great.' For a single man he was curiously intuitive around children.

'I put Chip to sit behind me so you can slide your seat back and stretch out your foot. It's about an hour drive to our first planned stop but there's no rush and we can take a break anywhere you like if you want to walk around or take pictures.'

'Thanks.' She decided to relish the novelty of being a passenger and did as he recommended. Taran didn't seem to mind answering her son's interminable questions so Sandy rolled down her window to let in the mild spring air and let her mind drift. All of a sudden the car juddered to a halt and her eyes flew open.

'It's okay. We've stopped at Baker Bluff to check out the scenic overlook. I almost woke you to see the redbud trees but you can catch them on the way back.'

'I slept?'

'Yes. I'm pretty sure you needed it.' His kind smile touched her. 'The redbuds are sensational and the cherry trees are pretty awesome too. I'm willing to concede that Edith had a point when she claimed there was nowhere prettier than Tennessee in the spring.'

'And the dogwoods aren't even out yet for a few more weeks. They're usually at their best around the end of April,' Sandy pointed out. 'They're probably my favourite. Of course, fall is hard to beat too and it'll be spectacular here on the Trace.'

'Perhaps we'll ...' His voice faded away and a fleeting sadness shadowed his gaze.

They both knew by October he'd be long gone.

'Are we getting out?' Chip pleaded.

'I hope so.' Sandy seized on her son's welcome interruption. 'I've only got a sore toe and I assume we're not planning to hike down to Jackson Falls?'

'Not today,' Taran promised. 'Have you been there before?'

'No but I've heard it's pretty.'

'We'll come again when you're up to it.'

Sandy didn't respond. She wished he would stop dangling possibilities in front of her because beneath the surface she was no more resilient than Chip.

They stood for a while looking out over the weathered split-rail fences and soaked in the incredible view. Today's deep blue cloudless sky cast a spell over the miles of rolling farmland, clothed in the bright greens and earthy browns of spring. An occasional silo or red painted barn broke up the natural landscape along with a sparse number of houses nestled into hollows in the land. They even spotted a group of wild turkeys in the field in front of them and several deer grazing in the distance.

'Shall we get going again?' Taran suggested. 'It's only about another fifteen miles to Fall Hollow and I thought we'd take a look around there first before eating lunch.'

'But I'm starving,' Chip moaned.

'I've got apples and raisins in the car so you can snack on those to keep you going.' He flashed Sandy a winning smile. 'You're welcome to some too.'

'Thanks, but I'm good.' Was it mean or simply self-preservation to wish he wasn't quite so thoughtful. She itched to find the flaw in this man apart from the obvious one that he wasn't planning to hang around Nashville any longer than necessary.

'Cool, Mr T.'

Back in the car, Chip crunched on an apple and popped raisins in his mouth all the way to their next stop.

'Can you manage the short paved path to the observation deck?' Taran asked.

'Yes, it's not a problem.' She let them go on ahead while he explained to Chip about waterfalls and how they were lucky that it rained last week because they'd be more impressive today.

'They're not quite Niagara Falls but they'll still be cool.'

She almost asked which waterfalls impressed him most on his travels but something held her back. Every time he allowed her another sneak peek into his life and thoughts it only made it harder.

'Savour this moment.' Taran's voice turned to gravel as he took hold of her hand, making Sandy's heart flutter. 'Don't look too far ahead down the road.'

Maybe he was right but embracing the challenge was a different story.

Chapter Seventeen

Taran doused his pulled pork with hot sauce and sunk his teeth into the gloriously messy sandwich.

'So how did the "Spice Street Sage" get his start?'

Sandy's question came out of the blue and he wiped a napkin over his mouth before answering. 'My dad moved us to New Delhi when I was about ten. It's one of the Indian regions renowned for spicy food. I made some local friends and wanted to fit in. When they challenged the pale gangly kid to eat pork vindaloo from one of the street traders he didn't back down and smiled through the sweat pouring off his face to convince them it wasn't a big deal. Their respect grew when I tackled chicken chettinad without blinking and I cemented my acceptance among them the day I finished a dish of phaal curry. It's made with bhut jolokia chillies. They usually get called ghost peppers and they're the hottest in the world.' He cracked a smile. 'I don't mind admitting I spent the next few days practically glued to a toilet and haven't risked eating it again since.'

'You must be mad.'

'Mr T, I want some of that stuff on my lunch.' Chip pointed to the sauce bottle.

'I'm not sure you'll like it,' Sandy said.

Taran needed to tread carefully. He was of the firm belief children should be encouraged to try new experiences and saw his childhood as a precious gift that way but maybe she didn't feel the same. They'd never really talked about it because she avoided the subject like the plague but surely Sandy could recognise there were positive aspects of their itinerant childhoods? 'How about I put a little on the side of your plate to dip your food in?'

'Okay.'

He shook some on the little boy's plate and Chip immediately dunked his sandwich in and took a massive bite. His cheeks turned pink but he kept eating until the sauce was all gone.

'That's good. More please.'

This time Taran shook the hot sauce straight on the pork.

'At this rate he'll become your mini-me.' Sandy's half-hearted complaint came with an indulgent smile.

There were more ways to win over a woman than buying red roses and chocolates. *Win a woman over? Seriously?*

'I'm finished eating. Can we play soccer now?' Chip sprung off the wood bench.

It'd been too pretty a day to be stuck inside eating and the summertime bugs that plagued Tennessee weren't out in force yet.

'We can go over there.' Taran pointed behind them to a wide swath of grass well away from the busy road. 'If it's okay with your mom?' He grazed Sandy's sun-warmed hand with his fingers and surprise flared in her eyes. 'You can watch us from here.'

Chip grabbed the ball and raced off. 'Hurry up, Mr T!'

'You're a glutton for punishment.' She gave him a puzzled look.

'This isn't punishment. Trust me.'

Trust him? Did he realise how much she really wanted to? Sandy should regret coming out here today but couldn't ignore her son's obvious happiness. Taran was disconcerted when she tried to dissuade Chip from trying the hot sauce on his lunch and deep down she knew he was right. It was important to expose Chip to a wider world outside of Rendezvous Lane but her own experiences made her wary. Sandy wondered if the tragedy of her parents' disastrous marriage and her own struggles were balanced out by some of the incredible sights she had been blessed to see. If she allowed herself to picture the blood-red sunrise over Uluru in Australia it still had the power to make her heart race. How many people were fortunate enough to learn to surf in Hawaii on Waikiki beach and gaze out over four countries from the top of the Zugspitze mountain on a clear day? Would she trade those experiences to have enjoyed a more peaceful, settled existence? Answering that question wasn't easy. Taran's observation about their past forging them and making them who they were today was deadly accurate no matter how much she tried to deny it. Perhaps when she came to terms with that she'd have a more focused vision of what she wanted from life now.

'Wake up daydreamer you've got two worn out men ready to hit the road.' Taran stood in front of her, his tawny eyes gleaming.

'Did you have fun?'

'I scored two goals against Mr T.' Chip beamed at her. 'Do you think my daddy would be proud of me?'

Her heart leapt in her throat.

'I'm sure he would.' Taran hurried to reassure him when he picked up that Sandy couldn't speak. 'You're smart and you're persistent.' He ruffled Chip's hair. 'And you took pity on this old guy who couldn't keep up with you. That shows you're kind and thoughtful which is more important than anything. I know I'd be … Any man would be proud to have a son like you.' The swift correction didn't escape her notice. 'Last one back to the car doesn't get to nap on the way home.' He swiftly grabbed her hand and interlaced his fingers with hers as Chip sprinted away.

They strolled along quietly and he stopped close to the car.

'You can beat me from here.'

'If I want to.'

Her teasing response brought back Taran's tempting smile.

'If you don't you'll have to drive Beth's tank back to Nashville.'

'Okay I'll give in.' Sandy limped on ahead and slammed her hand on the car roof. 'You lose.'

'Oh, I don't think so.' Taran's raspy voice set her body on edge and she dared not ask exactly what he meant in case he told her in no uncertain terms.

'In you get Chip.' She turned her back on him and settled her son in the back seat. Closing her eyes again on the way home would be a smart move.

Taran lazed in his grandmother's back garden and let the third ice cold beer trickle down his throat. The warm velvety darkness wrapped around him, perfect for sitting and thinking. He heard what he thought might be a mourning dove cooing its sad cry in one of the trees. He recognised Sandy's tentative dip into flirting before she did and if Chip hadn't been around he would have taken a huge risk and kissed her. The attraction simmering between them wouldn't take much to burst into flames but so far he'd resisted the urge to light the match.

Eight o'clock. Chip should be fast asleep by now because he'd barely roused when Sandy carried him inside after their tiring day out. He wondered how she'd react if he turned up uninvited with a bottle of wine to pave the way?

There was only one way to find out.

When she opened her front door, Taran realised he hadn't thought the idea all the way through. For a start he should have showered, shaved and changed out of his threadbare sleeveless T-shirt, running shorts and flip flops.

'Oh, what are you doing here?'

'I thought we might have a drink together.' He leaned against the doorpost.

'Isn't it a pretty evening, Taran?' Edith Beasley appeared

behind Sandy's shoulder and, before he could answer her, another half a dozen local women congregated around. 'Are you joining us?'

'Joining you?'

'No, he's definitely not.' Sandy sounded horrified.

'We're holding our Tangled Yarns group here tonight.' Edith's eyes sparkled. 'We're going to discuss *Lady Chatterley's Lover* and a man's point of view would be interesting.'

'We hear you're into gardening.' A blowsy woman with dyed red hair ogled him.

'Uh thanks that's very kind of you but I believe I'll be off and leave you to it, ladies.'

'Are you taking the wine with you? Spoilsport.' Edith teased him.

'Please feel free to enjoy it.' Taran thrust the bottle at Sandy and made a swift retreat, followed by a swirl of raucous laughter.

Sandy wished she could evaporate on the spot.

'Well Lordy be if that isn't the hottest thing I've seen since my oven caught fire. That man can come over and hoe my weeds any time he likes.' Brandy Charlton's ribald laugh set off the rest of her friends.

'Wine anyone?' Sandy desperately tried to steer the conversation in a different direction.

'Come on girl. Don't tell me that seeing that hunk in his X-rated shorts didn't get your blood flowing?' Jo-Ellen looked bemused. 'And those incredible tattoos – did you see the curled cobra heading down south?'

If she denied it too wholeheartedly they'd call her a liar. Taran was all of her worst nightmares rolled into one. Sandy could resist straightforward sex appeal these days because she'd matured enough to realise she needed more from life than an athletic bed partner. But a man who could make her laugh, provoke her with his intellect and arouse her with a simple sweep of his fingers over her hand? That combination made Taran more dangerous than a nuclear bomb. 'It was hard not to notice but don't y'all get any ideas. I'm not interested in—'

'Not interested?' Edith's disbelief spread around the group. 'We know you lost your man but life goes on. He wouldn't want you to be on your own forever.'

'I don't mean to be rude but you didn't know Andy and you know nothing about me. Please leave it alone.' She plastered on a bright smile. 'I've got pigs in blankets in the oven warming up and they should be ready by now … But please no hot dog jokes! They're very small ones and not worthy of it.' Sandy hoped that the touch of humour would redeem her to her friends.

Everyone collected their food and drinks from the kitchen then divided up in their usual way. The knitters who didn't read sat in the corner by the window where there was the most light while the readers who didn't knit gathered at the end, closest to the kitchen. That left Edith and Debra Parmer who pounced on the two comfy chairs in front of the stone fireplace in the middle of the room because they claimed to enjoy both hobbies. Of course, everyone knew it was really because they weren't about to miss out on any of the gossip that invariably ensued.

Now the serious business of the evening began.

'Did you hear about Mimi Irving's oldest boy …?'

Edith had started. The book probably wouldn't get a mention.

Chapter Eighteen

Taran grinned as he picked up the foil-covered pan from his front step. Ever since his humiliating experience in front of Sandy and the Tangled Yarns club he'd been swamped with attention from the women of Rendezvous Lane. Whether it arrived in the form of pies and cakes, tomato plants for the garden or dinner invitations, he was clearly the flavour of the month.

But none of it mattered because the woman he was most interested in had avoided him like the bubonic plague all week. Sandy was the main reason he told Rusty to add his name to the list of drivers for tomorrow's community outing to the Nashville Cherry Blossom Festival, held every year in April when the blossoms were at their best. If Sandy and Chip decided to give the annual festival a miss he'd console himself with trawling the range of Asian street food on offer. A decent bowl of spicy chicken bibimbop or miso ramen would go a long way to easing his aching heart. Oh God, that sounded like a bad country song, he thought. He'd been listening to far too many recently because he'd been too lazy to change the radio from Beth's favourite local station.

He was enjoying dipping into the "Southern Spice tour" when the mood took him because there was no set agenda. His social media followers loved the posts about his initiation into the Nashville hot chicken scene and he'd dropped hints already about visiting the cherry blossom festival. Taran eased back from his laptop and rolled his stiff shoulders. He was getting low on milk and a brisk walk to buy some at the shop around the corner would give his legs a much-needed stretch. When he showered this morning after his run he'd been reminded that his hair was growing shaggier by the day. Jake had mentioned using a barber's shop a block away from Rendezvous Lane so he could wander by and check it out. If they could fit him in without an appointment he'd let them hack it off before he couldn't see out from under it. He logged off and hurried downstairs to grab his wallet and keys.

'By the time I count to ten you'd better be out here with your shoes on.' Sandy was standing on her front step and yelling back through the open door.

'Is something wrong?'

'Oh it's you.' A frown settled between her eyes. 'It's nothing you need to worry about.'

'Sorry, I'll leave you alone.'

'No, I'm the one who should be sorry.' Sandy's voice throbbed with exhaustion. 'I didn't mean to be rude. It's just me being a lousy mother again.'

'You're an amazing mother.'

'Not this week. I've taken my crappy work week out on Chip and that's not fair. I'm usually better at picking my battles and should've known I'd lose this one.' She grimaced. 'Chip hates having his hair cut so I put it off as long as possible. It's school picture day on Monday and Andy's mother wants an up-to-date photo that she can show off to her friends. It's not much to ask when her only child is dead and her grandchild is four thousand miles away.'

'Maybe you could wait and take some when you see each other next?'

'That won't be anytime soon because I can't afford to go there and she's not well enough to travel here on her own. Andy's dad … doesn't want anything to do with us because he blames me for losing his son. Quite rightly too.' Sandy stared him down.

Perhaps one day she would pluck up the courage to tell him the whole story so he could make up his own mind. For now he kept his mouth shut.

'Thanks.'

'What for?'

'Not spouting the usual "comforting" spiel.'

'You're welcome.' He hesitated for a few seconds. 'I might be able to help with the haircut problem.' Taran smiled. 'Don't worry I'm not offering to wield the scissors myself.' He flicked his fingers through his thick messy hair. 'I was on my way to check out Jake's barber over on Parker Road. If they can't fit me in I'll make an appointment for another day.'

'I'll see what Chip says but I don't suppose he'll—'

'Is that you Mr T? Yay!' The kid raced out past his mother. 'Can we play?'

'Not right now. I'm just off to buy some milk and see if I can get a haircut.'

'Mommy told you to say that didn't she?' A mutinous expression wiped out his smile. 'I'm not going.'

'That's fair enough but I honestly can't play now.' Taran crouched down at eye level with the little boy. 'I'm not lying or trying to trick you – milk and a haircut really is my plan.'

'Do they hurt where you have it cut?'

'Hurt?'

'When he was three a hairdresser nicked the back of his neck and he's never forgotten it,' Sandy explained.

'Wow I'm sorry,' Taran said. 'I can't promise that won't happen but it's not very likely. I'm really old. I'm thirty-seven and it's never happened to me.'

'Never?' Chip sounded dubious.

'Nope.' He straightened back up. 'You can walk there with me if you like?'

'Will you make me have mine cut too?'

'No, of course not. If you decide you want to give it a try that'll be fine.' Taran saw the wheels turning in the boy's head.

'All right.' Chip smiled. 'I'm going with Mr T. I'll see you later, Mommy.'

He saw Sandy struggle to keep a straight face before she gave in and smiled.

'All right but make sure you hold Mr T's hand all the way there and back and do what he tells you.'

'I will.'

Taran held out his hand to Chip. 'Off we go, kid.'

Sandy gazed at the picture Taran had sent to her phone: a selfie of him and Chip with smart new haircuts. Tears stung her eyes at the sight of their matching mischievous grins and raised thumbs. Her kitchen timer pinged and she hurried to rescue her chocolate chip cookies. To keep from worrying how things might be going she had baked. Her go-to stress reducer these days would make Andy laugh because when they were together she couldn't boil the proverbial egg. The combination of a tight budget and her determination to do what she considered regular mommy stuff drove her to learn to cook.

'Look Mommy look!' Chip burst into the kitchen. His face was shiny with excitement and he spun around several times before wobbling to a halt in front of her. 'I didn't make any fuss did I, Mr T?'

'You certainly didn't.'

'It's really smart.' Sandy swallowed hard. The new shorter cut emphasised his resemblance to Andy and showed more clearly the man he'd one day become.

'I smell cookies.' Taran sniffed. 'My favourite. Liver and onions.'

'Don't be silly Mr T they're chocolate chip. Like my name.' Chip giggled. 'It's really Charles but no one calls me that except my grandma in England. My daddy's name was Andrew Charles Sutton.'

When they moved here it was simpler to let people assume Andy's surname had been Warner because it saved tricky explanations she didn't have the strength to give. She could see the time coming when she'd be forced to rethink that decision and probably sooner rather than the later she'd hoped for.

'That's a fine name.'

'Who's for a glass of milk?' The sooner they got off the topic of Andy the better.

'Are you going to the Cherry Blossom Festival tomorrow?' Taran asked.

'Yes, why?' Sandy almost choked on her coffee when he admitted he'd volunteered to drive. Every year the community organised a car pool to drop off the older residents who couldn't handle the long walk from the parking areas. Then they would all meet up to enjoy the festival together.

'I want to ride with Mr T.' Chip stuffed a second cookie into his mouth.

'Well I—'

'You're both welcome to join me.' Taran's eyes twinkled, reeling her in again. 'The other ladies will have to fight over the remaining seat. I can't imagine why but I appear to be popular these days.'

'I've no idea.' Sandy's face flamed. The Tangled Yarns' ribald comments were stuck in her brain. 'That's enough cookie eating for now or you'll spoil your dinner.'

'Yes ma'am.' Taran wagged his finger at Chip. 'We'd better do what your mom says or we'll be in trouble.'

'I didn't mean you.' She wandered over to toss the rest of her coffee in the sink.

'What's fair for one is fair for all, right Chip?'

'Yeah, Mommy says we have to treat everyone the same.' The fact he'd taken her words to heart pleased her but that still left her in a mess where her tempting neighbour was concerned.

'I must be off anyway.' Taran joined her at the sink.

As he leaned around to rinse out his milk glass she became acutely aware of his warm musky scent.

'See you tomorrow,' he murmured against her hair. 'Sweet dreams.'

She'd give him sweet dreams.

Chapter Nineteen

With Chip hoisted up on his shoulders and one arm looped through Sandy's arm, Taran felt more carefree than he'd done in years. They were taking a shortened version of the official Cherry Blossom Walk that the Nashville mayor and Japanese Consul led earlier in the morning. It had been a challenge to escape on their own because Edith had wangled the last space in his car but her bad feet stopped her joining them now so they left her chatting to some of her friends who also wanted to take it easy.

'I suppose you've been in Japan for cherry blossom time?' Sandy said.

It had surprised him to discover that Nashville planted over a thousand cherry trees during the last decade and today's spectacular clouds of pink and white blossoms was bringing back an unexpected pang of memory. 'Yes, I was in Tokyo fifteen years ago when it was *mankai*, that's full bloom time. Did you know the Japanese have a word for watching the blossoms? How cool is that? *Hanami* is their tradition of gathering with their friends and family to enjoy a picnic or barbecue under the cherry trees.'

'I'm sure it's amazing. Is there any chance you remember what you ate?' Her eyes danced with mischief.

'Japanese cuisine is on the mild side for my tastes but Tokyo was where I first tried Tantanmen. It's originally a Sichuanese dish.' Taran rattled off the ingredients. His mouth watered talking about the spicy sauce, minced fried beef, chilli peppers, chilli oil, Sichuan pepper and noodles. 'Are you both ready for lunch?'

'Oh yeah,' Chip piped up in an instant.

'Maybe they'll have some of that stuff you were drooling over.'

He shrugged off Sandy's sly suggestion. It might sound obsessive if he admitted he'd checked out the festival food offerings online last night. 'It's possible one of the food trucks serves it.'

'It's possible? I bet you know the name of the truck and exactly where it's located.'

'Maybe.' The confession made her laugh. 'But there are plenty of places to choose from. If we all try different stuff then Chip gets exposed to more ...' A subtle change in Sandy's expression shut him up. 'Sorry.'

'It's okay. I know you mean well.'

'But parenting is hard enough without other people sticking their oars in.' He lifted Chip off his shoulders and set him back down on his feet. 'I get the hint.'

'There you are.' Edith bustled over to join them. 'The Naylor boys are saving a couple of picnic tables so we can eat lunch together. I sure do enjoy seeing the trees and we've watched some of the cute dancing but I'm not much for all this foreign food.' She patted Chip's head. 'I'm sure we can find us a good ole hamburger somewhere. This little lad doesn't want any of that weird noodle stuff.'

Taran struggled against laughing out loud. These festivals were designed to help promote understanding of different cultures but today's faced formidable opposition in the unwavering form of Edith Beasley.

'Chip loves to try different foods,' Sandy said, her heightened colour betraying her annoyance.

'I'm gonna eat the same as Mr T. He picks good stuff.'

Chip's declaration made him smile. 'Let's see what we can track down. The trick is to follow the good smells.'

'The smells?'

'Yeah, if the smell makes your mouth water it probably tastes good too.'

'How about we find you a seat, Edith and we'll bring you

back a hamburger so you don't have to walk around any more?' Sandy said.

'You're a good girl. A plain cheeseburger and fries will do me. Mind you bring plenty of ketchup and I'll have a small Mountain Dew to drink.' Edith glanced around. 'I'll be over with Debra don't you worry about me.'

Sandy grabbed Chip's hand. 'Come on boys.'

Taran liked the sound of being one of her boys.

'Hi Sandy, I haven't seen you around much lately. I suppose you've been busy?'

Jake's probing question made her blush. He'd come to stand behind her in the long queue to buy home-made lemonade when she left Chip and Taran deciding what they fancied to eat. Sandy had laid down the law and warned them not to choose anything too spicy for her. If she hadn't been irked by Edith's attitude she would've been happy to join her in one of the juicy hamburgers she'd already bought and taken back for her neighbour. 'Oh just the usual.'

'Yeah?' He gave her a long thoughtful stare. 'It looks like Chip's taken to your new boyfriend.'

'Taran is a good friend. That's all.' That wasn't completely true but the last thing she wanted was to be rude and tell Jake it was really none of his business. After she moved into her house, the Naylor twins were always quick to offer if she needed any help. Rusty and Jake's parents were the first to move into Rendezvous Lane and the family had lived there ever since. Rusty worked at a local glass factory after high school but continued to live at home and eventually took care of his parents until they died. He once confessed to her that he was christened Adam but because of his surname and the red hair he used to have, his mates at school labelled him Rusty. Jake had gone to college and law school in Atlanta but after a brief failed marriage to a fellow lawyer he moved back in with his twin brother.

'I expect you'll see this as sour grapes but you might want to be wary of getting involved with him.'

'I'm not a naive teenager, Jake.'

'Poor old Beth told me once that she hadn't seen hide nor hair of him in decades. What does that say about the man?' Jake gave her a questioning look.

'Beth told you that? When? At the spring party you said that no one here knew he existed. Was that a lie?'

'That's not exactly what I said, Sandy.' He looked awkward, shuffling from one foot to the other. 'Beth told me in private one day when she was feeling a bit low. It hurt her to see other folks with their families around them. She hasn't seen her daughter in forever either and her son only comes once a year for a duty visit.'

Sandy couldn't help feeling hurt. She considered Beth to be a good friend and hoped that the older lady did the same in return but this opened her eyes to the knowledge that they'd both been keeping secrets.

'You're next,' Jake said.

'Sorry?'

'Lemonade.'

Sandy quickly placed her order. She needed to make something clear. 'Look I appreciate your concern but—'

'It's not simply concern on my part and you've gotta know that,' Jake said. 'I'm pretty sure you're probably not interested in me that way or we would've got somewhere by now but … I can't stand back and watch Taran Rossi make a fool of you. If nothing else at least think about Chip.'

'How dare you!' Sandy turned on him. 'My life revolves around my son and you know that.'

'You gonna take your drinks, sweetheart?'

She realised the stallholder was talking to her.

'There's other folks waitin'.'

Sandy apologised and took the three plastic cups on the

counter. She stalked off towards the picnic tables and fought to regain her composure. The last thing she needed was Taran picking up on her mood and finding out about her confrontation with Jake. She stuck a straw in one of the cups and sucked down the cold tart lemonade in an effort to lower her temperature a few degrees.

Taran enjoyed puzzles but this one wasn't much of a challenge. One minute Sandy joined them wearing a painted on smile and shortly afterwards Jake returned, perched on the furthest bench away and glowered at his lunch. They must have had a disagreement and if he were a betting man he'd guess it was over him. Although she wouldn't appreciate being warned off, Jake's disapproval would sink in anyway.

'Does that match up to the real thing?' Sandy pointed to his plate of spicy beef and noodles. He'd chosen a mild chicken dish for her which she appeared to be enjoying.

'I'll find out and give you my verdict.' He stuck his fork in and took a big bite of the Tantanmen.

'It's awesome, Mommy.' Bright red chilli oil dripped down Chip's face. 'Can you make this at home?'

'I'm not sure. If we can find a recipe I'll give it a try.'

A brief flash of envy surged through Taran. If he'd been stupid enough to pose the same question to his mother she would've given him a puzzled frown and told him to ask their cook. 'I've seen it being made, Chip. We could have a go one night.'

'Cool.'

'Is anyone else ready for home?' Edith clapped her hands to get everyone's attention. Soon it was established that she wasn't the only weary one and Taran and the other drivers were ordered to fetch the cars.

'Chip will be happy to stay here with Edith and I'll walk back with you.' Sandy jumped up too.

An hour ago her eagerness to join him would've raised his spirits but now he was wary of her motive. 'Fine. If you want.'

'What's wrong?' she asked.

'You tell me.'

'You're too smart. Come on let's walk.'

Halfway to the car, Taran stopped and turned her to him, stroking his fingers over her face while he counted the new freckles scattered over her sun-warmed skin. Maybe his timing was off but he couldn't tamp down the urge to kiss her a moment longer. He tried to ignore the crowds milling around them and the thumping Japanese karaoke music that almost drowned out any attempt to hear each other speak. Sandy's eyes flared with surprise when he slipped one arm around her waist and pulled her close.

'What are you doing?'

'This.' Taran swept his tongue over her lips in a soft kiss then deepened it when a gentle moan escaped the back of her throat. He forced himself to pull away and conjure up cooling thoughts before he embarrassed them both. After weeks of wondering what she'd taste like and how she'd feel in his arms now he knew. A dangerous combination of sweet and sexy – and he wanted more – much more.

'Oh wow.' She sounded as dumbstruck as he felt. 'I didn't plan to—'

'Neither did I if that's any consolation.' He chuckled. 'At least not in the middle of the Cherry Blossom Festival.' His voice turned husky. 'But it's been there between us. You know that.' *Would she try to deny it now he'd finally brought it out into the open?* 'I'm guessing Jake tried to warn you off?' Taran's observation hit home and she blushed. 'I suppose we ought to keep walking. They're going to wonder where we are if we don't get back with the car soon. Is it okay if I come over tonight after Chip's in bed so we can talk?'

'Just talk?' Her coy, teasing smile made him want to kiss her again but he ignored the temptation this time.

'That's up to you.' *What did he have to lose by laying the truth out there?*

'We'll see. You can come by later.' Sandy peeked at her watch. 'We'd better hurry up or everyone will guess what we've been up to.'

She wouldn't appreciate him pointing out that her shiny face and sparkling eyes gave away their secret without any words needing to be said.

Chapter Twenty

Sandy often took a second shower at the end of a long busy day but normally slipped into her pyjamas afterwards. She stood in front of her closet in a panic. If she didn't hurry up, Taran would catch her with a damp towel wrapped around her.

She popped on a decent set of white lace underwear, soft lilac yoga pants and a white cotton camisole. It worked until she glanced in the mirror where it struck her as too bare and obvious, so she draped a purple pashmina around her shoulders. After brushing her hair until it shone she sprayed on a light floral cologne and added a touch of rosy lip gloss. All of her good intentions had flown away on the cherry blossom scented breeze when Taran kissed her. Kisses told a woman a lot about a man and that one spoke volumes. One touch of his firm, warm lips and she'd sizzled all the way to her toes. The blatant longing in his gleaming tawny eyes had given her the mad urge to throw off all of her inhibitions and it would be only too easy to lose sight of why she turned on Jake like a mother tiger.

My life revolves around my son and you know that.

In some ways her old friend was a typical lawyer and he'd picked the right words to push her buttons. Jake had zeroed in on her wariness of starting a long-term relationship with a man whose passport contained more stamps than the local post office.

The doorbell rang and she took her time going downstairs.

'I was afraid you'd changed your mind and were going to leave me loitering out here like a creepy local stalker.' Taran's warm smile faded. 'Did I hit it on the mark?'

'Perhaps.'

He brandished a wine bottle. 'Do you still want to talk?'

'I don't know what I want.' Hot tears pricked the back of

her eyes. Over his shoulder she spotted Edith peering at them from across the street. 'You'd better come in.'

Taran glanced around too and flashed a quick smile before following her into the hall. As soon as she closed the door behind them his sexy good humour disappeared.

'If it suits you better I can disappear out the back door and hop over the fence.' He gave her a searching look. 'Or we can hash this out? You decide.'

'Stay.' She brushed away a tear.

'Oh, sweetheart.'

Sandy's resolve crumbled. 'Kiss me.' He didn't need asking twice and swept her into a bone-crushing hug before dragging them into a long hot kiss, setting all her senses on fire. She gestured towards the stairs and pressed a finger against his lips. 'Shush. Don't say anything more. Not now.' It was possible she'd regret this later but Sandy didn't think so. Inside her bedroom she locked the door in case Chip woke up and came looking for her then ditched the pashmina. She had a momentary flutter of nerves but quickly peeled off everything except for her bra and panties. The gold flecks in Taran's eyes grew brighter and he silently followed suit down to his black boxer shorts.

'Are you sure about this?'

The new rough edge to his voice ramped up her desire. 'Absolutely. Why? Have you lost interest?'

'Hardly.' He tightened his arms around her waist and the press of his rock hard body against hers made Sandy groan. 'I was struggling to be a gentleman.'

She teased her fingers through the soft golden curls matting his broad chest. 'Don't try too hard.'

Taran's long supple fingers stroked around her back to unhook her bra. 'That's better.' He abandoned it to the floor. 'Much better.' His molten eyes burned into her.

'Take me to bed.'

*

Taran trailed his hand down the smooth curve of her back and Sandy sighed against his touch as she roused from sleep.

'Again?' She gave a warm throaty laugh and her eyes fluttered open. 'Any objection?'

She reached back to the bedside table and tossed another foil packet his way. He'd been forced to suppress a satisfied smile earlier when she admitted that she hadn't been with another man since Andy but had picked the condoms up the other day at the chemist "just in case". Normally he'd have been better prepared but Taran hadn't wanted to offend her by assuming anything.

'Not in the least.' This time he intended to slow things down and explore every tempting inch of her but that failed when she wound herself around him like a coiled snake, breathlessly encouraging him to hurry. At the end he captured her cries in his mouth and they lay wrapped together, gasping for breath until he was afraid of crushing her. He peeled away and gathered Sandy in his arms. The awareness of his musky scent lingering on her skin jolted Taran back to reality. Where did they go from this? His feelings for her ran far deeper than the fact they'd clicked in bed but he wasn't sure she'd want to hear that.

'Don't panic. I'm not expecting a marriage proposal because we've had amazing sex.' Sandy tugged the sheet back up. 'That was a whole lot of fun but it's late and probably best you go home now.'

Fun? Normally he'd be relieved at the perfunctory dismissal but he damn well wasn't. 'We haven't had a chance to talk properly ... about Jake's assumptions.'

'Fine, if you still want to talk we can talk.'

Sandy's offhand manner confused him because she'd made it clear she wasn't into casual sex. He'd assumed that by taking this bold step with him he meant something more to her than simply "fun".

'Be honest with me please. You regret this ... us ... already.'

'That's not true.' His protest made her shake her head.

'Don't lie.'

'I'm not lying.'

'Then why did you shut down? I saw it in your eyes.'

He didn't try to defend himself because he'd scare her off if he admitted the truth.

'Jake was right. My little boy worships you and that's my fault. I've been selfish because *I* ... wanted you so badly.'

Her hitching sob tore at him.

'I'll tell you the same thing I told Jake. My world revolves around Chip and he always comes first with me.'

'I know that but—'

'There is no "but".' The last vestiges of her softness evaporated. 'You're gonna go. We both know that. It doesn't matter if it's next week or in three months' time. You warned me from day one. I should've listened shouldn't I?'

Taran wouldn't waste his breath arguing. That was all true until she and Chip turned his life upside down. Now he wasn't sure of what he wanted any longer and that unsettled him. The last thing Sandy needed was for him to make promises he might not be able to keep. He swung his legs out over the bed and picked up his clothes. A thick silence wrapped around them as he got dressed. 'Do you think you could get a babysitter one evening next weekend and we can talk through this some more?'

'What's the point?'

He took the fact she sounded sad rather than angry as a hopeful sign. Like a bolt of lightning, it struck Taran he might be going about this the wrong way. If there was the slightest chance they could explore the possibility of some sort of long-term relationship that wasn't a decision to make on his own. 'Please. It's not too much to ask is it ... after this?' Taran gestured towards the crumpled bed and watched the colour rise in her face. 'Could I call you later in the week to find out if you've been able to arrange something?'

'I suppose.'

'Thanks.' That sounded so inadequate but there was nothing else he could say right now that she wanted to hear. 'I'll see myself out.'

Chapter Twenty-One

Sandy lured Lashonda over to her cubicle by promising to share the last peanut butter cookies from her secret stash.

'It's gotta be tonight, right? I mean Taran said he'd call later in the week and it's Thursday now.'

Her friend's smile broadened to Grand Canyon proportions. 'Y'all are idiots. You had toe-tingling sex—'

'I didn't say it was anything of the kind.' The lie made her face burn.

'You don't need to spell it out.' Lashonda munched on a cookie. 'I could smack Jake from here to Christmas for sticking his nose in.'

'He's my friend and was looking out for me.' Sandy felt obliged to defend him.

'How old are you? Sixteen or thirty-six?' She brushed a few stray crumbs off her emerald blouse. 'Why don't I pop around to your place after Chip goes to bed? We haven't had a girls' night for ages and I've got a bottle of chardonnay begging to be drunk.'

'Won't Harry miss you?'

'Shush.' Lashonda tutted. 'You know we've got to be careful around here.'

Williamson Homes was typical of most large companies and discouraged workplace relationships, especially between managers and staff.

'Sorry.' They both knew there were other unacknowledged challenges the couple faced that should be irrelevant in the twenty-first century but still existed. 'I'd love you to come over. Why don't you join me and Chip for dinner and we'll bare our souls when he's asleep? I warn you it'll only be frozen pizza and salad.'

'Sheeesh what a let-down. You know I normally fix myself a gourmet five course meal after slaving away here for eight hours.'

She couldn't help laughing. Neither of them planned on doing debt collections for the rest of their working lives but at least their enduring friendship made it bearable. For the first time since Saturday night, Sandy's glum mood lifted. She hadn't been able to get out of her head the dismay plastered all over Taran's face when she passed off their lovemaking as unimportant. In truth the intensity of their connection had shaken her to the core and she'd panicked. It'd been self-preservation.

Her friend swiped the last cookie. 'See you later. It's time I got back to listening to more lies.'

This wasn't a job for the soft-hearted. Day in and day out they heard the same stories. The customer's payment was in the mail. They couldn't get the money together this month because they had to pay for their grandmother's funeral. Of course the best one was the fervent denial that the person they were looking for lived at the address. Sandy used to let it eat at her but over time she'd been forced to harden her sympathetic nature. She picked up the phone again and prepared to ruin someone else's day.

'It's not a problem, Uncle Bobby.' Taran was following his grandmother's instructions. Beth called him in tears the day before and told him if she had to stay another hour in cold dreary Maine she'd rather roll over and crawl into her grave now and be done with it.

'I talked the doctor around until he agreed it was fine for me to come home if I've got someone living in the house to help out and make sure I don't overdo it. Overdo it? I wish I could.'

He listened impatiently as Bobby droned on about the inconvenience of the tedious road trip necessary to move his mother back to Tennessee. She refused to fly, saying she'd managed eighty-five years without going up in the air and wasn't about to start now.

'How about if I fly up to your place, pick up a one-way car rental and drive her back?'

'You?' Bobby scoffed.

'Why not?'

'Mother told us you didn't have any time for family so why are you bein' so helpful?'

The brutal truth knocked the breath from him and it took a few seconds for Taran to pull together again. Becoming more aware of other people's perceptions of his attitudes and lifestyle was forcing him to take a long, hard look at himself these days. 'Look, I've made the offer Uncle Bobby. Take it or leave it.'

'I warn you now it'll take you a goddam age. Took me five days when I brought her up here. We stopped at every darn coffee shop and restroom between Nashville and Portland.'

'That doesn't matter. I'll get back to you as soon as I know when I'm arriving.'

He'd been in Rendezvous Lane for a month now and the change of scenery would do him good. It wasn't much of a challenge compared to booking a multi-country tour of Asia; Taran soon had his flight booked for the next morning and two different routes planned out for their road trip back, depending on how fast his grandmother wanted to get home.

Should he ring Sandy to tell her about his plans and ask her to check on the house while he was gone or give her the news face to face? He suspected she'd be relieved to wriggle out of their planned conversation. Taran probably wouldn't be invited in over the doorstep but the miniscule sliver of hope lurking inside him made him shower and shave just in case.

Sandy poured the dregs of the wine into Lashonda's glass and debated the wisdom of opening another. It hadn't taken much for her to pour her heart out and she was a little surprised when her friend came firmly down on Taran's side.

'I'll never regret taking a chance with Harry. You know that Jake is hardly an innocent bystander because he fancies you like mad.'

That all made sense but the worry of how this could affect Chip wouldn't leave her alone.

Lashonda chewed on a cheesy pizza twist. 'Has there been any gossip at work about me and Harry?'

'I haven't heard any but you know I don't socialise much with the others and they all know we're best friends.'

'He's invited me to lunch on Sunday to meet his mother. They've lived together since his daddy passed away.'

'That's good isn't it?' Sandy ventured to say. 'The invitation I mean not that he lives with his mother although that's not a bad thing.' There were deep frown lines etched into her friend's forehead. 'What's bothering you apart from what to wear?'

'Do you really think she'll welcome me? What if she's a real traditional southern lady who wants someone for her son who's more—'

'White?' They knew each other too well to dance around the elephant in the room. 'If she is that way she'll be the one who loses out.' Sandy grasped her friend's hand. 'Harry won't give you up. Not now.'

'What makes you so sure?' Lashonda's dark eyes turned sombre.

'Because I've seen the two of you together. He won't let his mother, nasty gossip or work rules break you up – and you won't allow it either if you've got an ounce of common sense.'

'What about you and Taran? Are you goin' to let the best thing that's happened to you in years get away?'

She wasn't the one planning on leaving the area but they both knew there was more to it than that. Sandy startled as the doorbell rang. 'Oh God what if it's him? What am I going to say?'

'How about you answer the door first? I'm happy to disappear if you want.'

'No. Don't you dare move!' Sandy hurried across the room and flung the door open. 'Oh hi.' Taran stood there looking awkward.

'I thought I'd take a chance and stop by.'

'You'd better come in. Lashonda's here by the way.'

'That's okay. I don't want to interrupt your evening and I can pass on what I need to say standing here.'

'I thought you were going to call and plan a time for us to meet. This feels a bit like an ambush.' Sandy's voice rose.

'Hey we're not only on different pages today but different books.' A gentle smile creased his face. 'I'm happy to come in but I can't stay long because I've still got to pack.'

'Pack?' Sandy's legs turned to jelly. 'You're leaving already? Is Beth well enough to come home?' Taran's firm hands grasped her shoulders and the distinctive scent of his musky soap and bergamot shampoo surrounded her.

'Yes and no.' His voice turned husky. 'Let me say hello to Lashonda and then I'll explain. I can't miss seeing my spice buddy again.'

'Of course.' She struggled to pull herself together and led him inside. 'Would you care for a glass of wine? We were about to open another bottle.'

'We were?' Lashonda grinned. 'Well hi there, Taran. Fancy seeing you here.'

Sandy couldn't help smiling when he slumped down on the sofa and gave her friend a wary glance.

'So that's all I came over to say.' He took a large swig of chardonnay. After he'd rattled off his plans a touch of colour had returned to Sandy's face. Perhaps he should've felt guilty for scaring her but instead it sent his spirits soaring because he saw it as proof she cared about him. 'Beth is pretty miserable and she's convinced her doctor she'll get back on her feet faster back home with me helping her out. Uncle Bobby's third wife hasn't exactly made her welcome.'

Women told each other things so he was pretty sure Lashonda knew what was going on between him and Sandy and he almost sensed sympathy from her which he wouldn't have expected. Up until now he'd been convinced that although she liked him well enough she wasn't convinced he was good for Sandy. Taran stood up and set his empty glass on the coffee table. 'I'd better be off. You've got a set of house keys right?'

'I should do. I'll go and check. They should be hanging by my back door.'

When Sandy disappeared Lashonda grabbed his arm.

'Make sure you sort this out as soon as you get back and don't you dare mess her around.'

'Yes ma'am.' The swift reply earned him a sly grin.

'The keys are there.' Sandy returned to join them. 'Let me know when you and Beth are arriving and I'll get a few groceries in.'

'Thanks.' They walked across to the door together. 'I love the dress by the way.' The exotic green and gold fabric swirled around her body and showed off her tempting curves.

'Lashonda said I'm channelling my inner African warrior princess.'

The first laugh he'd heard from her all night sneaked out. 'In case I haven't made it clear, I admire your spirit. Your lack of ordinariness.'

'I'm a regular suburban mom who works in debt collection. It doesn't come much more ordinary than that.'

One day he hoped she'd see herself through his eyes as a vibrant, smart, funny woman with endless potential who was doing an incredible job of raising her son alone. Taran cupped her chin with one hand and kissed her. The scent of her skin was ingrained in his senses from Saturday night and he inhaled it again now, an intoxicating mix of cool lime and musky heat.

'That's enough.' Sandy eased away.

'Is it?'

'It needs to be. At least for now. Have a safe journey and I'll see you when you get back.'

'And then?'

'Until we've had that chat neither of us wants ...' She glanced away.

'Maybe you can get together with Jake before then and be as ordinary as you like with him.' Sandy's eyes widened and he wished he could retract his bitter words. 'I'm sorry. You didn't deserve that.'

'No, I didn't.'

'I really am sorry.'

Convincing her to give him another chance after this might be harder than climbing Mount Everest in a snowstorm but Taran wasn't a man to give up easily. Not when something or someone meant a lot to him. And Sandy did. Proving it to her was his next challenge.

Chapter Twenty-Two

'Mommy, Ms Beth is home!'

Chip wriggled out of Sandy's grasp as she unbuckled him from his car seat. He took off running which left her with no choice but to follow him despite the fact she'd prefer not to be facing Taran wearing her crumpled black suit and too tight heels that made her feet throb. Her gaze homed in on his thick tawny hair, gleaming in the sunshine. He was standing with his grandmother and solicitously holding her arm while Beth checked out the front of her house.

'Well aren't you a sight for sore eyes?' Beth beamed at Chip. 'I swear you've grown a foot since I went away.'

Her little boy stared down, then back up again and shook his head. 'No, Ms Beth I've still only got two.'

Taran caught her eye and they both struggled not to laugh. This is what she missed as much as the sex. Raising Chip on her own left an aching gap where adult companionship used to be.

'Ms Beth means you've grown taller.'

'Oh. Then why—'

'I'll explain later.' Things that sounded literal but weren't, often confused her son. 'It's wonderful to see you home, Beth.' When Sandy hugged her, the older woman's new frailty became more evident. She was usually tanned from spending as much time as possible outdoors but her pallid skin was creased with a patchwork of fresh lines and she'd lost weight. For the first time she looked every one of her eighty-five years.

'If this boy hadn't come to rescue me I reckon I would've died.' Beth's warm brown eyes welled up.

'People and animals all die.' Chip sounded matter of fact. 'My daddy died and he's in heaven now but Mommy promised she won't until I'm really big and can look after myself.'

'Your mommy's right, sweetheart.' Beth patted his head. 'I didn't want to die away from my home though.' Her familiar smile returned and the knot of tension in Sandy's stomach eased.

'Let's go inside so you can rest.' Taran's suggestion made his grandmother snort.

'Don't be silly. It'll be time enough to rest when I'm … tired.'

Sandy guessed she'd come close to saying the D word again but didn't want to upset Chip.

'I'm longing to see my garden.' Beth smiled at her. 'Taran tells me I've got you and Rusty to thank that it's not an overgrown mess and all my plants pulled out in mistake for weeds.'

'He's exaggerating,' Sandy said.

'I'd never do that.'

Their eyes locked and the connection she kept fighting was there again.

'You'll find the groceries you wanted in the kitchen and of course the Tangled Yarns wanted to do their bit.' Sandy smiled and shook her head. 'I tried to warn them you might have new dietary restrictions but they dropped off enough casseroles, pies and cake to feed a starving army.'

'They're good souls.' Beth looked misty-eyed again.

'We'll catch up properly soon and if there's anything you want you only have to ask.' She hugged her friend again. 'It's wonderful to have you back home.'

'And me?' Taran said, his eyes sparkling like stars in the night sky.

Beth's knowing look made Sandy blush. No doubt they passed away long hours on the road from Maine talking about her. She'd freaked out after their impulsive lovemaking and dismissed it as "fun" in a failed attempt to defuse its powerful effect. Taran seemed determined to push aside her hard-won carefulness, and her reckless side kept prodding her to throw caution to the wind and enjoy his company without worrying about whatever future they might or might not have.

'Of course. Chip is particularly pleased you're back. Apparently I'm useless at soccer.'

His searing gaze swept over her. 'I can't imagine you being useless at anything.'

'That proves how little you know me.' She struggled to ignore the amusement hovering around his mouth. 'Come on, Chip it's time to go.' Sandy grabbed her son's arm and almost dragged him towards their house.

'Oh dearie me. You've certainly put the cat among Sandy's pigeons haven't you?'

His grandmother's twinkly smile made Taran laugh. The time spent together on the road had given them the opportunity to really get to know each other. He'd only retained fragments of memory from his few visits to Nashville as a small child, including the buttery deliciousness of his first proper southern biscuit and being frightened by a trumpeting elephant at the zoo. The picture of Beth he'd carried in his mind since then had been largely a creation of his imagination. Her surface sweetness masked a wicked sense of humour, an innate intelligence and huge curiosity about the world.

During their four day expedition the only time they stopped talking was when she drifted off for a nap, an event that made her fiercely cross when she woke up again. He'd discovered more about his family than his parents ever shared which gave him a deeper understanding of them and himself.

'Remember what I warned you in the car.' Beth wagged her finger in his face. 'That dear little boy thinks the sun shines out of you and Sandy's besotted too.'

'Besotted is a bit strong.'

'Any time we love we risk getting hurt. It's inevitable.' His grandmother smoothed her hand over his cheek. 'You're a good man and she needs one of those but you've inherited your parents' restlessness and I'm afraid you're gonna go off and leave Sandy behind to pick up the pieces.'

Taran couldn't lie. A lifetime commitment was something he still struggled to wrap his head around. He felt himself edging closer towards it with every day that passed but the idea still had the power to frighten him.

'Let's not fret over it today.' Beth said firmly. 'I want a tour of my garden first then you can fix me a decent cup of coffee.'

He'd seen Sandy's shock when she hugged his grandmother and longed to reassure her that Beth was a great deal stronger than she looked. She passed all her rehab tests with flying colours and the doctor had no concerns about her returning to Tennessee. Taran suspected she would soon regain weight away from the northern food she derided as bland and boring. When Beth saw the leisurely route he'd planned for their trip home she laughed herself silly.

'Good Lord, boy I'll have my ninetieth birthday on the road if we don't get a move on. I don't need to be babied.'

When he tried to disagree she shushed him like a disobedient two-year-old.

'We'll make a deal. You promise to keep driving until I tell you I'm tired and want to stop.'

He'd done as he was told and four days and twelve hundred miles later here they were.

'I can't believe I missed the cherry blossoms and the redbuds but at least I'm in time to admire these beauties.' Beth patted the trunk of one of the pale pink dogwoods framing her front porch. 'Let's go around the back. Are any of my iris still flowering?'

'The purple and white ones are.'

She beamed. 'I thought they'd wait for me. They're the Tennessee state flower, at least the cultivated one. The state wildflower is the passion flower but I don't plant any of those because it's a fast-growing perennial vine and can become a real nuisance if you're not careful.' Beth sniffed appreciatively at the air. 'You probably think I'm crazy but Maine smelled so … cold and bare. Can't you just sense everything growin'?'

They kept walking and Taran sensed the residual tension seep out of his grandmother's body. He let her soak in the pleasure of reconnecting with her beloved home without commenting on how alien this was to him. Was it sad that there was nowhere on the face of the planet he felt this strongly about? The bigger question was if he wanted that to change? Did it have to be one or the other or could he find a compromise between staying put and seeing more of the world?

'You're thoughtful. What's on your mind apart from how soon you can sneak off to see Sandy?'

'I was wondering what we could have for dinner.'

'You're a hopeless liar.' Beth prodded his arm. 'That pompous surgeon would turn his nose up at all of the good ole southern casseroles but if you think I'm passin' up Brandy's loaded baked potato casserole you're mad. You can fix some boring chicken and broccoli to go with it if you must.' She pointed to the grass. 'You're doin' a good job. Better than that useless lump next door.'

Before he could warn her to keep her voice down, Rusty leaned in over the fence grinning from ear-to-ear.

'Good Lord woman can't a body get a minute's peace around here. I might've known you'd be back to cause trouble.'

'Someone needs to keep you in line.'

His grandmother's face lit up. Taran guessed she'd missed the rapport with her neighbours as much as her garden and her own bed.

'I'll whip you and your hopeless brother into shape if it's the last thing I do.'

'Probably will be,' Rusty quipped. 'It's good to see you back on your feet again. I could get the gang together at the weekend for a get-together if you're up for it?'

Before he had a chance to protest that Beth needed to take it easy, his grandmother happily agreed to the crazy idea and gave Taran a look that told him to keep his advice to himself.

Chapter Twenty-Three

'You need any help with that, sweetheart?'

A strange man grabbed the other end of the table Sandy was attempting to set up. 'Thanks.' She shaded her eyes from the sun. 'I don't think I know you?' The man's slicked back dark hair, mirrored wraparound sunglasses, sharp suit and black wingtip shoes weren't traditional Rendezvous Lane barbecue attire.

'Nope but I'm more than happy to remedy that.' He stuck out his hand. 'Byron Cassidy, entrepreneur and property developer.'

Alarm bells rang in her head. 'Sandy Warner.'

'Looks like you're havin' a party?'

'We are but it's only for local residents.'

He smirked at her. 'I guess I'll be getting an invite to the next one then after I move in.'

'Move in? I didn't know anyone was selling.'

'I don't need them to. If things stay on track this piece of land will belong to me in another sixty days. I thought I'd better check it out before I sign on the dotted line.'

Sandy bristled but said nothing. She couldn't insist that it belonged to the community because legally that wasn't true. Walter Henderson, a distant relation of one of the original settlers of Nashville, bought this land in 1916 after a devastating fire wiped out a huge swathe of properties east of the Cumberland River. He developed Rendezvous Lane as it was today but left the park area untouched. She presumed it was still owned by the Henderson heirs.

'I'm thinking of building townhouses or condos, not sure which yet but I'm definitely gonna reserve one for me.'

'You'd never get planning permission.'

'Wanna bet?' His unpleasant laugh made her flesh creep. 'The mayor and council are huge supporters of expanding Nashville. In case you hadn't heard we're living in the new IT city.'

'But you'd be destroying all this.' Sandy waved her arm around.

'All what? It's a scrubby unused plot of land, ripe for development. The yuppies will lap this up.'

The encroaching gentrification of East Nashville would snatch another victim if Cassidy had his way and she doubted they could do anything to stop him. Of course everyone needed a place to live but Sandy couldn't understand why the very differences that lured people out of the crowded city was what they seemed hell-bent on eradicating once they arrived. This wonderful tight-knit community would vanish.

'Y'all will benefit because your property values will rise and you'll see new stores moving in. Wouldn't you like a decent coffee shop in walking distance? Maybe a couple of bars or restaurants? A clothing boutique?'

Sandy tamped down the urge to tell him where to shove his development. 'You're welcome to stay and join us. It'll give you a chance to chat to people and possibly get the community on your side.' She felt confident that would never happen in a million years.

'That's mighty kind of you Ms Warner.' Cassidy's oily smile broadened.

'No problem.' She spotted Rusty rolling an oversized grill out from his backyard. The developer could dig his own grave now without her help. 'I'll see you around again later.' Sandy disappeared to put the finishing touches to her vegetable platter and change out of her old jeans. The sixty-four thousand dollar question was what to wear? Too much effort would send up red flags to her sharp-eyed neighbours but maybe she needed to give Taran a subtle reminder of why he might choose to linger in Nashville? She poked her head around Chip's door. He'd been bribed with the promise of a new *Paw Patrol* car if he played quietly in his room while she helped set up the party.

'Is it time to go?' Chip bounced off the bed.

'Not quite. Give me ten minutes.'

'But I want to go outside now. *Please*. Mr Jake and Mr Rusty are there. I saw them from my window.'

'You'll have to wait.'

'You're mean.' Chip flung himself face down on the floor.

Sandy ignored him and hurried off to change; continuing the argument would get her nowhere.

Feeling sorry for herself was a wasted effort. Everyone knew life wasn't fair and she had so much to be grateful for. Sandy focused back on the here and now.

'That's for your benefit.' Beth poked Taran in the ribs.

Before he could ask what she was talking about, Sandy sashayed into view wearing a simple scarlet tank top and white leggings, both fitting everywhere they touched.

'Down boy.'

'You're evil.' Were grandmothers supposed to have this much fun at their grandchildren's expense? 'If you're not careful I'll drive you back to Maine.'

She snorted. 'I'd like to see you try.' Beth pointed to where several of her friends were settled on a row of folding chairs, set up by the food table. 'Help me on over there and then you can go beg at Sandy's feet.'

Taran refused to rise to her bait and tucked her arm through his to make sure she didn't trip on the uneven ground. He glanced back over his shoulder and caught Sandy staring straight at him. The gleam in her bright blue eyes made his body tighten and it took a disciplined effort to turn away. He plastered on a smile. 'Hi ladies, are you enjoying yourselves?'

'We sure are but we're better now you've arrived. You sure do brighten the place up.' Jo-Ellen winked at Beth. 'He's a handsome lad.'

Debra nodded over at Sandy. 'I reckon she stands a better chance than us.'

'It probably helps she's fifty years younger and her boobs aren't draggin' on the ground yet.' Edith chuckled.

'If you'll excuse me,' Taran said. 'I'll—'

'Oh we'd excuse you anything.'

'Do you need rescuing from these incorrigible women?' Sandy appeared as if by magic and laid her warm fingers on his bare arm. Her fleeting touch made him startle and Taran couldn't escape the vivid memories of her supple hands exploring every inch of him in bed.

Now he wasn't certain who he needed rescuing from the most.

'The kids need someone to supervise their games and Chip volunteered you.' She tilted a mischievous look his way. 'His exact words were "Mr T is awesome".'

The vulnerable boy who'd crawled into his heart could be more of a threat than this fascinating woman and that was saying something.

'I can hardly refuse after that ego boost.' He smiled at the group of laughing women. 'Behave yourselves.'

'Is he always this boring?' Edith asked his grandmother.

'Not at all. I promise.' Sandy leapt into the conversation and her sly comment made the whole group burst into suggestive sniggers. 'Come on, David Beckham.' She tugged him away.

'You're as bad as them.' Grumbling wasn't easy to pull off because a tantalising drift of perfume was tormenting him. Sandalwood and vanilla if he wasn't mistaken. 'Who's the suit? He looks like a shark searching for his next victim.' Taran pointed to a stranger who was hanging around the grills and chatting to Jake. The lawyer's deep frown and jabbing hand gestures didn't give the impression they were friends.

'Your description sums him up well.' Sandy looked worried and told him everything she knew about Byron Cassidy.

'Shit.' His brain raced. 'Why don't you prise Cassidy away and introduce him to Beth and her friends? He'll wish he'd never set foot here by the time they've had a go at him. While you're doing that I'll offer Jake an olive branch and see if we can swap ideas about how to safeguard this space.'

'We'll never raise the money to buy it.'

'Don't give up yet.' Taran slid his hand down the curve of her back. 'You rock this look by the way. Any chance I might get to enjoy it more closely later?'

'I'm not sure …'

He held her gaze. 'Don't give up on us either.' Taran wished he had simple answers to the million and one questions which must be lurking in her brain. He'd spent endless hours trying to sort out the confusion in his own head, becoming increasingly certain that he wanted a future with Sandy. 'Come on. Let's put our "Save Rendezvous Park" plan into action.'

'Our plan?'

'I'm in this with you.' He couldn't blame her for looking sceptical.

'Really?'

'Really. All in.'

'You better mean that,' Sandy said and frowned at him.

She knew he'd let down every other woman in his life. Telling her she was different wasn't enough. He needed to prove it but this wasn't the place for a heart-to-heart.

'If you're free you can come over to see me later.'

'I'll be happy to.'

'But this time we're talking first.'

Taran smiled at the prospect of what "second" might

involve but her serious expression didn't alter. 'That's fine with me. Time to introduce me to Mr Smooth I think.' He reached out for her and sensed a brief hesitation before Sandy slipped her small warm hand in his. That gesture lifted his spirits. If she wasn't bothered about setting off alarm bells on the local gossip meters he was in with a fighting chance.

Sandy had almost pulled away but right now she couldn't make herself care about what effect this small public declaration might have. By the time they made their way through the crowd to Jake there was no sign of their quarry.

'Where's Byron?'

'Byron? On first-name terms are you? I didn't believe him.' Jake's forehead knotted in a deep frown.

'What are you talking about?'

'Cassidy said you're supporting this godawful scheme of his.'

'Of course I'm not,' Sandy protested.

'I suppose he's in on it too.' He gave Taran a dismissive nod. 'Might have known.'

'Don't be an idiot,' Sandy jumped in. 'He hasn't even met the man yet and the only reason I buttered Cassidy up a bit was to dig more information out of him.'

'Really?'

'Yeah really. I thought if I let him loose here he'd sink his own ship. You know they'll all rip him to shreds.' She tried to explain where she'd been coming from. 'I hoped it might make him reconsider and pick somewhere else for his development scheme.'

'Sorry.' Jake's colour rose. 'I wish you'd told me.'

'I didn't have the chance. Where is he now?'

'I sent him away with a flea in his ear.' The awkward confession deepened her old friend's embarrassment.

*

129

'Let's not worry about Cassidy for a minute,' Taran intervened. 'The bigger question is what are we going to do next now we know what he's after?'

'We?' Jake glanced down at their linked hands. 'Speaking for her now are you?'

'Surely the more supporters we can rope in the better?' Sandy tried to reason with him while trying to suppress a small kernel of hope. Did Taran's talk about being part of any effort to save the park mean that he'd rethought his plan to leave as soon as Beth was fully recovered?

'For what it's worth I'd recommend having a community meeting as soon as possible. Lay all of this out and see what everyone thinks,' Taran suggested.

'Aren't you a genius?' Jake scoffed. 'We'd never have thought of that by ourselves. Good thing we've got you here to set us on the right track.'

Sandy had heard enough. 'We've got better things to do than listen to you being childish. And yeah I did say "we". When you come to your senses and want our help give me a call.' She stalked off, leaving Taran to catch up. 'You've got kids to play with.'

'Does that include the one we've just left?' He cracked a wide grin. 'Sorry. I didn't mean to be—'

'Equally juvenile?' They both burst out laughing and a flash of euphoria rushed through her. In her determination to give Chip a settled life she never meant to confine them to the boundaries of Tennessee. Maybe she and Taran could compromise and find some sort of middle ground. The idea of something long-term between them might not be so outrageous after all.

Chapter Twenty-Four

'I hate saying this but I should go.' Taran sighed. 'I'm not worried about shocking Beth because she's one of your most avid fans and encouraged me to come see you but I'd hate to upset Chip.'

'Me too.' Sandy's warm fingers rubbed over the soft stubble on his cheeks.

During the night they'd explored each other in a myriad of ways although that hadn't included as much talking as they'd promised. Now she knew the story behind each of his tattoos, those exotic lasting souvenirs of his travels. She studied the fiery Chinese dragon on his right bicep and the sleek lines of the Hawaiian shark on his left shoulder but eventually chose the vibrant peacock feather, the national bird of India, etched on his back and centred between his shoulder blades, as her favourite. In return, Sandy told him about the emergency appendicectomy she almost didn't survive in Tangiers and the worst job she ever had working in a German beer hall during Oktoberfest.

'What time does Chip normally wake up?'

She glanced at the bedside clock. 'We should be good for another hour.'

'It won't take me that long. There aren't any sexy clothes to peel off this time.' Taran's observation made her smile and he swiftly moved over her. After they turned each other boneless with pleasure they clung together and a deep emotion stirred him.

'I didn't mean to avoid the serious chat we promised to have.' He stroked her face. 'You lured me into bed remember.'

'You didn't take much luring.' Sandy's smile faded. 'There are things I need to tell you.'

'Will I want to hear them?'

'I doubt it.' Sandy looked wistful. 'You think I'm some sort of relationship expert but that's far from the truth.' She gulped. 'Around seven years ago I decided that the lifestyle I'd been born into was adversely affecting my choices. You might not agree but it's how I felt.'

'Any way of life can be destructive.'

'I did something dreadful. I decided on the kind of man I thought I needed in order to live a so-called "normal" life and set out to find him.' Her face tightened. 'When I bumped into Andy he fitted my blueprint to a T. The funny thing was while I wanted him for his ordinariness, he was looking for the exact opposite in me. Andy was tired of good little Home Counties girls with their family pearls and plummy voices and thought I was some sort of wild child which couldn't be further from the truth. Ironic isn't it?'

'But you made it work. You were expecting Chip and getting married?'

'It wasn't that simple.'

Taran wasn't sure how to respond when Sandy explained that Andy's upbringing wouldn't allow him to do anything other than propose when they discovered she was pregnant.

'I tried to be honest and I explained why I fell for him in the first place. He didn't … take it well and things were still tense between us when he died.'

'You deliberately got pregnant?'

'No!' Horror suffused her face. 'I'd never do that. It was a complete accident. We both wanted a family one day but not that fast.'

Sandy had put into words his worst fear. He wasn't convinced as many "accidents" happened as people claimed and always made damn sure no woman could ever accuse him of being careless. If she was to fall pregnant with *their* child, he wasn't sure how he'd react. He suspected his first instinct might be to jump on a plane out of Nashville. A therapist would no doubt claim that was his default reaction when things went wrong in his life. What no one understood was that his own father had been too wrapped up in his own life to pay Taran much attention and he didn't intend to repeat Jakub Rossi's mistakes.

'I know I'm not blameless but I offered Andy the chance to leave. I said I'd raise our child alone without making any demands on him.'

'But he didn't take you up on it?'

'No.' Her voice wobbled. 'There's more but maybe it's best left for another day. Take some time to process what I've told you.' Sandy's half-hearted smile didn't fool him. 'You know where I am.'

Taran couldn't shape the right words to ease her despair. When he made his own confession about Ingrid and Alexei she had no trouble in accepting his questionable behaviour so why couldn't he do the same in return? 'I'd better go.' He sat up and tugged his crumpled clothes back on.

'People who say honesty is always a good thing are fools.' Sandy's bitterness sliced through him.

Taran was pretty sure she was right.

Sandy only half-listened to Chip's excited monologue about the animated film they'd been to see. She hadn't had the energy for anything taxing and took him to the cheap cinema that showed older releases for two dollars a ticket. It had been depressingly easy to read the direction of Taran's thoughts in the early hours of this morning. It hadn't taken much to knock the idea that they were inching towards a more serious relationship to the kerb.

'Mommy, someone's knocking.'

She pushed up off the sofa and steeled herself before opening the door. 'Oh …' It took a moment to sink in that it was Jake, not Taran, standing there looking sheepish. 'Hi, what's up?'

'I came to apologise.' He switched his baseball cap from one hand to the other. 'Can I come in?'

'Of course.' Sandy swept the pile of magazines she'd been flipping through off the sofa, then had second thoughts. 'Chip, why don't you watch TV while I talk to Jake in the kitchen?'

'With cookies?'

'Yeah, with cookies.' Buttered popcorn at the cinema and now a sugar fix. She wouldn't win the mother of the week award this time around.

'Do I get cookies too?'

Jake's gentle teasing reminded her what she missed about their old friendship. 'You do if you're good.' He followed her into the kitchen. 'Tea, coffee or beer?'

'Whatever you're having.' He shrugged. 'Or nothing. Doesn't matter.'

She put the kettle on to boil and searched in the cupboard for a couple of clean mugs. 'You'll have to excuse the mess. I usually have a good clean through the house on Saturday mornings but we've been to the movies so I haven't had time.'

'Sandy, I didn't come by to rate your housekeeping skills.'

'What did you come for?'

'First to apologise for being a complete dick. I don't know what got into me.' Jake scowled. 'That's a lie. I do know and it's ugly.'

'I hope you're not talking about me?'

'No way.' The flush deepened in his ruddy cheeks. 'You know how I feel about you … and Chip. I thought we could be friends and hopefully more when you were ready.'

'But Taran came on the scene.' One of them might as well spell it out.

'Yeah.' Jake shoved his hands in his jeans' pockets. 'Rusty

is sick of me whinging and he kicked me 'round here. Told me not to come home 'til I'd sorted it out.'

'Clever man.'

'He never lets me forget he was born five minutes before me.'

Sandy touched his arm. 'Sit down and I'll bring our tea over.'

'Will it help?'

'It always does on the British TV programmes I watch but they're usually murder mysteries with a high body count so maybe they're not a good example.'

'I've missed this.'

His wistfulness took her aback. She'd missed their easy conversations too but it would hurt him if she admitted to enjoying the same lively banter with Taran but with a physical draw added in that she'd never experienced with Jake.

'I hope we can still be friends?' He sounded pensive.

'Will that be enough?'

'I'll have to get used to it.' Jake shrugged it off. 'Why don't we concentrate our efforts on saving the park area?'

'Great idea.'

'What do you think about rounding everyone up for a meeting mid-week?'

They settled down to talking details and by the time they finished Sandy felt that she'd successfully put right one small corner of her world.

Chapter Twenty-Five

'Remind me again why we're holding the meeting here?' Taran made his way around the room, setting down drink coasters to protect the furniture.

'Because I don't want to go out traipsing around of an evening,' Beth said.

Even if only one person turned up from each of the twenty houses on Rendezvous Lane it was beyond him how they'd all squeeze into his grandmother's cramped living room. When Jake sent out an email with the brief details of Byron Cassidy's redevelopment plans and suggesting a Wednesday night community meeting, Beth had volunteered to host it. It meant he'd spent the whole of today following her orders to scrub the bathrooms, polish everything that didn't move and then be her kitchen assistant while she baked two pies and three types of cookies. Beth was determined no one could claim her standards had dropped since having heart surgery. Taran wasn't stupid enough to point out that not everyone had a gullible grandson to order around.

'Off you go to smarten yourself up.'

'Me?'

'Do you want to crawl back in Sandy's good books or not?' Beth frowned. 'I still don't know what you did to rile up the poor girl.'

And you won't ever find out if I have my way, he thought.

'Wear that cream linen short-sleeved shirt and slap on some of the good smelling stuff you had on the other day.'

'I'm not a prize bull going to auction.'

Her eyes danced with mischief. 'Not much difference.'

It was easier to give in than stand there arguing. Twenty minutes later he was back downstairs freshly showered, shaved, splashed with cologne and dressed as instructed. 'Ready for inspection.'

'Oh my Lordy.' She turned pale. 'You look exactly like my dear old father.'

'Really? Do you have any pictures of him I can see?'

'Of course I do.'

He'd picked up his live-in-the-moment attitude from his parents but suddenly these things seemed to matter. 'I'd be interested in seeing them.'

'We haven't got time now but tomorrow I'll drag out all the albums and bore you to death for as long as you like.'

Tears clouded his eyes. If he hadn't taken some time out from his nomadic life he'd never have known this incredible woman. It forced him to wonder what else he'd missed out on over the years.

'It's all right, my love.' Beth squeezed his arm. 'This is a blessing to me too. When you reach my age you'll learn to let a lot of things go. Brooding over things in the past that we can't change is a big one. Don't be so hard on yourself and don't be too hard on other people either. We're all human and we all make mistakes.'

Did she guess what a jerk he'd been to Sandy? When she opened up to him and shared things he suspected she'd never told anyone else before, he'd panicked and thrown it back in her face. The ironic thing was that he'd been on the verge of laying out his feelings and exploring their possible future together.

'That's enough for now. Put the coffee on and open the wine. We've got work to do.'

'Remember our deal.' Sandy made Chip stand still and look at her.

'I'm allowed to eat two cookies and I must be quiet when you tell me to.'

Chip parroted her earlier words back at her. She hoped that most of the other parents would trade off babysitting duties so the meeting wouldn't be a complete madhouse. Sandy planned to settle her son in a quiet space with his books and toy cars so she could concentrate on what was being said. Another, much harder, part of her plan was to treat Taran as any other friend there tonight. Maybe she'd expected too much but his negative reaction when she told him about Andy and getting pregnant wouldn't leave her alone.

'Come on.' Sandy locked up and clasped Chip's hand.

They wriggled in through the crowd of people squeezed into Beth's living room and as soon as she latched eyes with the man in question, her willpower went the way of the dodo. Theoretically Taran's linen shirt and chinos were unexceptional but their casual simplicity emphasised his lean tanned physique and allowed the intricate tattoos that were visible to take centre stage.

'Right everyone. Find somewhere to sit.' Jake clapped his hands. 'If you haven't nabbed a slice of Beth's baked lemon pie already you're probably out of luck.'

'Pedro's here.' Chip pointed to one of his school friends. 'Can we play with my cars on the porch?'

'I suppose so but stay there so I know where to find you.'

'I need your help.' Jake grabbed her elbow. 'After I've done a quick intro would you take over and tell them everything Cassidy told you? Then I'll run through the ideas we came up with the other day and throw the meeting open for questions.'

'Sure.'

There were a lot of anxious faces and disgruntled murmurs by the time they finished and Jake's request for questions sent a flurry of arms shooting up into the air.

'My first question is who put you in charge, lawyer boy?' Lonnie Birch lumbered to his feet. 'You sure don't speak for me and I'm not the only one who thinks that way. What's wrong with gettin' a bit more life in this place?'

'You'd better mind your manners while you're in my home, Lonnie Birch.'

Sandy stifled a laugh as Beth's sharp reprimand shut the man up.

'I know you're not an official group but there's nothing stopping you having a vote is there?'

She could tell that Taran's suggestion irritated Jake. His resolution to back off where she was concerned was clearly a work in progress.

'We could have one vote to establish what the majority of the residents' views are regarding the possible development? And another to put Jake in charge, or not, of communicating the residents' views to Byron Cassidy?'

It didn't take long before Jake was put in charge of the new Rendezvous Lane Action Committee and there was a general consensus that they'd do everything in their power to stop the development plans.

'Beth tells me there are plenty of desserts left and y'all need to eat them up because the doctors say she's not supposed to.' Jake's announcement made everyone laugh.

Sandy smelled hints of bergamot and cinnamon then turned to find Taran standing behind her, putting her up close and personal with his glittering tawny eyes.

'I'd say that was a pretty successful meeting although … it's none of my business. Forget it.'

'Spit it out.'

'Fine.' Taran looked wary. 'Please don't get me wrong because I'm one hundred per cent on your side but I'm afraid I don't rate your chances of stopping Cassidy very highly. It sounds as though the Henderson heirs are ready to sell so why would he be rattled by a bunch of people with no serious clout or money behind them?'

Sandy wished he didn't make sense.

'What're you talking about?' Jake planted himself in front of them and scoffed when she explained. 'And you agree with him?'

Talk about being between the devil and the deep blue sea. 'He does make a valid point.'

'I'll take that as a yes.'

'It doesn't mean I'm ready to give up but we might have to be smarter in how we go about this that's all.'

'Yeah well you can put your views to the group and see what they say.' Jake stomped off towards the kitchen.

'He doesn't believe we can come up with anything.' Taran's eyes shone 'Do you want to call his bluff? What about a powwow at the weekend? We can talk about the development and … us … if you want to?' He looked downcast. 'I screwed up the other night. I know that. Will you give me a chance to explain? Please?'

'All right.' Under the circumstances she thought she'd kept her answer short and relatively sweet.

'Great. Where's Chip by the way?'

'He's playing out on the porch with Pedro.'

'Really? I thought I saw the kid going home with his father soon after the meeting finished.'

Sandy didn't stop to answer him and pushed through the small crowd of people still hanging around. She shoved open the wonky screen door and stared in horror at the empty space, her hand clasped over her mouth.

Taran caught Sandy as her knees buckled and held her upright.

'Oh my God where's he gone?'

'I expect he came back inside when Pedro left. He's probably in the kitchen stuffing himself with cookies.' He watched a hint of warmth return to her skin. 'Come on, let's track down the little devil.' Taran steered her back inside. 'You check the kitchen and I'll run upstairs.' It didn't take long to make a thorough search of the two bedrooms and the bathroom before returning to Sandy. 'No luck?' She was clearly on the verge of tears and he couldn't begin to imagine how frightened she was. That wasn't a hundred percent true but Taran pushed away a memory that still had the power to terrify him because if he went there now he'd be no use to Sandy. 'Should we tell everyone?'

'Tell us what?' Beth stopped talking to Edith and everyone else fell quiet.

'We're not sure where Chip is.' Sandy's voice trembled.

Taran explained what was going on and hoped she wouldn't tell him off later for interfering.

'We need to call the police,' Beth said.

'Hang on a minute, Granny. Sandy might prefer us to check a few places ourselves first.'

'That's a good idea. He's probably hiding around here somewhere.' Sandy sounded calmer.

'Jake, could you search the garden and Rusty, maybe you can run over to Pedro's place and ask if he or his father know anything?' Taran appreciated it when neither man argued.

'What about us?' Edith pointed around to the other Tangled Yarns who were still there. 'We're not goin' to bed until we know that dear little boy is okay.'

'How about y'all go to your houses and turn the lights on?' Sandy said. 'If Chip went outside to play and now he's frightened because it's dark it will show him the way home.'

'We can do that.'

After the other women disappeared, Taran wracked his brains for something to keep his grandmother occupied. 'We need you to stay here in case Chip's hiding somewhere in the house. He might be scared to come out because he thinks he'll be in trouble.'

'All right.'

He grabbed Sandy's hand. 'I bet we'll find him sitting on your doorstep.'

'You really think it's that simple?'

'Fingers crossed.' If Taran allowed his mind to stray too far down the path of something bad happening to Chip he'd be unable to function. Sandy needed him to stay strong.

Chapter Twenty-Six

Sandy jerked awake and felt the policewoman's disapproving gaze boring into her. How could a loving mother sleep when her only child was missing? She'd run increasingly awful scenarios through her head until she slumped in Taran's arms and briefly closed her eyes to make everything go away. The most important job she had since the day Chip was born, and until he was old enough to take care of himself, was to protect her son and she'd failed. No discussion about the community land was important enough to have put Chip's safety at risk. There were no excuses.

'Is there any news?' she whispered to Taran.

'No.'

He looked gaunt and exhausted. It was heart-breaking to see him and the other good men who were her friends treated as suspects by the police. In fairness they'd questioned the women as well but their focus was obvious. So far the police had established that the last person to see Chip was Luiz Ramirez when he collected his son from Beth's porch. He'd told Rusty that he tried to persuade Chip to go back inside but her strong-minded little boy refused.

'Mommy told me to stay here.'

Did something happen to make him change his mind or did someone change it for him? Sandy eased out of Taran's arms and wandered across the room to stare out of the window. At three o'clock in the morning Rendezvous Lane would usually be in complete darkness except for the occasional light from one of the insomniacs or those with young children. Now it looked like the middle of the day, bathed in floodlights and with a sea of emergency vehicles spread out around the area.

'Is there anywhere Chip wanted to go or something he

wanted to buy recently that you said no to? That might give us a clue to where he's gone.'

Taran's question almost pulled a smile out of her. There spoke someone who wasn't a parent. 'How long a list would you like?' The sweet garishly coloured marshmallow cereal she told him would rot his teeth. Chip's plea to go on an African safari after they went to the zoo. The brief glint in his eyes faded when Sandy finished her recitation. 'I appreciate you trying.' She rested her head on his chest. 'Remember he's not quite six and barely knows where Africa is on the map. I suppose walking to the shop in search of cereal is a tad more likely.'

The detective in charge of Chip's disappearance strode back into the room. 'Mr Rossi, I need you to come with me to answer some more questions.' Sandy hadn't taken to Toby Merino from the first time he entered her house and made it clear he was annoyed they hadn't called the police in earlier.

'Why?'

'We've come across some new information that might have a bearing on this case.' Merino's expression was grim.

'But I need him here with me.' Sandy clutched Taran's hand.

'We'll bring him back as soon as possible … assuming his answers are satisfactory.'

'Satisfactory?'

Merino's thin mouth flattened into a straight line. 'Yeah, satisfactory.'

'It's all right, they're only doing their job.' Taran kissed her gently on the mouth. 'They can question me as long as they like if it helps get Chip back to us. Call Beth and ask her to pop over. You need someone with you.'

Sandy nodded. If she tried to speak she'd break down.

'You trust me don't you?' His hoarse whisper sent shivers coursing through her body.

'Of course.'

'Then we're good.'

Taran left the room with the detective but after the door closed she couldn't help wondering why he'd needed to ask.

'Does the name Alexei Novak mean anything to you, Mr Rossi?'

He guessed what was coming next. It'd been bound to come back to bite him on the tail one day. Things would be misunderstood. Lost in translation. Taran would pay the price and so would Sandy. The worst thing about it was that by wrongly focusing on him it distracted Merino and his team from the search for Chip. If that proved the difference between saving the little boy or not there would rightly be no forgiveness where he was concerned. And Sandy? He could forget all about any sort of future with her then.

Taran pressed his hands into his thighs so the detective wouldn't see them shake. 'Yes.' Now he regretted turning down the earlier offer of a solicitor but if he changed his mind it would look bad. He couldn't win.

'He was five too when he went missing wasn't he? The same age as Chip Warner.' Merino slid a picture in front of him and he blinked back a rush of emotion at the sight of Alexei's toothy smile and shock of unruly dark hair.

'I was never charged with any offence.'

'Yeah well we all know how that goes.' Merino scoffed at him. 'There's a lot of scumbags runnin' around the streets who've never been officially nabbed but it doesn't make them innocent.'

'I was.'

'If you say so, sir.'

The detective's derogatory tone left Taran in no doubt he was in big trouble. 'I'll be happy to tell you the whole story and you can make up your own mind.'

'Isn't that generous of him, Sergeant Parker?'

'Sure is.' The younger officer gave a more conciliatory smile. Obviously he'd been landed with the good cop role. 'We're listening.'

Taran focused on the tired grey paint on the wall and ran through the whole story.

'So let me get this straight.' Merino's mouth turned up in a sneer. 'You were watching Alexei for your girlfriend, the little boy's mother, and took him to a street market but he disappeared while you were buying food at one of the stalls. You reported him missing and then claimed to the local police that shortly after arriving at the market there was a confrontation with Alexei's father and you suspected him of taking the boy.'

'Yes, that's correct.'

'We're talking about Havel Novak, a respected doctor and distinguished army veteran?'

He didn't waste his breath trying to explain that the man had terrorised his wife and young son to the point where Alexei clung onto Taran that day, terrified to see his father again.

'The same man who found his only child wandering around the crowded market in tears because you'd given him money to leave you alone while you were drinking at one of the cafes?'

'That was a lie.'

'So you say, sir.'

'What was Ingrid Novak's reaction?' Parker stepped in. 'She must've been upset. Obviously she was relieved her son was okay but who did she blame?'

'Me,' he muttered. 'And she was right.'

'First you claim you did nothing wrong and now you say you were to blame.' Merino's face jutted forward, inches away from Taran. 'Which is it?'

This must be how the police could wear people down. Right

now he'd almost admit to anything to stop the interrogation. If he couldn't convince them he'd never have harmed Chip or any other child he'd be headed straight for a jail cell. 'Ingrid was right to lose faith in me because I was responsible for Alexei that day. I took my eyes off him for a few seconds while I bought the palačinky crepes we both loved. But Havel Novak was very convincing at telling a good story and I was the young foreigner with no obvious means of support who was living with his ex-wife. Their divorce had been bitter and he'd lost custody of his son. He'd threatened to take Alexei away many times but never within earshot of anyone else.'

'The police must have had some doubts or they would've charged you,' Parker said.

'Exactly.' Taran seized on that. 'There were doubts about Havel Novak in certain quarters and in the end it came down to his word against mine.'

'Have you been in contact with Ms Novak since you left Prague?' Merino glared at him.

'No.' After that incident and Taran's decision to leave because he felt he'd done enough damage to Alexei and Ingrid's lives there hadn't been anything left to say to each other.

'Uh sir, you might want to look at this.' The young sergeant frowned and glanced up from his iPad.

The detective barely hid his impatience but peered at the screen.

'Shit.' Merino shoved one hand up through his greying hair. 'I guess you might as well read this.' The detective shoved the tablet towards him.

Taran bit back tears as he skimmed through the news article. Havel Novak had done what he threatened, and worse. The year after Taran left, Ingrid had taken Alexei on holiday to Croatia but Novak tracked them down. He attempted to abduct Alexei and fatally shot his ex-wife when she tried to protect her son. It was a struggle to hold onto his see-sawing emotions. Grief. Guilt. Anger. They all filled his head until he thought it might explode. 'So, do you still think Novak was a fine upstanding citizen?' he choked out.

Merino's grim expression didn't alter.

'Are you going to charge me with anything or can I go now? There's a little boy still missing while you're wasting your time here with me.'

'That story doesn't prove a thing as far as Chip Warner is concerned. You can go for now but we'll be watchin' you.'

The man didn't want to lose face but Taran could live with that. One thing he'd learned with maturity was when to step up and fight and when to back off. 'Thank you.'

Five minutes later he was huddled in the back seat of a taxi and headed back to Rendezvous Lane. He couldn't wrap his head around Ingrid's horrific murder and it tore him apart that poor Alexei was forced to watch. How did a child live with that? The burden of his own part in the tragedy weighed on him. He couldn't help wondering if Sandy would want anything more to do with him when he told her everything. It would be yet another black mark against him. Even more proof that she shouldn't consider putting her life and that of her son in his unreliable hands.

If Sandy asked Beth if she knew why the police were holding Taran so long it could imply that there might be a good reason. If she took one step down the path of doubting him in any way she'd lose her mind.

There was a flurry of noise outside and she clutched at Beth's hands. Her heart leapt in her throat and every single one of her worst fears flashed in front of her eyes.

'I've got good news, Ms Warner.' A smiling policewoman burst into the room. 'One of your neighbours found Chip safe and sound.'

For a second she felt light-headed and thought she might faint but then Sandy spotted Rusty Naylor and heard her son's high-pitched squeal.

'Mommy, Mommy.' Chip raced across the room and flung himself at her. 'I'm sorry. I know I was supposed to stay on the porch but I had to—'

'Shush, sweetheart it doesn't matter right now. Tell me later.' Sandy squeezed him so tight she was surprised he didn't protest. She inhaled his familiar little boy scent, a unique mix of innocence overlaid with a layer of grubbiness and noticed his dark blue eyes were heavy with tiredness. 'I think it's a long way past your bedtime.' The first slivers of pink were starting to sneak into the morning sky.

'Ms Warner, Chip ought to be checked by a doctor.'

'Not now.' She waved off the policewoman's suggestion. 'That can wait for a few hours. You can see he's fine. Right now he needs to rest.'

'All right. We're going to pack up here. We'll need some statements to wrap up the enquiry but that can wait until later too.'

'Thank you. Thank you for everything.' Sandy couldn't even begin to express her painful emotions in front of Chip or she'd frighten him.

'Will you be all right if I go on home?'

The deep worry lines she noticed etched into Beth's face reminded her that Taran hadn't come back yet.

'Of course. You go and get some sleep.'

'And you too, dear.' They kept up the pretence but neither of them would rest until Taran joined them again.

Chapter Twenty-Seven

'I'm home, Granny.' Taran trudged into the house and pushed the door shut behind him. He'd considered going straight to Sandy but all of her lights were off and he suspected they'd gone to bed.

'Oh thank the Lord. I'm in the kitchen.'

He found her hunched over the table with an untouched mug of coffee in front of her, her tired face grey and drawn.

'Did you hear they found our dear boy?'

'Yes the police told me. That's great.' He cleared his throat. 'There's something I need to tell you. I didn't do anything wrong but there's a story you need to hear. It's the main reason why the police held me all this time.' Taran rushed through the whole tale and puffed out a weary exhale when he was done.

'That poor little mite.' Beth grimaced. 'The man was pure evil to do that in front of his own son. You've got to wonder about some folk.' His grandmother patted his hand. 'Ingrid only did what any good mother would do so don't you go thinkin' for one moment she would've regretted saving Alexei.'

'Yeah but if I'd been there maybe—'

'If wishes were horses, beggars would ride.' She trotted out the old saying with a wry smile. 'What did I tell you the other day? The past is what it is and we can't do anything to change it.'

Knowing his grandmother was right and accepting her efforts to reassure him were completely different things. In his heart Taran knew he and Ingrid wouldn't have worked out together in the long-term but he still felt a huge sense of loss. It struck him like a bolt from the blue that Sandy's strength and resilience reminded him of Ingrid. Both women had overcome difficult odds to create good lives for them and their sons. At least Ingrid had done until Havel Novak put paid to her efforts in the most brutal way imaginable.

'Did Alexei have other family to take him in?'

'I don't know. I hope so. I've never dared to track him online in case …' Taran couldn't finish the sentence and clutched his head in his hands.

'Alexei going missing that day wasn't your fault, my love.' Beth patted his hand. 'Sandy will understand.'

'Will she?' He wished he had his grandmother's confidence. 'Yesterday I was terrified I'd let down Sandy and Chip too. I couldn't have lived with that.'

'Send her one of those text message things and let her call you when she's ready. You need to get some sleep.'

'So do you.'

'Did they feed you down at that place?'

'They offered but I didn't want anything.' Taran put a hand on his grandmother's shoulder to stop her getting up. 'I'll cook us breakfast.'

'Well all right but nothing spicy mind.'

The warning cheered him. If Beth was back to telling him off, the ordeal they'd gone through hadn't done any lasting damage. After they ate she didn't protest when he suggested they left the dishes until later. Taran offered her his arm to help her up the stairs.

'Will it bother you if I take a shower?' He needed to scrub away the lingering smell of stale coffee and hopelessness from the police station.

'No, I'll be out like a light when my head hits the pillow.' Beth stroked his cheek. 'You're a good boy and don't you ever forget that.'

He wanted to believe her.

The shower helped and he roughly dried his hair before

flopping on the bed. Things were all right until he closed his eyes and a carousel of faces rotated through his tired brain. As vividly as if he'd been there he saw Ingrid's horror as Novak's bullet sliced through her followed by Alexei's tear-stained face as he crouched over his dying mother. By far the worst because he didn't need to imagine it showed Sandy's hollow eyes following him from the room as the police hauled him away a second time for questioning.

Taran's phone pinged and he was scared to glance at the screen.

Come over now.

He tugged on a clean dark green T-shirt and jeans and shoved his feet into a pair of leather thong sandals. Taran rubbed his hand over his stubbly chin and abandoned the idea of shaving. Going straight to Sandy was far more important than how he looked.

She checked on Chip for what must be the hundredth time and resisted the urge to stroke his tousled dark hair, splayed over the pillow. The sight of her precious son sprawled in his usual starfish position with the Superman duvet kicked half off the bed shot a dagger through her heart. Would she ever take his safety for granted again? He'd fallen asleep as soon as she tucked him in but Sandy hadn't slept a wink so Taran would have to take her as she was with dark bags under her eyes and unwashed hair.

A quiet tap on the front door sent her hurrying downstairs.

Taran was one up on her because he'd showered judging by his damp hair but it hadn't eliminated the grey tinge to his skin or washed away the haunted shadows dulling his tawny eyes.

'Do I get a hug?' she whispered. Without a word he wrapped his arms around her and clung on tight, burying his face in her hair. 'Chip's fine.'

'I know. They told me.' His voice cracked. 'I'm so thankful.'

It struck her how vulnerable he seemed and almost afraid of her. 'Come in. I don't know about you but I need a strong cup of coffee.'

'That's fine but we have to talk.'

'Sure.' There was an urgency she didn't understand behind his words. She let him follow her into the kitchen and quietly fixed their drinks. Sandy set one mug down in front of him.

'I'm sorry, I should be fussing over you not—'

'It's okay. Really. Was it very awful at the police station?'

Taran's eyes darkened. 'Yes but the worst part was imagining what you must be thinking. Don't lie to me, Sandy. Please.' He gripped hold of her shoulders. 'You'd be inhuman if you didn't wonder what was going on when they took me off the second time and kept me for hours.'

Tears prickled her eyes.

'Listen to the whole story then make up your mind if I'm a man you can trust with your—'

'Love.' Sandy cleared her throat. 'I love you and so does Chip. Whether you want that love or return it is a question for another day but for now you're stuck with it.'

'Stuck with it?' He sounded stunned. 'I can't begin to imagine why you think I'm worthy of loving but—'

'Look we're both exhausted. I absolutely meant what I said but let's talk about it another day when we're both properly awake.' A tiny kernel of disappointment lodged in her stomach, not so much because he hadn't said the words back at her but because he thought so little of himself. 'I don't care if the police got the wrong idea about you but I knew you could never have had anything to do with Chip's disappearance. Now drink your coffee before it gets cold then tell me everything.'

He pushed the mug away. 'Forget about the coffee.'

Sandy's heart broke a little more for him as she listened

to his halting story. She understood far too well what guilt did to a person. 'And you seriously thought I'd turn against you because you took your eyes off Alexei for a couple of minutes? Do you think that Chip's never wandered off in a shop and I couldn't find him? What about yesterday? My mind was on Byron Cassidy and his redevelopment plan when I should've been paying attention to what Chip was up to. Did you come down on me like a ton of bricks for that? No, you took care of me and did everything you could to help. That's the measure of the sort of man you are.' She slumped in the chair. 'It happens to every parent. Every caregiver. All you can think of are those familiar names from the news – the children who've been snatched and either never seen again or their bodies dumped like yesterday's rubbish. You're convinced it'll be your child's picture on the front pages and you'll be crying in front of a room full of reporters with the police by your side as you plead for your child's return.' Tears trickled down Taran's face and she leaned over to brush them away, sighing when he did the same to her own damp cheeks.

'It tore me apart when I heard about Ingrid. I might've been able to save her if I'd been there. Beth says that's nonsense but—'

'She's right but I totally get where you're coming from.' Sandy shook her head. 'I should've told you before but you need to hear how Andy died. We were living in Paris when I got pregnant and I was horribly sick almost from day one. I sent him out late one evening to buy more ginger ale but while he was waiting to pay, an armed teenager burst into the small shop and ordered the owner to open the till. When the man refused the robber panicked and shot them both. Poor Andy died for a handful of scratch off lottery tickets, the only thing the boy had time to grab as he ran off.'

'Oh God I'm so sorry.' He wrapped his hands around hers

and clutched them to his chest. 'But you didn't "send" him. He chose to go because he loved you.'

'Love? Maybe he did but I'll never know now. I respected Andy, we were good friends and he was the father of my child but …' Sandy hesitated. She felt terrible saying this but Taran needed to hear the truth. 'I didn't love him the way I love you.'

'And I didn't love Ingrid the way she deserved but we can't force feelings that aren't there.'

'I've come to accept Andy's death was a tragic accident – at least most of the time – but it's different in Ingrid's case. She chose to protect Alexei because she loved him. I would do the same for Chip in a heartbeat. So would your mother.' Sandy noticed he gave her a strange look but said nothing. Maybe they'd revisit this conversation another day. 'Did they tell you where they found Chip and what he'd been doing?'

She hitched a smile. 'The little monster wanted to pee and instead of coming inside to use the restroom he ran out into the garden and went on the grass.'

'It's a man thing.'

'Uncivilised creatures.' Sandy shook her head. 'Chip wiggled the latch open on Beth's gate and wandered down the alley. I've always told him not to go out there on his own and he's not keen on the dark so I've no idea what made him so daring.' She rattled off the rest of Chip's story. 'He was going to creep into our back garden and surprise me but turned the wrong way and ended up in Rusty's garden instead. There weren't any lights on in the house so Chip sneaked into the shed.'

'I suppose he fell asleep?'

'Yes and of course he got frightened when he woke up.' She swallowed the lump in her throat. 'Rusty heard him crying. Can you imagine if—'

Taran shushed her. 'Don't go there. He's safe and none the worse for wear.'

'Alexei wasn't hurt either that day.'

'No thanks to me.'

Sandy grabbed his arm. 'You were no more to blame than I was.'

She decided to say what was on her mind. 'I know you told Beth you were afraid to google Alexei's name but don't you think it might be better to know? If you find out he's doing fine wouldn't that give you a measure of peace?'

'Maybe.'

Sandy sensed this wasn't the right moment to push him any further. 'Well I don't know about you but I could do with some distraction.'

'What did you have in mind?' A teasing smile hovered around his mouth.

'I'm pretty sure Chip won't wake up anytime soon.'

'Is that an invitation?' he asked.

'It certainly is. RSVP required.'

He dragged her over to sit on his lap. 'Taran Jakub Rossi would be delighted to accept.'

Sandy drew him to her and gave him a long lingering kiss.

Chapter Twenty-Eight

'Beth must be wondering what's happened to me and Chip's bound to wake up soon.' Taran twirled a lock of Sandy's silky blonde hair around his finger. 'Why don't you both come over for dinner later and give me a chance to show I can rival Rusty in the grilling department.'

'We'd love to.' She buried her head in his chest and clung on for a few more seconds.

'Mommy, I'm starving.' The doorknob rattled. 'Why is your door stuck?'

'Uh there's a problem with the lock. You go on downstairs and I'll be there in a minute.'

'I wanted a cuddle first.'

Sandy threw him a desperate glance.

'Will it be the end of the world?' he whispered. 'It's fine with me but it's your call.' Taran yanked on his abandoned boxers and T-shirt. She dragged her pyjamas back on with a resigned smile and opened the door.

'Oh wow, Mr T. Cool. Can we play?'

Finding him in Sandy's bed clearly wasn't a big deal. The availability of a playmate was far more important.

'How about we fix some food first?' Sandy's suggestion brought a big grin to her son's face.

'Okay.'

The three of them headed for the kitchen and Taran chatted to Chip while Sandy rustled up a quick lunch of tomato soup and grilled cheese sandwiches. For many Americans that combination was the comfort food of their childhood and Chip was no exception, judging by the way he wolfed it down. Of course he hadn't eaten since dinner last night so the poor kid must be ravenous.

'I'm done.' Chip swept a hand over his mouth to wipe off his milk moustache.

'I think some quiet time might be a good idea for the rest of the afternoon,' Sandy said.

'Why, Mommy?'

'Yes, why, Mommy?' He ruffled the boy's hair. 'We're not tired are we?'

'Nope.'

'Why don't we go outside and play while Mommy takes a nap?'

'But I want her to play too and she can't be tired because she was taking a nap with you.'

Taran's cheeks burned and Sandy turned decidedly pink too.

'He's right. I'm fine. How about we go to the park?'

'Yippee.' Chip waved his arms in the air. 'It's got a big green dinosaur to climb on but you're too big Mr T so you can watch me. We can take my soccer ball to play with.'

'I need to fetch my other shoes or I'll do your mommy's trick and hurt my toes.' He winked at Sandy.

'It's a pretty day so why don't you see if Beth would like to ride along with us? It'll only take about ten minutes in the car.'

'That's a great idea. I won't be long.' On impulse he kissed Sandy, not enough to embarrass Chip but far beyond friendly. He'd travelled around the world without a map or any planned route. He could do this. But love? Taran hadn't missed the lingering disappointment in her eyes when he didn't rush to say those three magic words. He'd never spoken them to any woman and had always intended to be one hundred percent sure if he ever did. Sandy deserved nothing less.

Sandy tilted her head to the sun and relaxed for the first time in days.

'This does my heart good.' Beth nodded across at Taran

and Chip who were kicking a football around on the grass. 'After yesterday they both needed this.'

'So did I. I've never been so frightened.' She clasped her old friend's hand. 'Taran told me everything about Alexei and poor Ingrid.'

'The boy blames himself for far too much.'

'I know how that goes.'

'What do you mean my dear?'

She fell silent, unsure how much to say.

'You know what they say a trouble shared is a trouble halved.'

Before she knew what she was doing, everything started to pour out and for the second time that day she told Beth everything about the night Andy died and the immense guilt she'd lived with ever since.

'Oh my Lord you poor girl. I'm sure Andy wouldn't want you to keep blaming yourself. Does Taran know all of this?'

'Yes I told him earlier and he was incredibly kind.'

Beth gave Sandy a shrewd look.

'Taran loves you both very much you know.'

She shrugged. 'He's very fond of us yes but love? Some men toss the word around casually and I respect him for not doing that but—'

'You need to have a little patience.' Beth pointed up to the massive oak tree they were sitting under. 'The person who planted this knew they wouldn't live long enough to see it grow to this size but they did it anyway. Taran's problem is that no one taught him the real meaning of love. Unselfish love. Taran's parents aren't bad people but they were always too caught up in their own lives. Oh they sent him to fancy schools and lavished money on him but they rarely paid him much attention and in the end that's all a child really needs to flourish.' Her eyes twinkled. 'I think you might be brave enough to take on the job.'

'Me? My upbringing was hardly stellar.'

'I guessed that.'

'How?'

'By what you don't say.' A thoughtful smile crept over Beth's face. 'You've learned about love the hard way. Losing Andy. Bringing Chip up on your own.'

She hated to destroy her old friend's illusions but it had to be done. 'I didn't love Andy... at least not that way. He was my best friend and would've been a great dad but what I feel for Taran is night and day different. And you know I'd lay down my life for Chip without a second thought.' This was tricky ground. She couldn't imagine Beth was anything less than a wonderful mother and yet she wasn't close to either of her grown children.

'Don't you go feelin' sorry for me, honey,' Beth chided her. 'My kids are leading the lives they want and they seem happy enough.' Her eyes twinkled. 'I'm not sure why Bobby keeps choppin' and changin' wives but he never was good at settlin' to anythin' even as a boy. Naomi's the same way when it comes to movin' around all the time. They sure didn't get that from me. If I have my way, I won't shift from Rendezvous Lane until I'm laid out in my coffin.'

She couldn't help laughing.

'What's so funny?' Taran flopped on the grass by Sandy's chair, stuck his hands behind his head and stretched out his long tanned legs. Chip flung himself down in the same position, copying his idol.

'I'll tell you later.' She leaned over and dropped a kiss on the top of Taran's head. 'How about a cold drink?' Sandy fished out a couple bottles of water from the cooler she'd brought along. She wasn't at all certain he'd appreciate being the subject of her heart-to-heart conversation with his grandmother.

'Mr T is going to fix me a spicy burger for dinner.' Chip could barely contain his excitement.

'I hope he'll do some plain ones for sensible folks who don't want their heads blown off.' Beth gave Taran a stern headshake.

'Of course, Granny.'

'Dare I ask what's in your head-exploding ones?' Sandy's question brought the dreamy expression back to his face.

'I usually throw in garlic, jalapenos, poblanos, red pepper flakes and habaneros but that would be overkill for this young guy so I'll tone it back a bit today.' Taran sat up. 'I reckon it's time to go home.' A tinge of heat highlighted the sharp slash of his cheekbones.

It took her from the ground up to hear him say the dreaded four letter H word and she noticed Beth's satisfied smile. Sandy remembered the oak tree. After they gathered up all their belongings, Taran made a grab for her hand and pulled her on ahead.

'That slipped out because it's a common expression but ... it's starting to mean something.' He looked awkward. 'I'm not sure what yet.'

'Beth advised me to be patient.'

'Can you be?'

'If you don't run off I can.' Sandy watched her words sink in.

Chapter Twenty-Nine

Damned if he hadn't enjoyed cooking with Chip last evening more than anything he'd done in a long time, excepting making love to Sandy which was in a separate category entirely. He clicked the "buy" button on his laptop. By tomorrow he'd have a set of safe knives for Chip to use because it frustrated the little boy yesterday when Taran insisted on chopping up the peppers. Sandy wouldn't have been pleased to discover her son minus a couple of fingers. Chip had loved helping to mince garlic in the special press and cheerfully stirred all the burger ingredients together in a large plastic bowl. He'd trotted alongside Taran to the grill and kept a close watch while he oiled the grate and slid the burgers on to cook before asking a whole bunch of questions.

'What's that for, Mr T?'

'It's a meat thermometer.'

'What's a meat therma thingy?'

'It tells us how hot the meat is inside because if it's not hot enough we'll get sick eating it.'

'Throwing up is yucky.'

'It sure is.'

Even though he dialled the recipe back it still had a distinct kick and when Sandy risked a bite she had to guzzle down a whole glass of ice water. Chip had ignored the sweat trickling down his face and polished his off in record time.

'Oh dear mini-me time again.'

Sandy's laughing comment had made the familiar fear trickle back in. If he could've been alone with her last night she would've reassured him but that hadn't been possible and his sleepless night was infected with the usual nightmares. He could try to push it away for now with a little work, his go-to solution to life's problems.

He checked the blog stats for his retrospective posts and was pleased to see one of his guest bloggers had been a big hit with her unique spring cocktails. Taran posted Instagram pictures of their 3-Alarm burgers, so called because he'd moderated his usual 5-Alarm recipe. The "Southern Spice Tour" slipped back into his mind. His grandmother was well enough now if he wanted to leave for a few days but he must only go for the right reasons.

'What are you up to in there?' Beth poked her head in around his bedroom door.

'I'm working.'

'I knew it wouldn't be long.' Her smile dropped away.

'This is my job remember.'

'Where are you off to this time? Russia. France. The Antarctic?'

'Uh, Texas for about three days. Is that allowed? I think you're well enough.' He shouldn't speak to her like that but he wasn't used to explaining himself to other people. It slammed into him like a speeding train that Sandy, Chip and Beth weren't simply "other people". They mattered to him and there lay the difference. 'Sorry.'

Her eyes misted over. 'I'm well enough all right but I've got too used to havin' you around.'

'If it's any consolation, I'm getting used to it too.'

'But the difference between us is you're not sure if that's what you want.'

The frank statement made him wince. 'I'm not a hundred per cent sure ... but I'm getting there.'

'Fair enough. When are you leaving?'

'Maybe on Monday but I'll talk to Sandy first.'

'That's a big step for you.'

Nailed again. She knew him better than his parents.

'You could offer to babysit tomorrow night. It's our May Tangled Yarns meeting. We always have it the first Saturday of the month and this time it's at Brandy's house. Sandy usually brings Chip along but you could look at this as—'

'A payback for my Texas trip?'

'I only meant it'd be a break for her.'

'Of course you did.' Taran suppressed a smile when she had the grace to blush. 'I'll follow your orders when I see her tonight.'

'As if I would try to tell you what to do.'

He kissed her cheek and laughed. 'Never.'

'What's up? Are you avoiding me?' Sandy followed Lashonda into the restroom.

'Nothing's up. I've been busy that's all.' Her friend rested her hands on the sink and sighed. 'I can't do this any longer.'

'What's wrong? Please tell me you haven't broken up with Harry?'

'Broken up?' Lashonda swung back around. 'The darn man only wants to marry me doesn't he?'

'But that's wonderful … isn't it?'

'Is it? Everything was going great and now he's spoiled it.' Lashonda pulled a small white box out of her trouser pocket. 'Look at that, will you.'

'Oh wow, it's gorgeous.' The huge diamond set in gleaming platinum twinkled under the fluorescent lights. 'I don't get it. I thought you loved him.'

'I do,' her friend wailed.

'Where is Harry this morning anyway?' She'd missed work yesterday following the trouble with Chip and it had just clicked that she hadn't seen their boss around.

'He's being interviewed for a new job. A good position with a bank here in Nashville.'

Sandy tried to be patient.

'He's doing that because of me. There've been some snide comments going around about us so he's being a gentleman and stepping away.'

'And you're not wearing the ring because …?'

'Harry's being his usual sweet self and letting me think about it. I love the man to death but ever since the twins' daddy cleared off when I was expecting I've got used to being independent.' Lashonda managed a faint smile. 'You think I'm an idiot don't you?'

'I wouldn't say that.'

'Yeah, only 'cause you're the best friend ever.' She sighed.

'What about Harry's mother?'

'What about her?' Lashonda frowned.

'I haven't heard much about how the two of you got on. What's she like? Would she be happy if the two of you get married?'

'Happy? She'd be ecstatic.' Her friend rolled her eyes. 'Maybelle thinks I'm the greatest thing to happen to him. She's a sweet lady and we have supper with her most Sunday evenings. My boys are all for it too. They love Harry and he's good for them. He never tries to play the heavy father figure but he'll offer kind gentle advice if they ask for it. You know how he is.'

'But you're having the collywobbles?'

'That about sums it up.'

Sandy admired the ring. 'I don't know how you can resist putting it on.' She grinned. 'I bet it fits perfectly doesn't it?'

'Maybe.' A rosy sheen tinged her friend's skin. 'Are you tellin' me you'd leap at it if Taran waved one of these around? You wouldn't think twice and wonder if you're doin' the right thing?'

Sandy didn't know how to answer. He hadn't even said he loved her yet so it was something of a moot point.

'I've promised Harry an answer by Memorial Day. Thank goodness it's the very end of May this year so that gives me about four weeks to talk myself in and out of it a million times.'

'It's your choice but try to imagine your life without Harry and decide if that's okay with you.' A deep sadness settled on her as she struggled to picture her own life without Taran. Unlike her friend she might not get the option.

'Aw honey.' Lashonda wrapped her arms around Sandy. 'Your man's not goin' to walk away.'

She wished for an iota of that same faith.

'Come on. It's back to the grindstone for us … and yeah before you say it of course it's crossed my mind that if I marry Harry I could kiss goodbye to Williamson Homes. I could find something I like better that maybe didn't pay as well because the responsibility wouldn't all be on me.' Her friend shook her head. 'That's a lousy way for a modern woman to think aint it, girl?'

'I'm pretty sure Harry would see it as giving you some freedom. If you really love someone you want them to be the happiest they can be.'

'So you'd be okay if Taran encouraged you to give up this place and the data entry work and take up your drawing and other art stuff professionally while he helped you financially?'

They'd spent endless hours over the years talking about what they'd do if they didn't rely on their monthly pay cheques. Sandy couldn't criticise her friend's line of thought when she didn't even accept help from Andy's parents to raise their grandson.

'Not so straightforward is it? I've never relied on any man and I'm not startin' now. If I say yes to Harry and this'—she smiled down at the ring—'pretty sparkler – I'm gonna pay my share of the bills and if I can't find another job that'll let me do that I'll keep ploddin' away here.' Lashonda checked herself in the mirror and wiped off a smudge of mascara. 'Heck, he'll be back soon and he'll change his mind if he sees me lookin' this bad so I won't have a choice to make.'

They both knew that couldn't be farther from the truth but

Sandy held her tongue while her friend pulled out a glossy red lipstick and did some touching up.

'That'll have to do.' Lashonda gave her a sly smile. 'Maybe over the weekend Taran will surprise you.'

'Oh he often manages to do that.' Sandy chuckled. She didn't spoil the moment by mentioning the distinct possibility that it might not be the good sort of surprise.

Chapter Thirty

'Is this to break us in gently before the "Spice Street Sage" kicks back into full gear?'

Sandy's blunt comment stung. When he made his babysitting offer, Chip had beamed at Taran and made him promise they could cook dinner together while his mother went out.

'You'll miss the action group meeting on Tuesday. Jake is seeing the Henderson's lawyer on Monday so he'll tell us what she had to say.'

He took that as a dig at his unreliability, showing how much his promises were worth. 'I'm sorry, that's the way it's worked out but you can catch me up when I get back.' Of course he could use the defence that this was his job but they both knew he'd made a choice. 'How are Lashonda and Harry? Perhaps the four of us could go out again.'

'They've got ... stuff going on." Sandy coloured up. 'This might not be a good time.'

'Nothing's wrong is there?'

She rattled off a succinct story about Harry's marriage proposal and Lashonda's reaction to it. 'I understand what she means about retaining her independence.'

'So do I but ...'

Taran needed to tread carefully. 'Isn't there a difference between complete independence and relying on someone in a trusting way? Trusting the other person has your back and wants the best for you. Shouldn't the best sort of relationship be a team effort where they help each other to fill their true potential?'

'Those are interesting words for a loner.'

He couldn't blame Sandy for sounding confused. 'So in

your book people aren't allowed to change? Are you telling me you're the same woman you were at nineteen?'

'Of course not.'

'But you are saying there's no hope for me? For us?' He grasped her arm and a waft of her familiar fresh scent surrounded him. 'Be honest. Please.'

'Fine. If you want honesty you'll have it.' Her sapphire eyes blazed. 'Do you know what Lashonda said when she was talking about you that brought me up short? "Your man's not goin' to walk away". Why is she so sure of that while I …?' Sandy's voice cracked.

'I can't blame you for not having faith in me.' A wave of sadness swept through him. 'I haven't done or said anything to make you feel differently.' She gave him an expectant look but before he had a chance to speak her mobile rang and she dragged it from her pocket.

'Oh hi Brandy.'

He picked up some of the conversation and saw what was coming.

'You're off the hook.'

Sandy's wobbly smile sliced through him.

'Brandy's sick so she can't host the Tangled Yarns tonight. I offered to have it here instead which means I won't need a sitter. Thanks anyway. I appreciated the offer even if I was a bit rude.'

'I promised Chip.' Taran folded his arms. 'I'm not going to let him down'

'He'll understand. I'll tell him you'll come another day.'

'Okay if that's what you want.' It would be a huge mistake to pressure her but he couldn't leave it there. 'One reason I've decided to take these few days away is to do some soul searching. I'm not making any rash promises because you'd be wary of believing them but I really want to make things work with you. It will take a massive change in my lifestyle and that's what I've got to figure out. Apart from anything else I still need to earn a living somehow but I can't lose what we've got. I've never felt this way before, Sandy. Never.' Sandy didn't resist when he stroked his hands around her waist. When he swept them into a deep kiss her body turned boneless in his arms. 'I'll fight for it. Fight for you.' It took all his self-control to drop his hands back to his sides. 'I'd better be off. Enjoy the Tangled Yarns tonight and I promise not to turn up half-drunk this time and—'

'Half-naked?'

'They enjoyed it. Why else did they all start fawning over me and baking more pies and cakes than I could eat in a month of Sundays?'

'Maybe they thought you needed feeding.' Sandy's warm laughter lifted his hopes.

'Right, because I'm so skinny and feeble looking.'

Her gaze lingered on him before she sighed. 'When you're back from Texas ... we'll see.'

There was so much he wanted to say but if he threw the words love and commitment into the mix at this point that would be reckless. He nodded and left it alone for now. And her.

Sandy hadn't felt this jangled up and out of sorts in a long time. As she'd expected, Chip had thrown a tantrum over Taran leaving and then she burned the tiny biscuits she'd taken the trouble to make from scratch to serve with country ham for the book club meeting.

Of course she hadn't got around to reading the book either but neither had anyone else. Sandy couldn't remember who'd suggested they read Moby Dick but plainly it wasn't somebody who'd been forced to read the dreary story in school. The general lack of interest in the book meant more time to gossip and she really wasn't in the mood for that.

'My boy's off to Texas on Monday for a few days and he bought me this so I can follow him.' Beth flashed around a new smartphone. 'He showed me how to check this Instagram thing and read his blog.'

Sandy's eyes stung. Taran showed his kind heart in so many ways.

'It's a pity you couldn't go with him.' Beth gave Sandy a pointed glance which made everyone stare at her.

'I've got to work and Chip's still in school.' That was deceitful because it implied that he'd invited them. 'Are y'all going to the park meeting on Tuesday?' Changing the subject seemed like a good idea.

'I doubt it'll be good news.' Edith looked gloomy. 'I bet the Hendersons will be happy to sell to the highest bidder. They aren't goin' to give a fig for us. Why should they?'

Sandy sat back and let the chatter swirl around her, at least it stopped them talking about her. On a normal evening no one was in a rush to break up the meeting but by nine o'clock there was only her and Beth left. 'Would you like me to walk you home?'

'Tryin' to rush me off? I thought you might whip up a fresh pot of coffee.'

'Of course I'd be happy to.'

'You're as bad a liar as my grandson.' Beth shook her head. 'Y'all must think I'm an idiot. One minute you're squished together like peas in a pod and now you're skirtin' around each other like a couple of nervous cats in a room full of rockin' chairs. His face was long as a fiddle when he came back from seeing you this morning and I don't think it's because you can't bear to be parted for a few days.'

There was no point pretending she didn't know what her old friend was getting at so Sandy rattled off the whole story including Lashonda's dilemma over whether or not to marry Harry.

'Oh honey.' Beth's gaze softened. 'I've been on my own for longer than I care to remember. My poor Wes went to be with the Lord when he was only forty and before Taran was even born. I'm as independent as any of you young women and I don't like relyin' on anybody for nothing but sharing the troubles and joys of life with someone you love isn't somethin' to sneeze at.' A gentle smile creased her face. 'Maybe young Taran's got more sense than I gave him credit for. It sounds as though he's having a good hard think about what he wants from life. I think our rolling stone might be ready to gather some moss.' Beth patted her hand. 'I know you've got Chip to think about and I don't want to see him hurt either but Taran sure loves that boy. Don't close your heart to him.'

Beth struggled up off the sofa. 'Don't bother with any coffee for me. It's late and I need my bed. I'll bow to common sense and let you walk me over.' She linked her arm through Sandy's

'I'll be happy to.'

Her old friend had given her a lot to think about.

Chapter Thirty-One

'Oh, what are you doing here? Aren't you supposed to be in Texas?' Sandy didn't look thrilled to find him on the doorstep.

'Would you believe me if I said I cancelled the trip to spend more time with you?' Taran noticed the corners of her mouth twitch with amusement. 'Didn't think so. When I did my research more closely I found several of the eating spots I want to hit are closed on Mondays and one is only open for business on Saturdays so it made more sense to reschedule. I'm leaving on Wednesday instead. Where's Chip? He usually races out when he hears me come.'

'He's on a play date with a friend from school so he won't be home until about seven. I've been making the most of the peace and quiet to do some work. My head's spinning from almost two hours of data entry.'

'And now?'

'I ought to fix dinner because I skipped lunch at work.'

Around her shoulder he could see charcoal sketches strewn across the coffee table. 'But you're drawing instead and now I've interrupted. Sorry.'

'It's okay.'

'No, it's not. You barely get a minute to yourself and you're so damn talented it's a shame.'

'How do you know I'm any good?' Sandy's eyebrows drew together.

'The day of the spring picnic I saw the sketch you did of me.' Her face turned beet red and before she could lay into him for nosing around he explained that when he fetched his wine bottle he'd noticed the drawing pinned on the fridge. 'Did you go to art school?'

'Hardly. I messed around some as a kid but I got more

172

serious when I saw the artists on the Left Bank in Paris working and selling their pictures. I started sketching tourist portraits or people's pets to pay for a bed for the night and a meal.' Sandy cracked a smile. 'I suppose you'd better come in. If you stay out here any longer you'll take root and I'm sure Edith has us in her beady sights by now.'

He followed her in, his attention landing on a set of charcoal portraits of Chip, hanging on the wall by the stairs. Presumably he'd been too distracted to notice them before. 'These are incredible.' He was no expert but had soaked up enough from his travels to recognise her gift. 'Do you use any other mediums?'

'I do some pastels and I enjoy experimenting with watercolours but I've never attempted any oils.' She pointed to a twisted metal representation of a tiger springing in the air, hanging over the bookcase. 'I made that when there were free classes at the community centre last year. I'll give anything creative a try.'

'You've no clue have you?' Sandy's luminous blue eyes lifted to meet his. 'You are one hell of a talented lady. These could pay your bills over and over again with no problem.'

'I can't take the risk. My parents ...' Her voice trailed away.

'Tell me more about them.' This was dangerous territory. Somewhere they hadn't ventured before. 'Sit with me.' He dropped down on the sofa and patted the cushion next to him. 'Were they ... reckless with you?'

'That's one way of putting it.' Sandy's expression hardened. 'Their marriage was volatile. I never knew what the atmosphere at home would be like from one day to the next and when I was a junior in high school my dad went AWOL from the army after a fight at the base. A soldier died.'

'So he's in prison?'

'He was but another inmate fatally stabbed him in the showers.'

'I'm sorry. What did you and your mother do then?'

'She wanted to bring me to the States but didn't have any money or any contacts here. Her family didn't want anything to do with us so she yanked me out of school and we went travelling. She picked up any low pay temporary jobs she could find but I was in the way. A nuisance.'

'Surely not.'

'She told me so often enough and we parted ways about a year later.'

He couldn't bear the pain laced through her halting words. 'Where is she now?'

'She died about ten years ago. Cancer.' Sandy's shoulders stiffened. 'Now you see why I'm determined Chip will never feel anything less than safe, secure and loved. I'll encourage him to follow his dreams but for now mine must wait.'

Anything he said would sound either trite or selfish.

'I'm not a martyr,' she continued and quirked a smile. 'I sell my drawings at local craft fairs or the flea market but it's a hobby nothing more.'

'How about I rustle us up something to eat while you … dabble in your hobby?'

'You aren't going to try and talk me around?' A mottled heat spread over her neck. 'I took it for granted you would.'

'Why?'

'Because you found a way to make a living from your passions.' Sandy shrugged. 'I assumed you thought everyone should do the same?'

'We're all different. What works for one person doesn't for another.' Taran held her gaze. 'And things change. People's perceptions change. I'm seeing a whole lot of things differently now.' He allowed himself to smile. 'Of course, that doesn't mean I'll give up trying to persuade you to pursue your art more seriously – just not today.'

Sandy's laughter bubbled out. 'You're stubborn aren't you?'

'And you're not?'

'Let's call us even.'

Her concession lifted his spirits. 'For the time being you need feeding so I'll go in your kitchen and whip up something to feed you.'

'And then?'

'Then?' Taran pretended not to understand but her eyes gleamed. 'We'll see.' One of their favourite phrases.

Sandy ran her finger over the drawing she did of Taran yesterday while he slept. He'd lingered after dinner until Chip came home and inevitably ended up spending the night. Normally a severe critic of her own work she had to admit she'd captured his intriguing mixture of strength and vulnerability. The shadow of his long dark lashes against the slash of his strong Slavic cheekbones. His tawny hair was starting to get unruly again and she'd tangled her fingers through the thick silky waves to draw him closer while they made love. Intricate details of the fierce Chinese dragon inked on his right bicep. All of those were there along with the twitch of a smile playing around his generous mouth.

She pulled out the narrow wood box she kept under the bed, full of all the special things she hung onto. The postcard sent to her in Madrid by Kurt, her first boyfriend when he returned to Germany. He'd professed his undying love and sworn to return the next summer. If he had done Sandy had been long gone. A dried purple orchid from the lei draped around her neck by Kahale, the Hawaiian boy who taught her to surf. The narrow silver ring twisted into a love-knot that Andy gave her in Paris.

It struck her that all of these gathered memories were part of her past which wasn't the place for Taran's likeness. If she was incredibly lucky it never would be. They'd reached a crossroads and both of them knew it. It'd taken huge courage on her part to admit she loved him partly because of guilt that the feelings she'd had for Andy paled in comparison. A comforting warmth swept through Sandy as she thought about all the ways Taran proved what he couldn't yet put into words and remembered Beth's plea for her to be patient.

The first official meeting of the Rendezvous Lane Action Committee would start in fifteen minutes next door at Jake and Rusty's house and if she didn't hurry up and get dressed they'd be late. Under her black leggings and a black and white check tunic she slipped on a plunging purple lace bra and matching panties. Just in case …

'Are you ready?' She popped her head around her son's bedroom door.

'I don't want to go.' Chip looked mutinous.

'I know but you can't stay here on your own.'

'I don't want to sit and listen to boring stuff.' He pouted. 'I want to play.'

It wouldn't help to remind him what happened the last time at Beth's. 'You can take a pad of paper and your colouring things. Mr T will be there.' Even that didn't bring out his smile. 'Come on or we'll be late.' Sandy steered him downstairs.

They made it as the last stragglers were rolling in. The décor was very traditional because the only changes the men had made since their parents died was to add the two brown leather recliners, set on either side of a new big-screen television.

'There's room for you here.' Taran jumped up from the sofa and beckoned them over. 'Why don't you sit on the floor under my feet, Chip?' He lowered his voice so only Sandy could hear. 'He'll be safe there if Jake needs your help.'

'Thanks.'

'He's a thoughtful boy,' Beth said with a smile, peering around from the other side of Taran.

Sandy couldn't help smiling back. His grandmother had become Taran's biggest cheerleader.

'Right, let's get started.' Jake clapped his hands. 'I'm afraid it's not good news.'

'Yeah, like we didn't expect that,' Lonnie Birch groused. 'This whole thing is a damn waste of time.'

'Ignore him. Get on with it.' Edith gave the man a sharp look.

Sandy's heart sunk as Jake went through everything he'd found out. On an easel he'd pinned up a picture that was an artist's representation of the four monstrosities Byron Cassidy intended to build on their park land. Tall, white, angular modern structures with an abundance of steel and glass. They were three stories high and totally at odds with the rest of the area.

'The land was willed to five Henderson family members,' Jake explained. 'Two of them would sell tomorrow because they want the money and don't care where it comes from. One is vehemently against the plan. The other two haven't made up their minds yet.'

'If we assume for a minute that they do decide to sell, how easy will it be for Cassidy to get planning permission?' Sandy said.

'Well first he'd have to get it rezoned because these aren't single-family dwellings. If he's willing to work with planning staffers to tweak the plans to their satisfaction and it gets recommended to the Planning Commission, I'm not saying it's a done deal but …' Jake couldn't quite meet her eyes.

'Stop bullshitting us.' Birch spoke up again. 'Everyone knows the Metro Council is approving projects similar to this all over the place. They'll hold a public hearing for show but behind the scenes we all know there'll be deals made and that'll be that.'

A large element of truth lay behind the man's blunt

words. The local news was full of stories about Nashville's phenomenal growth but little was made of the impact it had on existing neighbourhoods.

'So what you're saying is that our only real chance of stopping it is to persuade the Hendersons not to sell.'

It pained her to hear Taran spell out the hard truth.

'Yeah, pretty much.'

A sense of hopelessness filled the room.

'You're a defeatist lot.' Beth glared around at them all. 'The first thing to do is invite the five of them here for one of our neighbourhood get-togethers. We can't do much about the naysayers but we can butter up the one who's on our side and work on the two fence-straddlers.'

Sandy's admiration for her old friend soared. 'That's a great plan. Count me in.'

There were a few rumblings of disagreement but when Jake called a vote, the overwhelming majority came down on Beth's side. They decided to hold the party in ten days to allow time to fine-tune their strategy.

Taran lowered his voice to whisper in her ear. 'I'll see Beth home then I'll be back.'

'We'd better not tonight. You've got an early start tomorrow and it's a school and work day for us.' She hated seeing his face fall. 'We'll follow your travels through social media and see you when you get back.'

'Okay, I suppose one of us has to be sensible.'

He said it in such a mournful way Sandy burst into giggles. 'Oh, you poor thing. You'll survive.'

'Ah but will you?' Taran teased then gave her a big wink before turning to Chip. 'What do you want me to bring back from Texas for you?'

Her son's bright smile wrenched a knot in Sandy's heart. What would their lives be like if Taran came to the conclusion he couldn't make a commitment to them after all?

'I'm planning to get us some good Texas hot sauce and maybe a few Texas chiltepin peppers. They're the official state pepper and they'll add a good kick when we make our own barbecue sauce.' Taran grinned at her. 'They're about twenty times hotter than a jalapeno. Probably not for you.'

'We're in agreement there.'

'Good to hear.' Taran's bright gaze bored into Sandy before he turned his attention back to Chip. 'Don't worry, I'll pick up something good.'

'I know you will, Mr T.'

Her son's absolute faith struck home.

'Do they have *Paw Patrol* stuff in Texas?'

'Chip, you mustn't—'

'It's okay. I asked.' Taran pulled out a small leather notebook. 'Let me write it down so I don't forget.'

'I'd really like Marshall's fire truck with the long ladder. It's awesome.'

'That's far too expensive, Chip.' Sandy couldn't let him take advantage of Taran's generosity. 'That's a birthday or Christmas size present.'

'How about something smaller I can fit in my bag more easily?'

It was typical of his innate kindness to pick up on her awkwardness.

'Chase's rescue police cruiser?' Chip said. 'It's cool too.'

Sandy nodded at Taran behind her son's back.

'Sure. I'll look out for one. Out of interest, when is your birthday?'

'It's on the fourth of July. I share my birthday with America,' Chip bragged.

'How awesome is that!'

'You can come to my party.'

'Thank you. I'd love to.'

She longed to beg him not to make promises but Taran's

pained expression brought her up short. Perhaps she should take a leaf from Chip's book and be more trusting.

'Some of us need our beds.' Beth touched Taran's arm. 'Why don't you plan a date with this young lady on Sunday after you get back? This young man and I will be okay won't we Chip?'

'We sure will.' Her little boy beamed. 'Mommy got me the new *Paw Patrol* DVD and we can watch it together.'

'Is that okay with you?' Taran asked

She brushed a kiss over his warm cheek. 'Absolutely. I'll see you on Sunday.'

A hot blush zoomed up her face when he kissed her on the mouth. Sandy didn't think it was reckless to believe that Taran's kiss spoke of promises yet to be made. 'Come on, Chip it's bedtime.'

Chapter Thirty-Two

Sweat trickled down Taran's face but he dove back in for another bite of spicy link sausage, heavy on the red pepper and chilli powder. He'd skipped breakfast and pushed through the hot, humid Texas weather to run a punishing ten miles this morning. Even with his good metabolism he wouldn't survive seven barbecue restaurants in four days without a touch of self-discipline.

When he flew into Houston yesterday he picked up a rental car and drove half an hour outside of the city to be waiting on the doorstep of Blood Bros. BBQ for when they opened. That kicked off the Texas part of his "Southern Spice Tour". It exceeded his expectations and already his followers were lapping up pictures of his lunch of boudin sausage with Thai green chiles and smoked brisket fried rice. In the afternoon he tracked down a hotel for the night and took it easy for a few hours before hitting up the Reveille BBQ Co in Magnolia for their combo dinner plate of pepper brisket, pepper turkey and pepper beef ribs. As far as he was concerned it was hard to go wrong with that theme running through the menu.

Today he'd driven east of the city to Beaumont for lunch at Charlie's.

'More tea, sir?' The smiling bleached blonde waitress filled his glass when he nodded through a mouthful of food. 'This your first time here?'

'Certainly is. Have you worked here long ... Mary Lou?' He checked her name tag.

'Oh Lordy I'm part of the furniture. I was with the boss from when he started with a food truck before we set up a small eat-in place in the back of a convenience store. He bought this restaurant in 2012.'

'Did you grow up around here?'

'Yeah, my family had a smallholding out in the country and in those days I thought comin' into Beaumont was goin' to the big city.'

'Have you travelled much out of Texas?' People and their different lives interested him.

'No, honey but I feel like I have 'cause we get a good mix of folks through here from all over the place.'

Taran offered her one of his business cards. 'I'll advertise my stop here today on my blog and Instagram later.' It'd been a two-hour drive to get here but worth every mile. 'Texas is certainly spoiled for good barbecue joints.'

'We sure are. Where are you off to next?'

'I'm making my way across to Dripping Springs near Austin after this.'

'The Switch?'

He shouldn't be surprised that rival Texas barbecue spots knew each other. 'Is it worth the trip?'

'Some say so.' Her dark eyes shone. 'It won't match us but you won't go hungry.'

That was the closest the other establishment would receive in the way of praise. He pushed his plate away. 'I think that's all the damage I can do here.'

Mary Lou's gaze swept over him and her red and white check uniform strained at the seams when she leaned over the table to give him an eyeful of her generous cleavage. 'You could hang around here Mr "Spice Street Sage" until I get off at three to have a drink or whatever with me and still make it to The Switch for dinner.'

'I appreciate the offer but my lady in Nashville wouldn't be too happy if I took you up on it.'

'She's a lucky soul.'

Sandy would laugh when he rang up later and told her this story.

'You take care and have a nice day.'

'You too.' Taran left a generous tip and headed off in the direction of his next hotel and dinner. It was a four-hour drive but he'd break the trip to shop for Chip's toy. He could've ordered the car online but making the effort this way meant something he couldn't quite define.

Seven o'clock found him sitting in front of another plate of barbecue. He'd ordered The Switch's version of spicy boudin sausage which was fast becoming a new favourite with him. The menu described it as one of their Cajun/Texan specialities and claimed it tasted like the inside of a barrel of Tabasco sauce. They were spot on and the tingling in his mouth woke his taste buds back up. Taran couldn't help thinking that Chip would love the food here and Sandy would do her best to find something tame on the menu in order to humour their obsession with spicy food. He kept doing this. Missing both the boy and his beautiful mother. He'd seen a steam train ride advertised along the way that Chip would love and when he pulled off at a rest area, Taran found himself looking for a safe spot to kick a football around in.

A sort of flatness sneaked in that he wasn't used to experiencing when travelling and sampling new food. He could put it down to eating too much over the last couple of days but didn't believe that for one moment. Taran paid his bill and raced back to the hotel to call Sandy.

'Is this a bad time?'

'Not at all. It's a wonderful surprise. I thought you'd be too busy.'

'I'm never too busy for the two of you.'

'I'm pleased to hear it. Really.' He sensed her smile. 'Is Chip still up?'

'Yeah, he's had his bath and we're reading a book before bed. 'Now he's trying to tug the phone from me because he's realised who I'm talking to.'

'Mr T, when are you coming home? I miss you.'

He swallowed hard. 'I miss you too, kid. I'll be back in Nashville late on Saturday. That's only a couple more days.' Often when he was hanging around at airports and train stations he overheard people talking to their families and saying how much they longed to be home with them again. Taran would wonder why they couldn't make the most of the chance to be somewhere new outside of their ordinary lives but now he understood. He listened as Sandy resorted to bribery in the form of watching an extra TV show tomorrow if Chip let her have the phone back. Time to take a chance. 'In case you were wondering I'm missing you too. I'd have a lot better time if you were both with me.' There was a heartbeat of silence before she spoke again.

'I miss you too.'

'Good.' Taran corrected himself. 'I don't mean it's good that you're unhappy but …' He stumbled over his words. 'No one's ever said they missed me before.' It was a struggle to get his emotions back under control. 'Do you want to know everything I've been up to? I'll save telling you all about Mary Lou until last.'

'You've found another woman already? That's not what I want to hear.' By the lilt in her voice she found it amusing and not in the least threatening.

He rattled out a condensed version of his trip so far. 'I'm staying at a place called Dripping Springs tonight. The name came about because the original settlers needed to call it something in order to get a post office. They got their drinking water from the Milk House branch of the Edwards Aquifer which was a local gathering place for the Tonkawa Indians so a woman named Nannie Moss came up with Dripping Springs.'

'Well, aren't you a fount of information?'

'That's me.'

'Come on. Break me the bad news about Mary Lou.'

Taran chuckled. 'She was a very generously endowed waitress at Charlie's where I ate lunch and what she offered me definitely wasn't on the standard menu. I gently turned her down and said my lady back in Nashville wouldn't be too happy if I accepted. Was I right?'

'Do you even need to ask?'

'Not really but I reckoned it would be polite.'

Sandy's throaty laughter hummed down the line. 'And we know you're always that.'

'I try.' There was so much more he wanted to say but those were conversations to have face-to-face when he returned to Nashville. The first would involve telling Sandy that he loved her because now he had no doubts at all.

Logically Sandy knew other women must come on to him. Taran was a hot single guy travelling alone so it must happen all the time. That didn't mean she had to like it but at least they'd laughed about it together. 'No one tempts me these days apart from you.'

How did he expect her to answer with Chip laying on the bed next to her?

'Mommy, why is your face red?'

'Yes, Mommy why is your face red?' He parroted Chip.

Sandy fought to suppress another giggle. 'I must go. Enjoy the rest of your time in Texas.'

'I'll see you on Saturday.'

'I thought our date was Sunday?'

'Yep but that doesn't mean I've got to wait until then to see you again does it?' Taran asked. 'Chip will want his presents and there might be something for—'

'Your lady?'

'Are you bothered by me calling you that?'

'Not bothered exactly but it's ... something to talk about.'

She'd add it to the mile-long list. 'We'll see you on Saturday. Enjoy the rest of your trip and stay away from predatory waitresses.'

'Happy to obey, sweetheart.'

'You'll call again tomorrow?'

'Yes, I'll call.' Taran's voice turned husky. 'I'm happy that you asked.'

'Good.' Her throat tightened. 'Sleep well. I've got a story to finish reading.' Sandy glanced down at Chip and smiled. 'Well I did but my tired little boy's asleep.'

'Perhaps you should follow his example.'

'Not a bad idea.' After they said goodnight she wandered across the room to shut Chip's curtains and stared out at the velvety night sky. Sandy picked out the brightest star and made a wish. It might be childish but she thought they needed all the help they could get.

Hours later she was still awake and staring at her bedroom ceiling as the luminous red numbers on her alarm clock trundled towards three o'clock. She might as well get up and work on the drawing Jake asked her to come up with. He'd talked to all of the Henderson heirs and persuaded four out of the five to come to their Memorial Day shindig to kick off the traditional start of summer.

'I need a picture to rival the one Cassidy had of his appalling development plan. Maybe one of your charcoal sketches imagining what the space could look like if it belonged to the community?'

Sandy ignored any defeatist thoughts and set to work. Sometimes ideas flew onto the paper and this was one of them. Not much over an hour later she stared at the end result and was pleased with how it'd turned out. The watercolour pencils she used gave her the fine details of a pencil drawing but when activated by water turned into a form of watercolour paint with all its shades and nuances. In the imaginary creation, children were throwing a ball on the grass while their parents chatted and watched them from wood benches placed under large shade trees. A group of older people played boules in one corner and on the opposite side a large barbecue grill, several picnic tables and benches stood on soft grey paving stones sheltered by a gabled roof.

A surge of excitement shot through her. If Beth could remain positive at her age, Sandy wasn't giving up either. Not where it came to the Rendezvous Lane park. Or Taran Rossi.

Chapter Thirty-Three

Thank goodness he'd dragged himself out of bed this morning for another run. Most people focused on how many calories they were burning off while exercising but he'd been spurred on by dreams of the John Mueller Black Box Barbecue joint and black pepper coated brisket. Eaten from a trailer in a parking lot this had truly been going back to his street food roots. By the time he ate, wandered around the downtown historic district and arrived at his hotel, the social media hits for his travels were zooming off the charts. He hadn't only struck a chord with his American fans but people around the world who were interested in regional cooking. A glimmer of his old zest for discovering new food and new places had sneaked back in but he still couldn't wait to fly back to Nashville tomorrow. He was convinced that there was no reason why the best of both worlds wasn't possible. He'd love to reignite Sandy's travel bug and show her life didn't have to be a question of either/or.

His phone pinged with a new message and Taran frowned when he saw his mother's name pop up.

Your father suffered a mild stroke yesterday. He ordered me not to bother you and it doesn't appear to be serious but I thought you should know.

Bother him? If that wasn't a sad condemnation of their detached relationship he didn't know what was. He sent off a swift reply.

Thanks for telling me and keep me up to date. I'll come if you need me.

He and his parents didn't do 'needing' each other but perhaps there was a first time for everything.

Taran returned to studying the online menu for Miller's

188

Smokehouse to decide what to order for dinner tonight. It would be a toss-up between "El Gallo Picante" or "Fire in the Bowl", both loaded with enough spice and heat to make him a happy man.

A couple of hours later he conceded defeat after finishing the best food he'd tasted so far. He didn't have a spare inch of stomach space left to squeeze in one of the home-made desserts so Taran satisfied himself with buying Chip a Fourth of July themed T-shirt instead in the restaurant's gift shop. He also picked up two bottles of barbecue sauce for Lashonda and Harry – one original and one spicy – like them.

Time to call Sandy.

'I can't wait for you to see the drawing I've done.' Excitement coursed through her voice as she described the imaginary park she'd created.

He murmured a sort of vague approval because he couldn't bear to dampen her eagerness. It didn't seem to have occurred to anyone that even if by a miracle Cassidy's plan failed to go through, the Hendersons would receive other offers. His grandmother's neighbours were hard-working people but most lived pay cheque to pay cheque or were retired and scraping by on Social Security. They didn't have the sort of money needed to buy the land for the community. He'd considered offering to help from his own savings but that would still leave a huge shortfall and possibly offend people who'd become his friends.

'I thought you'd be more enthusiastic?'

'I am.'

'But?'

'We'll talk when I get back.' He waited for her to push but she backed off and changed the subject to Chip's parent-teacher conference at school.

'Ms Vestal said she'd noticed a positive change in him these last couple of months. He's much more confident, he's happier to answer questions in class and is making friends easier too. She asked if I knew what might've happened to cause the improvement and I said I couldn't think of anything but I wasn't being completely honest.' Sandy cleared her throat. 'You've made a difference to him.' Before he had a chance to protest she raced on. 'Please don't take that as any sort of pressure it's only what I see as the truth.'

He thought he'd moved past his old demons but it was still a struggle not to equate it with Alexei calling him táta.

'Oh, God I shouldn't have told you. Not when I can't see you. You're panicking now aren't you? I've dumped something on your shoulders that you're not ready for and I totally didn't mean to ...'

Taran heard a sob catch in her throat and ached to promise Sandy it would be all right.

'Good night, we'll see you tomorrow.'

She hung up before he could find something, anything to say that allowed for his sliver of uncertainty while still reassuring her of how much he cared about her and Chip.

Sandy took her mug of steaming camomile tea out onto the porch as the first pink slivers of sunrise sneaked into the sky. Was Taran awake early too and thinking about her because his sleep was disturbed by the abrupt end to their conversation last night? It'd been stupid of her to think he'd be pleased to hear about his positive effect on Chip's efforts to settle into school.

'The day Alexei called me táta, the Czech word for daddy, I packed my bag and left.'

It broke her heart that the tentative promises he'd made recently were clearly worthless when it came to push and shove. She'd invited him into her bed and her life and Chip worshipped him. How much more of a fool could she have made of herself? Sandy rested a hand on her stomach. Much worse if her fears came true. She'd managed to put her other vaguer symptoms down to stress until she barely made it to the bathroom this morning before throwing up.

She refused to make the same mistake twice and put Taran in the impossible position of feeling obliged to commit to a family life that he didn't want. Sandy had never been certain deep down that he was a hundred per cent convinced that she hadn't tricked Andy into fatherhood. If she tried to keep a possible pregnancy secret until after he left Nashville that wouldn't work when his grandmother lived next door and Beth wouldn't believe her if she claimed that Taran wasn't the father.

Maybe she'd be lucky and discover it was a false alarm. A picture of a baby who was the absolute image of him floated into her brain. For a few foolish seconds she pictured his deep golden eyes brimming with tears as he cradled his son or daughter, overcome with awe at the child they'd created together.

Sandy could hear Lashonda now.

'Grow up, girl and have some sense. I like the guy and anyone can see he loves y'all but a baby? That's another kettle of fish.'

There was only one thing to do. Buy a test. Pee on the stick. Find out one way or the other and then deal with it.

'Hey Sandy how's it goin'?' Jake slowed his car outside her house and yelled out of the window.

'Where are you off to this early?' It was a long standing joke between them that he chose entertainment law because most of his clients didn't surface before midday.

'I'm goin' on a date.'

Sandy wandered down her steps and out to the street. 'At this time of the day? I hope she's worth it.'

'I guess I'll find out. We're meeting at the Pancake Pantry in Hillsboro Village for breakfast. She suggested it. I suppose her thinkin' is that her whole day won't be trashed if it's a bust.'

'You're going on a blind date at six in the morning. You must be desperate!' Sandy regretted the words as soon as they left her mouth.

'We aren't all as lucky as you. Why are you looking so miserable anyway? I thought lover boy was coming back tonight?' Jake's eyes narrowed. 'Don't tell me he's dumped you and done a runner? I never could see him settling down here to play happy families. So much for his supposed support for the park project.'

'Taran hasn't dumped me and he's flying in from Houston later.'

Jake peered at her closely and frowned. 'Are you sure you're okay? You look kind of green.'

Before she could answer another rush of nausea swept through her and she lost her tea all over the pavement. Her friend hopped out of his car and when he touched her arm, Sandy burst into tears.

'Let's get you inside.' Jake slipped his arm around her and steered her towards the house.

'But you're—'

'Doesn't matter. It's a waste of time anyway. You're right. I'm never going to hit it off with a woman who's raring to go at the crack of dawn.' He looked sheepish. 'Unless it's for a better reason than pancakes.'

Once they were sitting at her kitchen table and she'd cried her way through half a box of tissues while blubbing out the whole sad story he stared at her in dismay.

'Pregnant?'

'I don't know for sure.'

Jake gave a wry smile. 'Of course you do. This isn't your first rodeo.'

He was right. An official test would only confirm what she'd refused to accept when she checked the calendar for the date of her last period.

'Hey, maybe I'm wrong and Taran will change when he discovers he's going to be a father.' His Adam's apple bobbed. 'I sure would if a woman gave *me* that sort of news.'

Sandy could hardly look at him. Things could've been so different. But she loved Taran with all her heart and nothing could change that.

'Mommy where are you? You weren't in your bed.' Chip's voice drifted down the stairs.

'I'm in the kitchen, sweetheart.'

Jake tapped in a quick message into his phone. 'That's me free. After you see Chip a minute I'll take care of him and you can go back to bed. You need flat ginger ale and dry crackers. If you haven't got any in the house I'll go out and buy some.'

'How do you know about morning sickness?'

He raised an eyebrow. 'I haven't been living in a cave the last forty years.'

'Mommy.' Chip raced into the room with his hair sticking up and face flushed from sleep. 'I'm starving. Can we have chocolate chip pancakes? Please.'

A rush of bile filled her mouth.

'Your mom's feeling a bit puny this morning,' Jake said. 'How about we fix us some food and let her rest a while?'

'Okay. And can we watch a show on TV.'

'We sure can.'

She didn't have the energy to object. Sandy grabbed a handful of crackers and a ginger soda from the fridge. The unacknowledged event must've made her put those items on her grocery list last week. 'Thanks, boys.'

Buried under the bedcovers, she struggled to push everything away and drifted off to sleep.

Chapter Thirty-Four

Taran hurried up the path and knocked on Sandy's door. Luckily his flight was on time and the traffic coming back from the airport wasn't too heavy so he'd said a quick hello to his grandmother and dumped his bags before hurrying next door.

'Oh, hi. Look I'm super tired so do you mind if we catch up tomorrow instead?'

Everything about Sandy seemed drained from her pale skin to her flat eyes and lank uncombed hair. 'Of course.' Disappointment flooded through him. 'Is there anything I can do to help?'

'Oh you've done enough.' She bit her lip and stared down at the ground. 'I'm sorry. Forget I said that.'

Taran's mind whirred. Something beyond his wary reaction to Chip's teacher's report or a lack of sleep on Sandy's part was going on.

'Call me tomorrow.'

'Are you sure?'

'Yes. Goodnight.' Sandy stepped back and closed the door in his face.

He wasn't sure what to do with the bag of gifts he'd brought but supposed they'd have to wait and headed back down the path.

'Off for good now I suppose?' Jake Naylor stood on the pavement glaring at him. 'I hoped you'd be man enough to prove me wrong but don't fret too much. We'll all rally around to help Sandy.'

'Help her with what? I don't have a clue what you're talking about.'

'You're trying to deny it's yours? Don't you think more highly of Sandy than that?' Jake sneered at him.

'What's mine?' An icy chill trickled down his spine.

'The baby of course.'

'She's pregnant?' Taran turned to stone. 'How the hell do you know that and I don't?'

'Because I hadn't plucked up the courage to tell you yet.' Sandy's shaky voice pierced through his anger.

'But you told him.' He swung back around to face her. 'Do you want to explain yourself?'

'Not out here.'

His grandmother's command stopped Taran in his tracks and he became aware that people were emerging from their homes to see what all the fuss was about.

'Jake, go into Sandy's house please and listen out for Chip in case he wakes up.' Beth was her usual no-nonsense self. 'We'll go into my place for a civilised conversation.'

He considered raising an objection to being bossed around like a naughty toddler and by Sandy's gaping mouth she felt the same way. Neither of them spoke.

Five minutes later the three of them sat around his grandmother's kitchen table.

'I know you're both mad at me for interfering but without a referee you'll say things you regret later.' Beth managed a tight smile. 'Before we start let's establish one thing. Sandy, was Jake telling the truth when he claimed you're expecting Taran's baby?'

It was hard not to admire his take-no-prisoners grandmother.

'I haven't done an official test but ... yes.' Sandy looked like a ghost.

'Why did you tell Jake before me?' He couldn't hold back his resentment.

'I didn't plan to but I was sick outside this morning in the middle of talking to him. He was kind.' She gulped. 'I had to tell someone and you weren't here.' Sandy slapped a hand over her mouth and raced over to the sink to be sick.

Taran came up behind her and slipped his arm around her waist as she slumped forward, clinging on to the edge of the counter until the heaving stopped.

'And don't you dare say I did this on purpose.' She pushed him away.

'Oh Sandy love he wouldn't do that.' Beth looked horrified.

'Yes he would because he thinks that's what I did to Andy,' Sandy snapped.

'That's not true. You told me it was an accident and I—'

'I saw the doubt in your eyes.'

Her quiet sadness tore at him but she was wrong. 'But how …?' Taran slid an awkward glance at his grandmother.

'There's no need to be shy around me.' Beth shook her head. 'Believe it or not I know where babies come from and how they get there in the first place.'

Sandy tilted her chin in the air. 'In case you've forgotten, the first time we had sex I told you I wasn't on the pill because I hadn't been with another man since Andy died.' Her face flamed. 'You had problems with the condom. There's your "accident".'

'So you're how far along?'

'Four weeks. I'm counting from the second week of April because after that we were more careful so that means we'll be ringing in the New Year with a new baby. It's uncommon to get sick this early but some people do.' She exhaled a resigned sigh. 'I did with Chip.'

'Well I think it's wonderful.' A huge grin creased his grandmother's face. 'I can't wait to cuddle my great-grandbaby.'

'It's all right.' Sandy sounded defeated. 'I don't expect anything from you, Taran. I know you've had some changes of heart recently but I'm not sure it's altered your views on family and commitment. You never wanted this.'

'Neither did you,' he protested. Her expression altered and all of a sudden he sensed her pitying him.

*

196

Sandy managed her first smile in forever. Taran was right and totally wrong at the same time. After Andy's death she closed the door on her dream of having another child but now she was getting used to the idea, Sandy welcomed it, challenges and all. Chip was doing fine without a father so there was no reason for this baby not to flourish as well. For a start it would have a doting great-grandmother and more honorary aunts and uncles than it could shake a stick at among all of her friends and neighbours. 'I know we've a lot to talk about but I honestly am exhausted. When you've had the chance to let the news sink in come and see me again.' She struggled to treat this like one of her difficult debt collection calls when she blotted out her natural sympathies and focused on getting a successful result. 'If you choose to be involved in the baby's life that's up to you.' Sandy patted Beth's hand and tears filled her old friend's soft blue eyes. 'I'm going to need a great babysitter you know.'

'I'll walk you home.' Taran squeezed her shoulder.

'There's no need.'

'I'll walk you home.' A ribbon of steel ran through his voice.

'Fine.'

Neither of them spoke and when they reached her front door, Taran grasped her arm.

'I get that you're tired but I'd really like you go in and thank Jake then send him away. I need to talk to you now, not tomorrow or next week.'

'Okay.'

'Thank you.'

'What for?'

'Not arguing.'

A shimmer of amusement danced in his eyes and for a fleeting moment she wondered if there was still any hope for them. Taran followed her inside and Jake immediately sprang up from the sofa.

'Oh hi, is everything okay?' He gave them both a wary look.

'We're good. Thanks for looking out for Chip.'

'No problem. I never heard a peep from him.' He glanced between them both. 'Right, well I'll be going then.'

'Yeah, it's been a long day.'

Finally alone they stood like statues.

'Can I get you anything?' Taran looked leery of her.

'A stronger stomach?' The miserable attempt to crack a joke failed. 'I meant what I said. I've done this once on my own and I can do it again.'

'What if I don't want you to?'

Sandy saw red. 'It's my body. I'm keeping this baby whether you—'

'That's not what I meant.' Taran's voice rose. 'Although if it's what you wanted … I'd support you. It's your choice.' He slumped on the sofa. 'What I'm trying to get across to you is that I intend to be around for our child. I take full responsibility and I won't let you down.'

She longed to argue and tell him she wasn't seeking another dutiful relationship but couldn't deny him the chance to be a part of their baby's life. Sandy wasn't naïve. Many other babies around the world had far worse starts but it still gnawed at her soul. The magic she'd shared with Taran would disappear in a mound of custody agreements, shared parenting plans and halved bills. She struggled to be grateful. 'Thank you.'

'Thank you? You have nothing to thank me for. I'm the one who knocked you up in the first place. That'll teach me to brag about being careful.'

Another wave of nausea swept through her. 'Please go,' Sandy begged. 'You can come over and see Chip tomorrow.'

'What about our date?'

'Date? What's the point?' She bit back tears. 'We're way past dating now.'

Taran scrambled to his feet. 'I'll go. If Chip wants to kick a ball around send him over tomorrow afternoon and I'll give him his presents then. It'll give you a break plus you obviously don't want me around.'

Want him around? Her body ached from wanting him so badly. She suspected it would only take one kind word to break through the wall she'd erected to protect herself. Sandy steeled herself not to reach out to touch the red tail of his dragon tattoo that peaked from under the arm of his tight black T-shirt. 'I would say thank you again but you'll tell me off.' That didn't soften his grim expression.

'Good night. I'll see myself out.'

Sandy stared at the floor and waited until the front door closed behind him before she allowed a flood of silent tears to wrack her exhausted body.

Chapter Thirty-Five

'Good Lord, boy, have you never heard of Sunday being a day of rest?'

His grandmother stood at the back door shaking her head at him. Taran set down the axe and wiped the sweat from his eyes. The temperatures were starting to crank up and in another few weeks summer would be in full swing. 'You wanted that dead holly bush taking out.'

'I sure did and I appreciate you gettin' on with it but take a break and I'll fix us a bite of breakfast.'

'I'm not hungry and I'd be lousy company.' He wasn't in the mood for another round of recriminations. After he returned from Sandy's last night, Beth couldn't understand why he wasn't rushing out to buy a diamond ring, ready to fall on one knee and propose to Sandy. She'd love nothing better than for him to settle in Rendezvous Lane with a wife, a ready-made son and a baby on the way. The sharp dose of reality he doled out meant they'd barely been talking to each other by bedtime.

'I don't care. Do as you're told.'

He recognised the glint in her eyes as a clear warning. 'Yes, ma'am.' Even his mangled attempt at a southern accent didn't brighten her sour expression.

'That's much better.'

'I need a shower first.' He trailed into the house behind her.

'Don't take too long. My biscuits deserve to be eaten fresh.' At last a faint smile curved the edges of her mouth. 'You haven't touched a thing since you got home. Your poor stomach must think your throat's been cut.'

Considering the amount of food he'd consumed in Texas he sincerely doubted that. It was the turmoil surrounding Sandy that killed his appetite.

Taran tugged a comb through his damp hair to make himself vaguely presentable. That nudged him to pull out his phone and scroll through to the pictures of he and Chip at the barber's shop. His resolve tightened. He wasn't letting the boy down any more than he'd abandon this new baby. If Sandy didn't want him as a lover he'd be forced to accept that but as for disappearing from their lives – that wasn't happening.

When he strolled back into the kitchen, Beth gave him a scathing look.

'If you scowl any harder you'll curdle the milk.'

'Did I tell you my mother rang while I was away?' Taran pulled out a chair and sat down.

'You know you didn't.' She frowned. 'Is Naomi all right?'

'She's fine but Jakub had a mild stroke. I think he'll be okay but she didn't go into a lot of detail.'

'I'm so sorry to hear that but I'm surprised she thought to tell you.'

'Yeah, me too.' He stirred a dash of cream into his coffee. 'I'm thinking of popping over there to check on him.'

'You're going to "pop" four thousand miles over the pond because you're a dutiful son who's so close to his folks?' Beth scoffed. 'It wouldn't be an excuse to put a bit of distance between you and Sandy I suppose?'

Taran felt his face burn. 'I can't win can I? You criticised me for being fancy-free and going through life alone but now I'm trying to be more mature and thoughtful that's wrong too.'

'I'm sorry, my love. I didn't mean to get at you.'

The deep lines etched in her face sent a powerful reminder that his poor grandmother was eighty-five and still recovering from serious heart surgery. So much for being mature and thoughtful. 'No, I'm sorry Granny.' He reached across and squeezed her hand. 'I'm a bear today and not fit to be around anyone. I'll go upstairs to do some work and stay out of the way.'

'Do you love Sandy?'

The out-of-the-blue question took him by surprise.

'It's a simple enough question. Do you or don't you?' Beth gave him a long hard stare, taking him back to being a little boy when he'd lied about breaking one of her china ornaments.

'Yes. I was planning to tell her yesterday when I came back but ...' He clenched his hands, struggling with a rush of emotion.

'Then tell her now. Let her know you love her and Chip and that you'll love the baby too.'

'She wouldn't want to hear it.'

'Rubbish.'

'It's too late now because she'll accuse me of saying it out of duty. That's how things were with Andy when she found she was pregnant with Chip. She told me yesterday she was already raising one child on her own and could do it again.'

Beth tutted. 'That's not the same as *wanting* to do it alone. You silly man. She didn't get a choice the first time because Andy died but you and I both know that Sandy didn't love him the way she loves you so there's your difference.'

Taran remembered imagining a flash of longing in Sandy's eyes when he claimed she didn't want him around. He'd debated taking a chance and telling her the truth about what was in his heart but in the heat of the moment the opportunity disappeared so he'd walked out. He did the same thing now.

'When is it too soon to go and see Mr T?' Chip hopped around on one foot.

'He said anytime this afternoon.' Sandy pointed to the large clock over the mantelpiece and smiled as he studied the numbers, talking to himself as he worked it out.

'Eleven o'clock.' His sigh throbbed with frustration. 'That's ages.'

Thankfully she felt less fragile this morning. For now she was putting off telling her little boy about the huge change coming to their lives and finding a way to explain any role Taran might play. 'Why don't we set up our painting things on the table? You could do one to take over for Ms Beth while I work on something to sell at the next flea market.'

'I suppose.' Chip tilted a smile, the absolute image of his father. 'Could we have popcorn?'

If she tipped out a small bowl of dry popcorn for herself before adding butter to Chip's bowl that might be okay for her stomach. 'Okay.' Sandy ruffled his hair. 'Come on let's get busy.'

An hour or so later she sat back and stretched out her neck. Chip was still hunched over the paper with his tongue poking out and a deep frown etched into his forehead. His teacher often complained about his short attention span but like so many people if something captured his interest the problem disappeared.

'Do you think Ms Beth will like it?' He held up his painting. 'It's you, me and Mr T outside our house.'

Sandy fixed on a smile when she saw the two larger stick figures holding hands with the smaller figure in the centre. 'I'm sure she'll love it.'

'Can we go now?' Chip begged.

'If I call to say you're coming you could walk over on your own.'

'Oh wow cool.'

He didn't realise the selfish reason behind her offer and Sandy exhaled with relief when Beth answered her phone so she wasn't forced to speak to Taran. A few minutes later she watched Chip run next door and thrust his painting in Beth's hands before he waved back at her and disappeared into the house. She'd been working on a charcoal drawing of the Parthenon in Nashville and should finish it up but flipped over to a fresh page in her sketch pad instead. Soon another picture of Taran emerged, captured when they were in bed together and so intimate and personal it sent a flush of heat pulsing through her body.

Sandy rested her head on the table and wept. It would be a cop-out to put her see-sawing emotions down to pregnancy hormones because that was only half the story. A sudden tap on the front door took her by surprise and she swiped at her swollen eyes.

'It's me.'

The sound of Taran's deep rumbling voice made her stomach churn.

'Chip needs something. Can I come in?'

She reluctantly opened the door.

'God, you look terrible. Have you been sick again?'

'No, I was ... It doesn't matter.'

'Yes it does.' Taran gently held her arm and steered her over to the sofa. 'Tell me what's up. I guess that's a bloody stupid question, right?'

'Yeah, but we're expert at those.' Sandy attempted to smile.

'I'm here because we wanted to kick a ball around and Chip's wearing flip-flops so I said I'd fetch his trainers.' A ruddy flush darkened his face. 'It's something of an excuse though if I'm honest. Is there any chance you'll reconsider and go on that date tonight? Please.'

'I don't think it's a good idea.'

'We need to talk. My grandmother's furious with me and rightly so.' His wry smile got to her. 'Chip's the only person who's still fond of me and that's because he's too young to know any better.'

Sandy hated to see him beat himself up this way.

'I know you're tired but we needn't stay out late.'

Before she would've made a joke about him wanting to whisk her off to bed but teasing of any sort and especially that kind was off limits now. 'Okay.'

'Really?'

'Yeah, if the offer's still open?'

'Oh it's open all right.' Taran stroked his warm thumb down her tear-stained cheek. 'I hate that I've made you cry.'

Denying it would be futile and an outright lie.

'If you don't mind, we'll keep Chip for the rest of the afternoon.' A faint grin pulled at his mouth. 'As the old southern saying goes, Beth is in hog heaven fussing over him. Take a nap or do whatever you want and come on over when you're ready to head out.'

'Thanks … and don't say I've nothing to thank you for because there's a whole bunch. Chip's shoes are by the back door.'

'I'll get them.'

After he left, Sandy wondered if she'd been foolish to agree to tonight but it was too late now.

Chapter Thirty-Six

It about killed Taran to sit in the crowded restaurant across from Sandy and not touch her, smelling the hint of patchouli and lime fragrance she favoured and watch her hands rested on her stomach to protect their child. He'd just finished explaining about his father's stroke and told her he was considering going to England as soon as possible. 'My gran says I'm only going to put some distance between us.'

'Do you think she's right?'

The flickering candlelight reflected off the tired shadows under her eyes but despite that there was a new glow to Sandy. He ached to be the man she and Chip deserved. 'I don't know.'

'Oh I think you do.' Her quiet sigh tore him apart. 'You sound like me when I tried to pretend I couldn't be pregnant.'

'I suppose there might be something in it.' Taran's admission brought a faint smile to her full glossy mouth. 'This might not be the right time or place to say this but I've skirted around it long enough. I love you. I love Chip. And I'm going to love our baby. We can find a way to make this work.' His blunt declaration made Sandy's jaw drop. 'Let's get out of here so we can talk properly.' Taran signalled to the waiter to bring the bill. 'We could go to a coffee shop or—'

'Back to my place.' Her shining deep blue eyes allowed him to hope.

'Back to your place it is.'

In the car the silence was an easy one, neither were in the mood for inconsequential chatter.

'I'll make us some tea and we'll sit outside,' Sandy said.

'Whatever you want.'

'Is camomile okay?' She grimaced. 'I'm trying to be good

and cut back on caffeine. It's only fair you suffer along with me.'

'Happy to oblige.'

Soon they were settled on her tiny back patio, using only the light seeping out through the kitchen window to gauge each other by.

'Don't you love that scent?' She sniffed the warm air. 'It's coral honeysuckle. Beth recommended I planted it because the flowers are such a pretty colour and the fragrance is second to none.' Sandy's sly glance shifted his way. 'She's a smart woman.'

'Yep, she certainly is.' Taran set down his tea. 'She nailed it when she asked if I'd actually spelled it out that I love you, Chip and our baby. Beth told me I was an idiot for believing your insistence about doing this alone. I'm surprised she didn't smack me around the head.'

'She probably would've done if she could reach.' Her brief glimmer of good humour faded. 'Did you mean what you said in the restaurant?' Sandy looked wary. 'If you simply trotted it out because you want to do the right thing I'm not going there again.'

'I didn't say it lightly and I meant every word. Everything fell into place for me when I was in Texas and I was longing to tell you as soon as I came back but it threw me when you said about the baby.' Taran grasped her warm hands. 'It doesn't mean I know how to follow through but I'll try my damnedest. I honestly feel I need to go see my parents although I can't put into words why it's so important. I don't want to leave you right now but I must if that makes any sense?'

'Yeah it does.' She rested her forehead against his. 'You'll come back to us.'

'Always.' The promise hummed in the air between them, as significant as any promise he'd ever made.

'That's all I need for now. Apart from one thing.'

'Name it.'

'Oh I will.' Laughter bubbled out of her. 'Take me to bed.'

'I'd love to but I've got two questions.' She looked puzzled. 'What about Chip? Shall I pop over and bring him back home?'

'There's no need. Beth said she'd tuck him up in her bed for the night and they'd be fine.'

It struck him that the two women had plotted this all out.

'What's your second question?'

'Uh, is it safe to ... you know ...' A whoosh of heat flooded his face.

'Yeah, it's perfectly fine. There's no indication this is anything but an uncomplicated pregnancy. And believe me if I felt sick tonight I wouldn't be offering. Unless of course you don't fancy me any more?' The humorous lilt to her voice didn't match her serious expression.

'Trust me. Not fancying you isn't an issue.' Taran pulled her over onto his lap. 'Trying to keep my hands off you all evening now that's been ... painful.' He stroked his fingers over her white silk tunic and she drew in a hiss of breath as he teased around the generous curve of her breasts. 'Are you this sensitive everywhere these days?'

'Come upstairs and find out.'

'Why the wicked smile?'

Sandy trailed a finger down Taran's snake tattoo. 'After your half-naked exhibition in front of the Tangled Yarns that evening Jo-Ellen asked me if I'd seen the curled cobra heading down south. Of course I denied it.' She gave a throaty laugh. 'Wow, I think I've turned into a snake charmer.'

'You must be a witch. I should be bloody worn out. Are all pregnant women this randy?'

'Are you complaining?' It hadn't been this way with Andy but Taran didn't need to hear that.

His lazy smile widened as he shifted over her. 'Does it feel like it?'

She tightened around him until his startling golden eyes flared and when they'd eventually wrung out every ounce of energy from each other they collapsed in a mess of tangled limbs and searing kisses.

Taran pushed a lose strand of hair from her face and traced around the contours of her mouth. 'Is it okay if I stay the night?'

'I ought to warn you that mornings aren't my best time. It could be a case of me violently heaving over the toilet instead of more hot sex.'

'I want to be here for both.'

'I'll have to set an alarm because it's a school day for Chip and I've got to work.'

'No problem. I've got a trip to plan.' Taran looked wistful. 'I wish you could come too.'

'So do I but you need to do this alone.'

'I know.' Frustration laced his voice.

Sandy tightened her arms around his neck and burrowed into his chest. 'Just remember you're coming home to us.'

'I certainly am.' He dropped a soft kiss into her hair. 'Home isn't the bad kind of four-letter word any longer, sweetheart.'

'I never thought I'd hear you say that.' Sandy couldn't stop smiling.

'You're not the only one!'

Even before the alarm went off Sandy threw up three times. She succumbed to Taran's urging and picked up her phone to ring Harry.

'I'm sorry but I'm not up to coming into work this morning I'm a bit off colour. I'm sure I'll be better again later.' She struggled not to think about the effect on her pay.

'Take care of yourself and um.' Harry cleared his throat. '... You know. The little one.'

'Lashonda told you. I should've guessed.'

'Yeah, but I promise I won't say a word to anyone else.' He lowered his voice. 'Congratulations. Taran's a lucky devil.'

Was that him being polite or did Harry want a family of his own? She couldn't ask him outright but Sandy knew her friend's plans for the future didn't include more babies. Sandy made a non-committal response and got off the phone.

'Tricky?' Taran passed her a glass of flat ginger ale with crushed ice, the most effective nausea suppressor she'd found.

'Harry's a good guy and an awesome boss and he was fine.' She told him about the baby comment.

'They must've discussed it surely before he proposed.'

'I suppose so.'

'How about I fetch Chip and bring him back here so we can get him ready for school. You can supervise if you're up to it and then I'll run him there in Beth's car.'

She almost asked if he was sure. It still felt a huge step to take these kinds of small things for granted. 'Thanks.'

'You're welcome.'

Sandy flopped back on the bed and smiled.

'I hate leaving her like this, Granny.' Taran tossed clothes in his backpack anyhow, nothing like his usual meticulous packing. 'She understands and everything and we're all good and that but I still feel guilty.'

'You know she's plenty of us keepin' an eye on her and we won't wait 'til she asks for help either.'

He'd no doubt Sandy's friends would come together and make sure she was all right while he was away. Seven days. That was a quick turnaround for such a long trip but right now it sounded interminable.

'Was Naomi pleased to hear you're coming to see them?'

He concentrated on sorting out his passport and travel documents while he decided how best to reply.

'Oh Lord you haven't told her have you? You're a dumb boy sometimes.' His grandmother dissected his reticence like a skilled surgeon.

Taran felt an irrational sense of disappointment. He'd thought she would understand. The small boy who had fought for his parents' attention before eventually giving up was still buried inside him and he wasn't sure he could cope if Naomi told him it wasn't convenient or necessary for him to visit.

'Only sometimes?' The self-deprecating aside failed and he received the famous Beth Parsons frozen-solid-at-five-paces glare. 'I reckoned on phoning when I touch down in London.'

'Do it your way.'

He gave in. 'I'll ring from the Nashville airport this evening. Okay?'

Beth's scowl softened.

Taran zipped his bag shut. 'That'll do. I'm off to pick up Chip.' He'd offered to bring the little boy there to play after school so Sandy could work later to catch up on some of the time she'd missed through being sick. Chip had already negotiated a book on castles and a toy London double-decker bus as his souvenirs. The kid was catching on. Sandy's only request was simple.

'Come home safe.'

Chapter Thirty-Seven

'We'll visit your father in the morning. This late in the day he gets very tired.'

Taran guessed the truth behind his mother's smooth explanation. Jakub Rossi didn't want his son seeing him at his worst. It'd been three years since they'd all met and Naomi had changed. There were softer edges to her thin, wiry body and setting aside the strain caused by his father's recent poor health she appeared more relaxed and content than he remembered.

'I could do with some fresh air,' Taran said. The dragging tiredness from the journey pulled at him and if he didn't stay active he'd crash far too early and be awake with the seagulls.

'Do you want to take a stroll down to the harbour?'

'Yeah, why not.' He'd been surprised when they arrived at the compact grey stone house that bore little resemblance to the opulent homes his parents had lived in around the globe. It nestled along with half a dozen other similar properties at one end of St Lanow, a tiny village clinging to the rugged north Cornwall coastline.

'We could pop into the Smuggler's Arms for a drink.' Two blobs of heat lit up his mother's cheeks. 'I told a few of our friends that you were coming and they'd love to meet you.'

'That would be great.' They were being too polite with each other but he wasn't sure how to get past that. 'While we walk you can tell me more about what happened to Jakub.' He started using their Christian names when he was about twelve when Naomi in particular preferred strangers not to realise she was old enough to be his mother.

Out of the blue his mother linked her arm through his and gazed up at him. 'When did you get so tall?'

'Uh, I stopped growing at about seventeen.' His answer

blew open the distance between them again and a shadow dimmed her golden eyes, the mirror image of his own.

They wandered along a narrow winding lane enclosed by ancient hedges and the soft air carried the scent of newly-cut grass in the nearby field. Naomi touched one of the delicate white flowers jutting out in a glorious profusion.

'Aren't they beautiful? I think Queen Anne's lace is so much prettier a name than cow parsley. Margy Poltair used them in the church flower arrangements last Sunday and when the light streamed in through the stained-glass windows I'd never seen anything more lovely.'

'You go to church?'

'We wanted to fit in when we moved here. Make it clear we weren't fly-by-night second home interlopers. Put down roots.'

'Why?'

The road opened out along with the view and his mother's mouth curved in a gentle smile. Taran stared out across the calm blue-grey sea where the last edges of daylight caught and glittered like fiery diamonds.

'Does that answer your question?'

He could argue that she'd seen more spectacular views but likened it to his own recent desire to belong somewhere and to someone. 'There's a special woman I want to tell you both about ... and a few other things.'

'If all goes well your father will be home on Thursday. Save it and talk to us together.'

Taran tamped down a flare of frustration. 'Okay, let's get that drink.'

They strode down the short steep hill to the tiny harbour which appeared to be the centre of St Lanow.

'This is our only shop. It sells the basics and it's got a post office tucked in the back corner plus an owner who knows and passes on any item of gossip worth listening to.' Naomi stopped outside a small, squat building, the windows covered with posters advertising the week's special offers. 'In your great-grandparents' time they could buy everything they needed here but now we've got to drive into Newquay.' She pointed to a road leading away from the harbour. 'Tamsin, your great-grandmother lived in a little cottage up there.'

'That's incredible. You'll have to show me another day. How did she come to meet Frank? It was during the war, right?'

'I didn't realise you knew anything about them.'

When he explained that he'd asked Beth to show him all the photographs his mother looked astonished.

'The story goes that Tamsin went with a few of her friends to a tea dance at a church hall in Newquay. It was close to St Mawgan which was the airbase taken over by the US Army Air Force in 1943. The local girls wanted to check out the Americans.' Naomi's eyes sparkled. 'The lure of stockings and chocolate was enough to make a lot of run-of-the-mill Americans extraordinarily attractive to young women ground down by rationing and four years of war.'

'That makes sense.'

Taran and his mother lingered by the harbour wall watching men tie up their boats for the night and take down the signs for trips around the bay and mackerel fishing.

'Poor Frank had never been out of Tennessee before.' Naomi chuckled. 'He was as redneck as they come and bowled over by the sassy Cornish girl who was determined not to spend the rest of her life in St Lanow.'

'She must be where we get our adventurous spirit from.'

'I suppose so but it's curious to me that when she settled in Nashville she wasn't interested in going far. They only came back here once to see her family.'

'Granny misses you.' Taran wished he'd phrased that more tactfully when the light left his mother's face.

'Yeah, I know and I miss her too.'

'I don't understand why you don't visit? Money isn't an issue so what's stopping you?' He'd seen his grandmother poring over her treasured family photo albums night after night with tears in her eyes. 'She's eighty-five and not in great health.'

'I'm well aware of that and I don't need a lecture from you on family duty,' Naomi snapped at him. 'Let's go get that drink.'

He was hardly the only one to blame for their lack of closeness but Taran kept his mouth shut and followed her across the road to the Smuggler's Arms. As soon as they stepped inside they were swallowed up in a swarm of people who wanted to shake hands with him and ask after his father's health. For now he'd go with the flow and see how things panned out.

'It's hard to explain, Chip but where Mr T is staying in England it's the middle of the night now.' Sandy's explanation made her son frown. She'd received one brief phone call to say he'd arrived in Cornwall yesterday, his mother was fine and they planned to visit his father soon.

'Do you think he's bought my castle book yet?'

'I don't know. He said he hoped to visit one and take pictures for you.' Her son's latest obsession was King Arthur and the Knights of the Round Table, sparked by stories Taran had told him. It amused her because the closest Tennessee had to anything medieval was the castle at Triune, about a half-hour's drive away from them, where a local man decided to start building a replica of a Welsh border castle in 1970 and was still adding to it.

'Cool.'

'Off you go and brush your teeth. I'll be up in a few minutes.' A wave of exhaustion swept through her but at least it wasn't nausea. It helped that she hadn't needed to cook dinner this evening again although she was slightly afraid by the time Taran returned they'd be knee-deep in casseroles. The Tangled Yarns and her other neighbours seemed to forget they were only feeding her and a small boy.

Her phone jangled to life with a video call request from Taran.

'Hello, sweetheart.' The grainy picture cleared enough for her to gaze on his tempting smile. 'Did I catch you at a bad time?'

'No, Chip's getting ready for bed. I'll keep you to myself for a few minutes then take the phone upstairs with me so you can chat to him. We were just talking about you ... and castles of course.'

'Don't worry I won't forget the book he wants.'

'More important than that how are your folks?'

'Talk about a long story.'

He shoved a hand through his messy hair and she recalled the way she'd run her fingers through its silky thickness on Sunday night. No doubt he'd say it was due another cut but secretly she preferred it longer.

'My father's doing okay and he should be home from the hospital tomorrow. It's absolutely beautiful here you'd love it.'

'You'll take me one day.' Sandy's confident statement brought his smile back out. 'Were they happy to hear about ... us?'

'I started to tell Naomi that I'd met someone but she insisted I wait to give her the full story when Jakub gets home. She's worried about my father so I didn't want to push.'

Sandy fought to hang on to a smile.

'You think I'm a coward.'

'No. I'm hormonal and tired that's all.' That wasn't a lie. Under the circumstances she probably wasn't being fair to him. She knew enough about Taran's strained relationship with his parents to know this wasn't an easy time for him either.

'I love you.'

'I know and I love you too.' She eased off the sofa. 'Let's go say goodnight to Chip.'

Chapter Thirty-Eight

Taran's breath caught in his throat when his father entered the house, leaning on his mother's arm. Vulnerable. He'd never used that word to describe his father before today. Jakub's short stocky build, swarthy complexion and shock of thick dark hair were still clear indicators of his Polish/Italian heritage but he appeared shrunken and unsure. Last week his mother found him collapsed in the garden and called for an ambulance when she saw his droopy face and heard his slurred speech. The hospital's prompt treatment prevented the mild stroke from escalating and his doctor was hopeful of him making a full recovery. For now his speech was still halting and the right side of his body was weak.

'Why don't you take a nap before dinner?' Naomi suggested.

'I'm sixty not ninety.'

That sounded more like his brusque, no-nonsense father.

'I'll make us all some green tea and bring it out on the terrace.'

Taran suppressed a smile when he caught Jakub scowling. The doctor at the stroke centre had banned him from the thick dark espresso he relied on to get through the day except for one rationed cup. 'Shall we walk out together?' Taran hesitated before offering his father his arm.

'I suppose.'

They slowly made their way to the small brick patio, his father's hesitant steps nothing like his usual brisk pace. The terracotta pots of colourful flowers and bright red sun umbrella brought a touch of the Mediterranean to this corner of Cornwall and they settled down in two of the white wood chairs that were softened by squishy yellow cushions. 'It's a lovely spot. It'd be hard to tire of this view. I can see why you've settled here.'

'Can you? Really? Is our little rolling stone ready to gather some moss?' The effort to speak clearly tired his father.

'That's one reason why I came. I wanted to talk to you both.'

'Have I missed anything?' Naomi arrived to join them and set down a Chinese red lacquer tray on the glass table.

'Only that the boy didn't travel all this way out of concern for me.'

'That's not what I said,' Taran protested.

His mother poured out three mugs of tea and passed them around. 'Now Jakub, you need to let him explain.'

It wasn't easy to work out how best to approach everything he needed to say but one of Sandy's favourite songs came to mind. She had, what was to him at least, an inexplicable love for *The Sound of Music* and knew all the music off by heart. The beginning was usually the best place to start. Twenty minutes later their tea was cold, his father's expression had turned to stone and his mother's eyes were glassy with tears.

'So, you blame us for your wandering ways. What about the advantages that came with your upbringing? Think of all the places you've been and experiences you had that other children could only dream of.' Jakub scoffed.

'We're going to be grandparents!' Naomi's smile couldn't be broader.

'I don't blame you for anything and I truly am grateful for everything you exposed me to growing up.' Taran tried to reassure his father then grinned at his mother. 'Yes you're definitely going to be grandparents.'

'But you said … damn. The words won't … come fast enough.' Jakub slammed his mug down.

'You're not supposed to get agitated,' Naomi chided.

'I'm sorry, my sweet *kochanie*.'

The Polish endearment touched Taran and their deep love for each other struck him all over again as his mother wrapped her arms around her ailing husband. As a child that same closeness made him feel excluded although he guessed they'd be shocked if he said that aloud.

'Let our boy put your mind at rest first and then I want to hear every single thing about Sandy, Chip and the sweet baby we're going to have.' Naomi gave him a sad look. 'I know I was a lousy mother.' She gripped his father's arm. 'We weren't the best parents. Oh you had everything money could buy, the best nannies and a tip-top education but—'

'Not our time and attention.' Jakub managed to form the words. 'You will be different with your child.'

'But will I know how?' The anguished question stunned them into silence.

'Oh sweetheart.' Naomi sighed. 'You're a kind-hearted, thoughtful man and you'll love that little boy or girl with everything you have. We were too wrapped up in ourselves but you'll learn from our mistakes.' A faint smile brightened her sombre eyes. 'You'll make your own mistakes and that's inevitable because we're human and it's what we do.'

'Sandy and I still have a lot to work out.'

'We've been married for thirty-eight years and we're still workin' it out.' She laughed. 'That's what keeps it interesting.'

'Why don't you make another pot of that nasty tea?' Jakub wrinkled his nose. 'I will pretend it is … decent coffee. Then you answer your … your mother's questions.'

Taran's spirits soared. He was happy to bore them to death with every detail of life in Nashville and his plans for the future.

'What's put the smile on your face because, sure as God made green apples, it can't be work?' Lashonda had glanced up from her desk. 'Must be the lurve god.'

'Yep, Taran rang while I was eating lunch.' Sandy couldn't hide her happiness.

'I wouldn't call a yoghurt at your desk lunch.' Her friend opened her drawer and pulled out a plastic box. 'Here, have one of my ham sandwiches. I made too many.'

'I better not stop. Our awesome new boss won't turn a blind eye like Harry used to.'

'Yeah, tell me about it.'

The atmosphere in the office had suffered since the sharp-tongued Patricia Hayes took charge. Harry's kindness had make the job more bearable because he knew how to get the best work from people without grinding them down. Since he started his new job last week, two people had quit already under Patricia's strict new regime. Sandy had dragged herself into work several days when she felt lousy rather than incur the woman's wrath.

'Come over for dinner tonight so we can have a good natter,' Sandy said.

'I don't want you puking trying to cook for me.'

'Don't worry, my neighbours are keeping me well stocked. Feeding you won't be an issue.'

'Good afternoon, ladies.' Patricia appeared out of nowhere. 'Is there a problem I can help you with Sandy if Lashonda is too busy?' She gave the clock a pointed look.

'No thanks. It's solved.' Sandy almost exploded with giggles when her best friend stuck out her tongue and made waggly bunny ears behind their boss's retreating back.

Nothing could dampen her spirits today, even being questioned by Chip's teacher about why he'd refused to paint a summer beach scene like the rest of the class.

'He insisted on painting a garden instead. The picture showed him playing soccer with what looked like a large ape. I didn't ask about the ape.'

Taran would laugh himself silly when she passed on that little fun nugget. Now she planned to enjoy a relaxing evening.

'What's it going to be?' She pulled various dishes of food from the fridge. 'Chicken pot pie, Western baked beans or cheese enchiladas.'

'Enchiladas.' Her little boy didn't hesitate. 'With tons and tons of hot sauce.'

'Sounds good to me, kid.' Lashonda and Chip high-fived.

'Fine. I'll eat the pie.' Spicy Mexican food wasn't her favourite at the best of times and certainly not these days. It was a misnomer to label her problem morning sickness because she never knew when it might strike.

After they heated up their food they sat around the kitchen table. Half way through eating her meal a tightening cramp pulled at Sandy's stomach. She grasped the edge of the table as sharp pains stabbed through her belly. 'I've got a bit of a headache.' Despite Sandy attempting to sound normal, her friend looked concerned. 'I think I'll go lie down for a few minutes.'

'Good idea,' Lashonda said. 'Chip, seeing we're about done eatin' how about you take a cookie in the other room and I'll come in there too after I help your mom clear up.'

'Cool.' He grabbed one of the butterscotch oatmeal cookies Brandy Charlton had left on the doorstep and raced out of the kitchen.

'What's up?'

Sandy grimaced and told Lashonda the truth.

'We need to get you to the emergency room. I'll get Beth to pop over and sit with Chip.'

'What will I tell him?' She struggled to stand up and winced as another cramp hit her. 'Oh no.' Red dots were blossoming in the crotch of her jeans. 'He doesn't know—'

'I'll make somethin' up.'

Several hours later she lay in a hospital bed hooked up to a raft of monitors and tried to convince herself that the news from the doctor was encouraging.

'Your pelvic exam looked good and the amniotic sac is intact. The ultrasound was clear too. Until we get the results of your blood tests and the hormone levels in particular I can't say any more.'

Another message from Taran popped into her phone. She'd ignored his earlier texts because she couldn't lie to him and didn't want him worrying when he was so far away and couldn't do anything to help.

'I've brought you a decent nightdress.' Lashonda bustled into the room, waving around a sliver of purple silk. 'No one wants to be seen in one of those ugly hospital numbers.'

'Sure you wouldn't like to paint my nails to match?'

'I'll be happy to. You're soundin' a little brighter now. Any news?'

Sandy shook her head. 'I haven't had any further bleeding so that's good.'

'It sure is. By the way, Chip is fine. I told him you'd eaten something that made you sick and the doctors are giving you medicine to fix you up.' Her friend frowned. 'Beth's a bit on edge because Taran keeps calling her. The poor man's convinced you're upset about something because you haven't responded to any of his messages.'

'I can't.'

'You need to be honest and tell him what's goin' on rather than let him think the worst.'

'What's worse than this?' Tears brimmed over and dripped down her face.

Lashonda perched on the bed and wrapped her warm arms around Sandy. 'Having doubts about whether you still love him is what's worse.'

'It's the middle of the night there now. I'll wait.'

'You really think he's going to sleep a wink for worryin' about you.' She shoved Sandy's phone at her. 'If you won't call him I will.'

Taran picked up on the first ring and by the time she'd finished telling him where she was they were both upset.

'Oh, honey I'm sorry I'm not there. I'll try to change my flight and come back a day early. That's the quickest I can make it from here.'

'But your folks—'

'Will totally understand.' His voice turned husky. 'We've talked more than we've ever done before. I'll tell you all about it when I see you.'

'That's awesome.'

'Remember I love you so much.'

'But if we lose the baby ...' Sandy couldn't put her fear into words.

'I pray we don't lose him or her but if that happens we'll get through it together. I'll still love you. I'll still love Chip and want the three of us to make a life together.'

Another rush of tears bubbled out of her.

'I'll be there as soon as I can.'

'I know you will.' And she did. Taran had swept away the last of her doubts.

Chapter Thirty-Nine

Taran stood with his parents on the breezy station platform, waiting for the London train to arrive. For lunch they'd eaten delicious Cornish pasties – home-made by his mother, the same woman who barely knew where the kitchen even was when he was growing up.

'As soon as your father's well enough to travel we'll come to Nashville.' The colour rose in his mother's face. One of the conversations they had yesterday touched on why she'd stayed away for so long.

'Every time I see my mom I feel bad about not living closer to help her out so it's easier to deal with the guilt long distance. Now I realise that's cowardly and selfish.'

'Granny will be pleased.' Taran knew that "pleased" wouldn't come close to covering it but didn't want Naomi to feel worse than she already did. Beth was all they had left because his paternal grandparents died before Taran was born and Jakub had lost touch with his relatives in Poland and Italy.

'Here's the train.' His father grasped Taran's arm. 'Travel safe … you tell us how things are with … with Sandy when you … get an update.'

Jakub's stumbled words were partly due to the after-effects of the stroke but he was clearly overwhelmed with emotion too.

'They'll be the making of you.' Tears sparkled on his mother's dark eyelashes as she gazed at him and Taran sensed her imprinting his image on her brain.

'You're right.' Every cloud had a silver lining and although the relationship with his parents hadn't always been easy they were on a better track now. Second chances weren't granted to everyone.

The three of them exchanged hugs and tears stung Taran's eyes as he eased away. 'Next time I come to Cornwall I'll bring them with me.'

'We'd love that.' Naomi stroked his cheek. 'Off with you.'

He hitched on his backpack and jumped on the train. This would be the most interminable journey he'd ever endured. Four hours on the train. An overnight hotel stay in Reading. A bus to the airport and then a nine-hour flight across the Atlantic. Taran settled into his reserved seat and pulled out his phone. He hadn't spoken to Sandy yet today because of the time difference but she answered immediately and they managed to chat for a few minutes before the dodgy signal put an end to the conversation.

'You okay, mate?'

Taran became aware of the young man sitting opposite talking to him.

'I don't mean to stick my nose in but you seem a bit upset.'

He swiped a hand over his damp cheeks and managed a weak smile. 'Yeah I was but I think it's going to be okay.' Before he could hold back he poured out the whole story. By the time Taran reached the part about the news looking more encouraging and that Sandy hopefully wouldn't lose their baby he suspected he'd totally embarrassed the stranger.

'That deserves a beer.' The man fished a couple of cans out of his bag and passed one over.

'Cheers.' Taran smiled to himself. Sandy would laugh and call that such a guy way to wrap up an awkward conversation.

Sandy clutched the sheets to stop herself from smacking the smug-faced young doctor. He'd explained that one of the groups of women more prone to threatened or actual miscarriages were those "of advanced maternal age". Seriously? At thirty-six?

'Twenty to thirty per cent of all pregnant women will

experience bleeding in the first twenty weeks of pregnancy and half of those will carry their babies to term.'

'So it's a case of wait and see?' She heard the wobble in her voice.

'Pretty much I'm afraid. Overall your blood test results were good although your progesterone levels were borderline so we'll give you an injection to give those a boost. Some doctors recommend bed rest although the benefits aren't proven so I'm hesitant to do that.' The doctor's tone softened. 'This might sound blunt but maintaining this pregnancy is unlikely to be down to anything you do or don't do. Some things are out of our hands.'

'What about sex?' Lashonda asked.

'For heaven's sake that's the last thing on my mind.'

'Not at all. It's a perfectly reasonable question.' A smile pulled at his thin lips. 'Once your symptoms disappear it will be fine to resume sexual activity although you might consider saving the Fifty Shades variety for later.' He hesitated. 'I understand how frightening this is for you.'

'No you can't. Not really.' Lashonda turned on him. 'I'm sure you do your best but at the end of the day you'll never be on the business end of losing a baby. I know what it's like and it sucks.'

Sandy's head spun. 'You … you never said.'

'I know. I never meant to keep it from you but you know what it's like for something to hurt too much to talk about.'

She nodded and choked back tears. They had few secrets from each other but she'd always been too ashamed to be completely honest about her relationship with Andy.

'I lost a baby very early on in the pregnancy about four months after the boys were born. Things were already shaky with their daddy and the timing would've been lousy.' Her dark eyes looked haunted. 'It still hurt like hell.' She tapped her head. 'Up here was the worst.'

'Your friend is right.' The doctor nodded. 'Some women benefit from therapy to talk through their fears but that's up to you. My recommendations for you are the same I give all expectant mothers. No alcohol, smoking or illegal drugs and minimise your caffeine consumption. Consistent and comprehensive prenatal care is the best thing we can do for your baby.' The smile reached his bright green eyes. 'My prescription is to go home and hug your little boy, take a nap, eat a healthy dinner and have an early night. When your partner comes home let him fuss over you because this experience will have scared him too although he might not show it.'

'Thank you.' She wiped at her damp eyes. 'Oh these damn hormones.'

'Come on, kid let's get you out of here.' Lashonda hitched Sandy's bag on her shoulder. 'Hop in.'

Sandy grimaced at the wheelchair.

'It's hospital regulations as far as the front door. Sorry.' The doctor shrugged.

'Harry will drive around to the pick-up lane to meet us.'

A few minutes later Sandy savoured the soft May sunshine on her face. Statistics weren't her thing but she'd cling to the fact that their baby was clearly a fighter. She climbed into the back seat of Harry's black Cadillac and sunk into the luxurious tan leather with a sigh of relief.

'Do I look terrible?' She touched her straggly hair. 'I don't want to frighten Chip.'

'You're a touch on the pale side that's all,' Harry reassured her.

'I considered telling Chip about the baby when I get home but I've decided to wait until Taran gets back so we can do it together.'

Sandy gripped her mug of tea and stared at the sunrise from her front porch.

Slashes of pink and gold light coloured the early morning sky and the birds had started their dawn chorus. Taran's flight was due to leave London in about three hours and she had the sinking suspicion time would drag slower than a turtle competing in a marathon until he arrived in Nashville.

Apart from the miscarriage scare another worry niggled at her. While Taran was away she'd done something reckless that might come back to bite her. He always shut down the conversation when she brought up the subject of Alexei Novak and although he would never admit it she suspected this was hurting his ability to move on. It hadn't been difficult to find the young man's Instagram account and when she scrolled through the pictures she found lots of the handsome dark-haired Alexei with his arms around his grandparents at a stunning lake house. The most recent post stunned her into taking action. It showed him holding up a university acceptance letter and when she zoomed in to read the details, Sandy knew she'd no choice but to reach out to Alexei Novak. The question was when to tell Taran and how would he react?

'Come back inside and eat some breakfast.' Lashonda came to join her. She and Harry had insisted on staying the night after they brought her home from the hospital yesterday. 'Your little one needs the calories.'

'Fine,' Sandy murmured. 'I'll do as I'm told.'

'That makes a change.' Her friend's warm laughter was infectious and they wandered into the house arm in arm.

She managed to force down a turkey sausage biscuit and some freshly cut melon then pushed away from the table. Chip and Harry were squashed together on the sofa, watching her little boy's favourite show.

'He's good with kids.'

'Yeah.' Lashonda's eyes narrowed. 'Are you sayin' that for a reason?'

She couldn't be anything less than honest. 'I thought Harry

sounded envious of Taran when he first congratulated me on the baby.'

'We've touched on that subject already.' Lashonda patted her left hand. 'There won't be any sparkly ring goin' there until I'm sure of a lot of things and that was one of them. I know I'm still plenty young enough but I just don't want to start all over again and Harry's happy with that. We're interested in adoption or being foster parents though. There are lots of kids out there who need good homes.'

'That's an awesome idea.' Sandy found herself shooed towards the living room.

'Put your feet up or I'm packing you off to bed. You know I'm not happy about you and Chip goin' to the airport on your own later. I wish you'd change your mind and let us give you a lift.'

'I'm fine. You heard what the doctor said. I don't intend to do anything stupid but I can't wrap myself in cotton wool for the next seven or eight months either. I'm only about six weeks along and that would drive me crazy.' She tried to reassure her friend. 'I've already booked an Uber car and they'll drop us off right outside the arrivals area. I won't have to walk far and I'm pretty sure Taran's strong enough to carry his own luggage after we meet up. Okay?'

'I suppose.'

'Is there room for one more?' Sandy smiled at Harry and Chip who quickly made a space for her on the sofa. A few hours watching mindless cartoons should help pass the time.

Chapter Forty

'Are you ready, Mommy?' Chip begged. He'd nearly driven her crazy running in and out of the kitchen all day to study the clock after Lashonda and Harry left. She'd booked their car for five o'clock, although that was far too soon because after Taran's plane landed he'd still have to clear Customs and Immigration.

She'd subtly deterred Beth from joining them by asking her old friend to cook dinner for them all.

'Taran hasn't had my chicken and dumplings in forever. He used to love them as a little boy.'

Sandy doubted the bland recipe – an old-fashioned southern staple – was still one of his favourites but he'd wolf it down to please his grandmother.

'Mommy.' Chip tugged on her arm.

'Sorry, yes I'm ready.' She glanced at her phone. 'Our driver is here now. Let's go.'

She took it as a good omen when they were dropped off right outside the door.

'Don't mess up my sign, Mommy.' Chip hopped along beside her like a hyperactive kangaroo. He'd spent all afternoon turning a large rectangle of bright orange poster-board into an unmissable welcome sign. All Sandy was allowed to do was trace the outline of the letters for Chip to fill in. Apart from that the enterprise demanded copious amounts of glitter, scraps of fabric and glue.

ONE, TWO, THREE WE LOVE MR T

They picked a spot where they should be visible when Taran arrived and settled down to wait. Half an hour later Chip was sitting cross-legged on the carpet and resting against Sandy's legs with the poster lying next to him.

'How much longer, Mommy?'

'I don't call this much of a welcome.' Taran's deep rich voice boomed out of nowhere and he strode towards them laughing.

'We didn't see you!' She drank in the sight of him. The smile might be a little tired around the edges but that didn't matter when he was standing in front of her, more handsome than she remembered, staring at her "that way" and back where he belonged. The hours they'd spent video chatting and peering at each other on tiny screens paled in comparison. Of course what she really wanted was to be hugged and kissed until she couldn't think straight but that would have to wait.

'You missed it!' Chip wailed.

Sandy swept the poster up and shoved it into her son's hands.

'Wow, is that for me?' Taran's eyes were suspiciously bright.

'No one else is called Mr T.'

Her little boy's declaration made them both smile.

'They sure aren't. Let me have a good look.' He scrutinised it carefully. 'You've done an awesome job. May I keep it? I'd love to put it up in my bedroom.'

Chip's wide grin threatened to split his face in two.

'Hang on a second and we can do a swap.' Taran unzipped his backpack and held out a wrapped present. 'One castle book as promised. Tomorrow I'll tell you all about the incredible one I visited and show you lots of pictures.'

'Cool.' Chip ripped off the paper, flipped open the first page and let out a delighted yell as a 3-D castle popped up.

'It shows you all the different parts of the building and what they're for.'

'That's perfect,' Sandy said.

Taran's voice turned raspy. 'I think it's time to go home.'

No words ever sounded so good.

Taran prised the book from Chip's hands, set it quietly on the bedside table and slipped out of the room, leaving the little boy to sleep and dream of brave knights, soaring stone turrets and giant catapults. His mother's advice jumped to the forefront of his brain.

'Take things slow with Sandy. She's had a massive scare about the baby and will be shaky inside even if she doesn't appear that way on the surface.'

He strolled downstairs and offered to make tea.

'Only a week in England and they've got you converted?'

'I'm not sure I'll ever be a huge fan but I thought you could do with a cup.'

'Leave it for now and sit down.' She patted the seat next to her. 'You've been back for nearly three hours and I'm still waiting for a proper kiss. I excused you while Chip was around and we were eating dinner with Beth.' A teasing smile lit up her face. 'All bets are off now.'

Taran brushed his lips over her warm mouth and tamped down the desires surging through him as her perfumed softness wrapped in a teasing cloak around him.

'Is that the best you can do? I'm not gonna break. Why are you treating me like a shy teenager on his first date?'

He swallowed the emotions threatening to cut off his ability to speak. 'My mother warned me not to minimise how the threat to our baby has affected you.'

Sandy's eyes shone. 'I appreciate her concern and your … restraint.' Matching red-hot circles bloomed on her cheeks. 'You need to hear everything that happened and all the information and advice the doctor shared. I couldn't tell you the full story over our video chats.'

Taran relaxed when she nestled into him and restricted himself to a few brief questions while she spoke. 'And you've had no more problems?'

'No, but I'm still worried.'

'That's nothing to be ashamed of. I'm scared too.' Taran slipped one hand down to rest on her still flat stomach.

'It'll be sad if we're too frightened to enjoy this pregnancy.'

He tightened his arms around her and told her about the conversations he had with his father. One thing in particular that Jakub said stuck in his mind.

'You and Sandy need to be honest with each other. I've admitted to your mother how badly this stroke frightened me and she's done the same in return. I've been forced to face my own mortality but on the plus side it's put everything else in perspective.'

'The mental side is the biggest challenge isn't it?' Sandy echoed his own thoughts.

'Yeah, I didn't appreciate how much I love this baby already until …' He couldn't finish the sentence.

'I'm the same. I couldn't believe the surge of relief I felt when the doctor showed me the baby moving on the scan.'

'Wow I can't wait to see that.' Taran choked up again.

'But we've got each other and that's huge.' A flicker of sadness crossed her face and he guessed she was remembering Andy.

'It's all that matters.' Now he gave her the kiss she'd asked for and she melted in his arms.

'Is there any chance of sharing your bed tonight?' Taran quickly qualified the question. 'I simply want to hold you and wake up with you.' He cracked a smile. 'Frankly I'm too jet-lagged to perform anyway so you're not in any danger.'

'That would be wonderful.'

They made their way upstairs and when he watched her sleep later Taran was swamped with an overwhelming sense of rightness. He silently swore never to take her or their love for granted. Whatever it took he'd strive to be the man Sandy needed and deserved. It wouldn't always be easy, nothing worthwhile ever was but with her love he felt he could do anything.

'Goodness me, when you sleep you really sleep.'

Sandy's lilting voice seeped into his brain and he eased open one eye and caught her amusement. 'I suppose the other times I've been here I didn't do much sleeping.' The inference behind his comment deepened her smile.

'Are you hungry?'

His stomach rumbled. 'There's your answer. I'm starving.'

'Beth's chicken and dumplings didn't stay with you? They woke me with heartburn in the middle of the night.'

'I ate enough not to offend but under-seasoned chicken and gluey lumps of dough don't really hit the spot.' He shuddered. 'Of course if you tell her that I'll deny every word.'

'My lips are sealed. Don't worry I won't be whipping them up for you anytime soon because I'm not super fond of them either.'

Chip's excited voice drifted in through the bedroom door.

'Are you ever gonna wake up, Mr T?'

She buried her head in his chest to stifle her giggles.

'I'll be down in five minutes, Chip'

'I'm watching the clock.'

'Are you pleased I taught him to tell the time?' Sandy whispered.

'He'll never be a problem where I'm concerned.'

'I know that.' She pressed a kiss on his mouth. 'It's one of the many reasons why I love you.'

'Many? You going to tell me all about them?'

Sandy's eyes glittered. 'What a vain man. I suppose you want to hear you're the hottest thing on two legs? That I've never laughed or had so much fun with any other man?' Her smile fell away. 'How about that every hour felt like a month when you were away? And when I was stupidly afraid to tell you I might lose our baby because I had the tiniest nugget of doubt that it was the glue holding us together?' Big, fat tears trickled down her cheeks. 'You told me then that if that happened we'd get through it together. That you would always love me and Chip and want the three of us to make a life together.'

'I meant every word,' Taran whispered.

'I know.' A sigh slipped out of her. 'I'd love to stay here in bed with you all day but we've a little boy waiting for us downstairs and in case you've forgotten it's the Memorial Day barbecue tomorrow. We get our chance to wow the Henderson family and show them how awesome Rendezvous Lane is. If the stars align and a miracle happens they'll give up the chance to make a small fortune from selling the land because they're generous warm-hearted people.'

Taran grimaced. 'Can't believe it slipped my mind.'

'I've got lots to do today to get ready.'

'You're not supposed to be overdoing it and—'

'Look I've been swamped with casseroles and advice while you were away and although I appreciate everyone's concern and especially yours I've got enough sense not to do anything dumb. Jake, Rusty and the Tangled Yarns have everything planned for the barbecue event and the only thing they're allowing me to do is supervise. If I try lifting one finger they'll probably chop it off.'

Later he'd make sure to thank everyone, but he'd do it on the quiet so she didn't feel ganged up on. 'Fair enough.'

'I'm impressed. You managed to say that without flinching.' Sandy yawned and stretched out in the bed. 'I think I'll take a shower. You can talk castles with Chip and fix breakfast for us all. That should satisfy your nurturing tendencies for a while.'

He kept his answer to a long, lingering kiss. Smart men knew when to let the woman they love have the last word.

Chapter Forty-One

Sandy glared at the rain beating against her kitchen window. Rain to kick off summer season in Nashville. Seriously? She had organised the Memorial Day barbecue with military precision. Except for making a Plan B in case of bad weather.

'Now what the f—devil are we goin' to do?' Rusty wilted under Beth's stern glare. Taran's grandmother didn't consider anything less than the world coming to an end an excuse for bad language.

'We move it indoors of course.'

'But that defeats the whole point of showing the Hendersons how we use the land and we don't have a house big enough to hold everyone.' Sandy hated to put the damper on her old friend's unmatchable optimism.

'They're not gonna appreciate getting soaked are they?' Beth ran blithely on. 'The boys can still grill outdoors under a tarp. That's not a problem is it?' She fixed her eagle eyes on the Naylor twins who meekly nodded their agreement. 'We'll pick say three houses to make food and drink available in and people can meander from one to the other. Luiz, can you set up some kind of games for the kids at your place?'

'Yeah, I suppose—'

'Good man.' Beth cut him off with a broad smile. 'Jake, we'll make your house at Number One the headquarters where we display the boards showing our plans for the park. Sandy, you and Taran are in charge of the food, sharing it around and topping up as necessary. We'll rope in a couple of the teenagers as your runners.'

Sandy poked Taran's arm to hint that he should attempt to talk sense into his steamroller of a grandmother but he gave her a resigned look.

'I bet you anythin' the weather clears up by mid-afternoon

and we'll drag them outside then.' Beth's stern gaze swept over them all, daring anyone to disagree.

'I bet you anything it doesn't,' Sandy whispered in his ear.

'Oh ye of little faith.' Beth wagged her finger. Her eighty-five-year-old ears were functioning in tip-top form.

'Sorry.' Later she'd get revenge for the smirk plastered all over her lover's face.

'Chip can come over to my house and help me and Pedro.' Luiz gave her a hesitant look. 'If that is okay and you trust me to keep him safe?'

With everyone watching she couldn't ask the million and one questions racing around her head. 'Of course, that would be a great help and he'll love it.' She crouched in front of Chip and reiterated the rules three times before hugging him and sending him off with a bright smile.

'Well done.' Taran squeezed her hand. 'You're awesome.'

Sandy pulled him to her for a lingering kiss. 'We'd better get busy before your grandmother catches us slacking.' The warmth flooded into his golden eyes. Tonight she might not be able to resist indulging in far more than a kiss.

Taran focused on his assigned task, making sure the Donaldson kids delivered fresh burgers and hot dogs to the three different locations instead of sloping off to chat to their friends or curl up in a corner glued to their phones. Every time he caught a flash of Sandy's peacock blue kaftan he bit back the urge to tell her to sit down and rest. That was a touch hypocritical of him because he couldn't forget the open invitation in her enigmatic smile earlier and wasn't sure he'd have the strength to resist her when they were alone.

'I need your help.' Rusty sidled up to him. 'We've got a bit of a problem over at my place and you might have better luck than me diffusing it.' A deep flush ruddied his face. 'Jake won't be any help because he caused the mess in the first place.'

'Sure, I'm happy to give it a try. I must tell Sandy first and nab someone else to do my job or she'll be hauling crates of sodas around behind my back.'

'Like trying to pin down running water isn't it?' Rusty chuckled.

'Yeah, you could say that. I'll be over in five. Promise.' He buttonholed Jo-Ellen's husband Pete to keep an eye on things before tracking down Sandy. 'Rusty's probably fussing over nothing but I'll go and see.'

Mother Nature had paid attention to his grandmother and slivers of blue sky were poking through the clouds. Sounds of a loud argument drifted out through the open front door as he stepped inside the Naylors' house. The overriding voice belonged to Byron Cassidy and if Beth heard him she'd swat the foul-mouthed man around the head.

'If you think gettin' into Kayla's pants is gonna stop my development you're up the creek without a paddle.'

This didn't look good. Cassidy grabbed a fistful of Jake's shirt and hauled him off his feet. By his glazed expression, the lawyer must've knocked back a few beers and Taran took a guess he'd flirted with Kayla, a statuesque brunette and one of the Henderson heirs who displayed a cleavage to rival a Playboy bunny.

'It's none of your business if I decide to sleep with Jake.' Kayla's glossy red mouth curled into a satisfied smile. 'You sweet-talked me into bed to try to get my vote on selling the land to your company so what's the difference?'

'How about we go somewhere quiet to sort this out?' No one took any notice of Taran.

'For heaven's sake Kayla, don't turn this into a circus. Granddad wouldn't be happy.'

He recognised Jimmy Henderson from the pictures he'd seen; the gangly redhead was another of Emory Henderson's heirs.

238

'Oh for God's sake grow a pair.' Kayla sneered at her cousin.

Taran picked out the other two heirs who'd accepted today's invitation from the gaggle of people gathered to watch the excitement going on. Sandy had marked out Mary Lou Henderson Whitford with her clichéd southern big hair and colour coordinated outfit as the toughest nut to crack. The older lady was determined to fund her retirement with the proceeds of Cassidy's buyout and he guessed she came today to push her viewpoint. Their last visitor was the young gum-chewing bleached blonde, draped over the arm of the sofa. Vivian Henderson Whitford was refusing to sell in order to put one over on her family who she usually preferred to have as little to do with as possible. Carter Henderson, the oldest of the heirs, had flatly refused their invitation and was one hundred percent behind selling the land.

'Cassidy would do anything to get his hands on Granddaddy's land.' Kayla threw a withering glance at Vivian. 'Even you if he thought it would change your mind.'

'You cow.'

Taran placed his body between the two irate women. 'Calm down, ladies.'

'She's no lady.' Vivian scoffed at her cousin.

'Could we try to be civil please?' The women fell silent and returned to glaring at each other. Taran focused his attention back on Jake. 'Why don't you go outside and get some fresh air?'

'Who the hell do you think you are ordering me around?'

'Someone with a tad of common sense, bro. Let's go.' Rusty grabbed his brother's arm.

The sooner he could clear the room of curious observers the better. 'The weather's improved so why don't you all go and get things kicked off in the park?' Taran's suggestion had the hoped for effect and people started to move away. He expected someone to complain that he was an outsider with no right to take over but no one spoke up. It was time to put his money where his mouth was.

Sandy struggled to concentrate as Edith rattled off her supposedly secret recipe for devilled eggs before the head of the Tangled Yarns scuttled off to tell someone else. Everything was going smoothly since they moved the party outside but she couldn't see any of the Henderson family watching the Rendezvous Lane residents making the most of the park. Rusty had given her a brief rundown on what had happened at his house and she itched to discover how things were going but Chip was back with her now and she couldn't leave him unsupervised.

This was exactly what she'd envisaged. The grills had been fired up again and a mouth-watering aroma wafted around in the soft early evening air. Families and friends were clustered in small groups happily chatting away while the kids played tag, threw a football or had their faces painted by one of the teenage girls. The Thankful Bluegrass Band were on the makeshift stage and singing a wide variety of old favourites. It was typical of Nashville that no one made a big deal out of the fact that white-haired Thaddeus Morton who'd played fiddle with all the greats from Bill Monroe to Earl Scruggs and Alison Krauss was performing alongside the silky-voiced Sophia King whose only musical credits came in the form of singing lullabies to her small children.

'Sandy Warner sitting down and behaving? That's not like you.' Jake slumped on the vacant chair next to her. 'You want to come with me to see how Henry Kissinger is doin' over there?' He hitched a finger towards his house. 'Your man thinks he's brokering peace in the Middle East.'

'At least he's sober enough to make an effort.'

He looked taken aback. 'Oh God, here they come. I'm off.' Jake lumbered to his feet.

Taran, accompanied by the Henderson family and Byron Cassidy were heading their way. From what she could see no one appeared in need of medical treatment and an occasional smile bounced between them so that gave her a smidgen of hope. Taran strode out in front of the group and hurried over to her.

'I've thrown out a few suggestions which they haven't dismissed out of hand but they're not exactly leaping on them either so I've no idea if they'll come to anything. I did manage to get them listening to each other's views, apart from our friend Cassidy who's a time bomb waiting to explode. I suspect one of them tipped him off about what we were trying to do here today and that's why he turned up.'

'We need to get the family mingling and take on Cassidy alone.' She tugged his hand. 'Come on, introduce me to everyone and let's try to work a miracle.' It didn't take long to convince the Hendersons to take themselves off and enjoy the party and Sandy had a swift check around to see where they all ended up. Kayla, the family's glamour girl, was drinking beer straight from the bottle and hanging on Rusty's every word. Jimmy had settled down in front of the band and was singing along and tapping his feet. Beth and the Tangled Yarns had swept Vivian into their group and appeared to be fascinating her with their stories. Mary Lou was the biggest shock. She'd literally rolled up the sleeves of her white lace blouse and was throwing a softball to a group of the younger girls.

Sandy decided to put the flies, honey and vinegar adage to work. Vinegar hadn't worked so she'd try a dose of Southern charm. 'Isn't it wonderful to see everyone enjoying themselves, Mr Cassidy? Is that something you can put a price on?'

'I'm a developer. A businessman. Putting prices on things is what I do.' His exasperation showed in his florid face. 'What y'all don't get is if I don't buy this land someone else will and come up with a more disruptive idea for its use.'

She couldn't see how it could be much worse but held her tongue. 'If you found another piece of land where it wouldn't break up an existing community wouldn't that be a win all around? For a start you wouldn't have to deal with the hassle we're going to cause … and believe me we will cause it.' Cassidy blanched as she reckoned up their plans for petitions, protests, a media blitz and hounding every single politician in the state legislature to make their opposition heard loud and clear. 'Don't underestimate us.'

'And don't underestimate *us* either.' Mary Lou suddenly appeared and nodded around at the three other Henderson heirs. 'We don't appreciate being taken for fools and pitted against each other. I suspect my cousin Carter won't change his mind but we only need a majority to do what we like with the land. We have a proposal we believe would meet the approval of our esteemed ancestor.'

The breath caught in Sandy's throat and she clutched Taran's hand.

Chapter Forty-Two

Taran could hardly believe what Mary Lou was saying. One of his suggestions had sunk in because he'd hit on the one thing this long-time Nashville family valued above money.

'Emory Henderson was a remarkable man and ahead of his time in providing quality homes for working people.' Mary Lou's pride shone through. 'In the 1950s "affordable housing" wasn't the fashion it's becoming these days but Emory was an avid sportsman and a supporter of preserving Tennessee's outdoor spaces. We believe it would be an incredible legacy to form a land trust so this portion of undeveloped land could never be built on but be kept in perpetuity for the residents to enjoy.'

'You're kidding me, right?' Cassidy looked aghast. 'You're willing to give up a tidy sum of money to benefit a bunch of people you don't know from Adam?'

The old lady gave him a withering glance. 'I believe everyone will be happier if you leave and let us get on with celebrating the "Emory Henderson Memorial Park".'

'This is your doing, isn't it?' Sandy whispered. 'You're a genius.'

He could be modest and protest but when a woman looked at a man as if he'd hung the moon for her, Taran was human enough to enjoy it.

Mary Lou's raised voice had clearly carried because the people around them started to point and smile, chattering avidly among themselves. He noticed Edith Beasley making a beeline for the Tangled Yarns group and saw his grandmother's face light up as Rendezvous Lane's most efficient gossip spread the good news. There was really no public information system needed while Edith was around but Taran spotted

Jake running across to where a local band was singing and grabbing the microphone.

'In case any of y'all missed hearin' it – there's good news.' Jake's gruff voice echoed around the park. 'The good Henderson folk aren't goin' to sell this land. They're puttin' it in a trust for all of us to enjoy and no property leeches are ever goin' to stick their ugly buildings up here!'

Loud cheers went up and everyone was high-fiving and laughing.

'He'll tell me I'm blowin' hot air because it was a community effort and I'm not sayin' we didn't play our part but I still reckon we need three cheers for Taran. Without his persistence we couldn't have pulled it off.'

If Sandy hadn't given his hand a reassuring squeeze he doubted he could've held back the tears stinging his eyes but he managed to smile and nod at Jake. Everyone started to cheer and he was soon surrounded by people, embarrassing him with their good wishes.

'Come and play football, Mr T. *Please.*' Chip tugged his arm. 'I've been waiting for hours and hours.'

He could've hugged the little boy for rescuing him. Taran addressed his friends. 'Sorry. I'm on a promise and a certain kid's been patient long enough. I'm just more than happy to have been able to help.' He looked down to grin at Chip. 'I'm all yours now. Let's go, and show them what we're made of – if it's okay with your mom?'

'That's typical. Desert me. And see if I care.'

Taran smooched a kiss on her cheek. 'I'll make it up to you later.'

'You'd better.' She shooed them away. 'I'm going inside where it's quiet to call Lashonda because I'm going around the bend waiting for her to ring me.'

'I almost forgot it's decision day, right? Maybe Harry's planning to take her out for dinner tonight.'

'No, they were having a lunchtime barbecue at his house with his mother and Lashonda planned to tell him then.'

'Any clue which way she'll go?' Taran asked.

'She's gone back and forth like a boomerang ever since he popped the question.' Sandy sighed. 'I don't get it. You either want to marry someone or you don't. Surely it shouldn't take weeks to think it over?'

However he answered could doom him and judging by the heat flooding her face their thoughts ran on the same lines.

'Mr T, everyone's waiting to play.' Chip sounded fed up.

'Just let me say one word to your mom.'

'One.' The boy's stern admonition made them both laugh.

He touched Sandy's smile and stared into her eyes. 'Later.'

Was it a good or bad omen when her friend didn't answer? She debated leaving a message but Lashonda would see her number show up in her missed calls so that would have to do.

You either want to marry someone or you don't.

Would she be as certain if … Sandy cut off the thought, unable even to finish the sentence in her head. Andy's proposal had come as a casual suggestion rather than a grand romantic gesture.

'I want our child to have my name and we make a pretty good couple so what do you say?'

Her acceptance had been equally pragmatic but because he died before they could be married she'd never know now whether it would've worked out.

Should she take a step back and think harder about her future with Taran? Sandy stroked her fingers over her stomach. Was she risking her children's future because she was head over heels in love? She wandered out to her back gate and watched Taran and Chip for a few minutes over the fence. A delicious warmth spread through her when they stopped and waved, beckoning her over.

'I thought we'd find y'all still out here.'

Lashonda and Harry crossed the grass towards her and their beaming faces told her everything she needed to know.

'I've put him out of his misery and he's stuck with me now.' Her friend giggled. 'I'd drag him out to dance but he's a typical white boy with the rhythm of a block of wood.'

'Who're you calling a block of wood?' Harry tried and failed to sound offended.

'You, my darlin' man but it's okay because you've got more important attributes.'

Sandy held up a hand. 'I don't need the gruesome details.'

'There's nothin' gruesome about it.' Harry snuck his hand around Lashonda's waist and kissed her.

'Do I get to see the ring?'

'You already have.'

Harry's laconic response should've embarrassed her.

'It's okay I know you two are tight.' He grinned at Sandy. 'I'm pretty sure if you didn't approve she wouldn't be wearing the thing. But I'm happy she is and nothing else matters.'

'When's the big day?'

'Have we missed something?' Taran slid to a stop next to her with Chip fast on his heels, gasping for breath. Sweat slicked Taran's face and he pushed at the thick strands of hair sticking to his skin.

A trickle of desire sneaked through her as his deep golden gaze locked onto hers.

'How would you feel about being my best man?' Harry asked. 'Seems fitting when we've become quite a foursome with these two ladies.'

'I'd be honoured but don't you have any older friends who maybe expect to be asked?'

'Not really. I don't count work colleagues and I've lost touch with the guys I hung out with in school and college.' Harry winked. 'I'll be happy to return the favour when it's your turn.'

'Oh well in that case we've got a deal.' Taran shook Harry's hand and they did the man shoulder slapping thing.

'Was that your way of proposing to Sandy?' Lashonda shrieked.

Everyone around them turned to stare and Sandy's world spun on its axis as Taran's seemingly casual words sunk in.

'How about we go inside?' Taran needed to get her to himself right now. This definitely wasn't a conversation that needed an audience.

'But we're supposed to be—'

'I'm pretty sure they'll get on fine without us.'

'Chip can show us where the drinks are and we'll hang with him awhile.' Lashonda flashed them both a wicked smile.

'That would be great.' He whisked Sandy away before she could protest, taking care to avoid his grandmother and the rest of their curious friends.

In Sandy's quiet kitchen, Taran settled her at the table and offered to make tea.

'I'm allowed one decent cup of coffee a day so I'd like to claim it now.' Sandy shook her head at him. 'If I wasn't pregnant it would be a gigantic glass of chardonnay or maybe a whole bottle of gin.'

'I didn't mean ... No, I absolutely did but ...'

'Shush.' She leaned over and kissed him.

'Coffee. Please.'

Taran did as she'd asked then sat down too. He peeked at Sandy while she sipped her coffee, unsure whether the silencing order was still in place.

'Okay.' Sandy set her mug down. 'Do you want to explain whether you got carried away after Harry asked you to be his best man or ... actually meant to propose to me?'

If he was totally honest with himself and Sandy he hadn't

progressed past a general plan to ask her to marry him sometime in the future.

'I need the complete truth whether you think I'll like hearing it or not.'

'Harry took me by surprise but in a totally good way.'

'Yeah, there's been a lot of surprises going on today.' Sandy's wry smile raised his hopes. 'Don't stop there.'

'I told you that my trip to Texas crystalised a whole lot of things for me. I still enjoyed eating my way around a new place but at the end of the day it sucked being in another random hotel room and away from you and Chip.'

'Have you forgotten what you said not long after we met though?' Her lingering stare made him uneasy. 'Doesn't all this settled stuff drive you crazy? Those were your very words. I couldn't bear it if you woke up in a few years and resented us for clipping your wings.'

'Oh Sandy, we can make a life here together and fly too.' He cracked a smile. 'Literally. I stupidly assumed I had to choose between having a family and home of my own or continuing to travel but that's rubbish. We can do all of those things together and that's what I want.' Taran shook his head. 'When I visited my parents in Cornwall I discovered the labels I'd slapped on them didn't fit any longer and neither did the ones I'd put on myself.'

'So you want to slap a new one on?'

He struggled to keep his voice steady. 'Are you going to spell out exactly what you mean?'

'Husband. Father. Family man.'

Sandy's gentle, measured words settled in his heart.

'They all sound awesome to me.' Taran couldn't help shaking his head in amazement. 'Was that the most laid-back proposal in the history of mankind? I'm not even sure who ended up making it?'

'Does it matter? It's our unconventional streak coming out.'

'Shall we go back out there and break the good news before my poor grandmother suffers another heart attack?'

'She won't be surprised. I suspect Beth knew weeks ago where we were heading and she's been waiting for us to catch up.'

'I don't have a ring for you to show off yet but we'll put that right soon.'

When he got out of bed this morning he hadn't expected to end up engaged to this beautiful woman. It touched him when Harry asked Taran to be his best man because until now his lifestyle meant friendships were discarded with very little regret when he moved on again. The icing on the cake was the equally improbable fact they'd managed to save the park for the generations of Rendezvous Lane residents still to come. 'Come on, let's go and find Chip. We need his approval first.'

'You have such a generous heart. The awesome way you love Chip too is a huge reason why I'm marrying you.' Sandy flung her arms around his neck and plastered him with kisses.

'I'll enjoy hearing the other reasons later and I might think up a few of my own if you're lucky.' Taran's voice thickened with emotion.

'Oh I'm lucky all right.'

'Ditto.'

Chapter Forty-Three

Fourth of July

'I'm going to be a big brother?' Chip's face lit up. 'Really?'

'Yes, really.' Sandy smiled.

'Wow, that's awesome. That's the best birthday present ever … although my new bike and the Paw Patrol fire truck were great too.' He wrinkled up his nose. 'Will the baby have to share my bedroom? He'll mess up all my things.'

She struggled to keep a straight face. 'The baby will sleep in our room at first until he or she is a bit bigger and then we'll fix up the spare bedroom for them.'

'She? I might have a sister?' Chip looked horrified.

'It's possible.' If she dared catch Taran's eye now it would be impossible not to laugh.

They made the decision to share the news with Chip today mainly because she had passed the critical twelve-week stage and although they knew there were still no guarantees both of them felt easier in their minds. It also struck them as the perfect way to wrap up such a special day which started far too early with Chip bouncing on their bed and begging to open his birthday presents. After they cooked his favourite chocolate chip pancakes for a late breakfast it was a time for them all to get dressed for Lashonda and Harry's wedding. When Sandy wrangled him into the cute blue and white sailor suit she reminded him of the gift Harry had promised if Chip did a good job as ring bearer – a signed David Beckham jersey.

It reduced Sandy to happy tears to see her friends' obvious love for each other at the ceremony and she caught Taran wiping his eyes when he thought she wasn't looking. Although she missed seeing Lashonda at work these days she was thrilled that Harry had homed in on her friend's gift for turning life lemons into sweet lemonade and persuaded her to take a counselling course. It would qualify her to help troubled people to make the most of the hand they'd been dealt, especially other single parents. The biggest challenge of the whole day came when it was time to leave the reception and she had to practically drag Taran and Chip away from the Hattie B's food truck. Harry had hired the retro red vehicle to do the catering and Sandy fully expected it to make another appearance at their own wedding in October.

They'd plumped for later in the year to allow Taran's father more time to get his strength back but also because she wanted to hold their simple ceremony in his grandmother's garden and the weather would be perfect then. They planned to hold the reception in their park which was already taking shape with the barbecue area installed and several benches set under newly planted trees. In their minds there was no better place in which to celebrate with their family and friends than the spot that in many ways brought them together.

'Look there's the first firework!' Taran pointed to a burst of gold exploding in the sky. 'Do you want to sit with me Chip?'

Sandy's heart sang as her little boy jumped on Taran's lap and snuggled into him. She would never forget his reaction when they told him they were getting married.

'Does that mean you'll be my daddy? I know Andy is my daddy too but I want a real one here to play with forever.'

Even now remembering those poignant words made her throat tighten and her eyes sting.

'It's ice cream time Mommy. You promised we would when the fireworks started.'

They'd decided to skip birthday cake and enjoy their favourite ice creams while they watched the traditional Nashville Fourth of July display from the comfort of the back garden.

'I'll get them.' She slipped into the house and collected three mini-Magnums – two milk chocolate ones for Taran and Chip and a dark chocolate raspberry for her.

While they laughed, ate, and gasped at the extravagant display in the sky Sandy couldn't help remembering the first time they shared ice creams this way and the fantasy it stirred in her mind of the family they could be.

'The fireworks have finished and I think someone is ready for bed.' Taran scooped Chip in his arms and stood up.

'But I'm not tired.' Chip protested, rubbing his eyes.

'Well I am and so is L'il Pea.' Sandy rubbed her belly. They'd come up with the fun nickname for their baby and she hoped they wouldn't get tempted to use it when he or she arrived. 'Who do you want to put you to bed?' She already knew the answer because her little boy had quickly worked out that Taran was a sucker when it came to reading bedtime stories – never refusing Chip's pleas for "just one more Mr T".

The three of them went inside and she left them to it while she got to bed as quickly as possible. Sandy was surprised when Taran joined her a few minutes later.

'Chip fell asleep before I finished the first book.'

'You sound disappointed.'

He stripped off and slid in next to her. 'Hey I'm in bed with a gorgeous, sexy woman what could I possibly have to be disappointed about?' Taran stroked her belly and gave her a questioning look.

Now her sickness had subsided, she knew from experience there was a small window of time before the weariness of late pregnancy kicked in and intended to make the most of it. 'It's very strange but I'm not tired any longer.'

He flung back the covers, undressed her with his golden eyes and then his searching hands. All bets were off.

Taran was enjoying the rare lie-in. Because they were all late to bed last night Chip had overslept this morning and wasn't awake and looking for them yet. 'I know that look.' He stroked Sandy's cheek. 'You've got something on your mind.'

Learning to communicate better was a learning process for them both. When he brought up the question again about abandoning her data entry work to give more time to her art Sandy had been prickly. Only after they spent hours going over the pros and cons did she reluctantly agree to give it a try. Now a couple of months later the online store they set up was already a big success.

Tiny frown lines furrowed her brow. 'Have you thought any more about finding Alexei?'

'Of course I have but what's made you ask that now?'

'No particular reason.' Her face turned bright pink and a trickle of defiance ran through her voice as though she dared him to accuse her of lying. She was up to something and he needed to gently put a stop to it.

'I've decided it's best left alone. For his sake as well as mine. He was only six years old when I left so he's probably forgotten me by now.'

'Do you honestly believe that?'

'Let's just say I hope so.' Taran prayed he was right. Surely the less the young man remembered about his early childhood the better? He couldn't see that dragging up the past would help either of them.

'All right. I won't mention it again.'

Sandy and he were equally persistent, which sounded better than stubborn, and Taran was sure he hadn't heard the last of this particular conversation.

Chapter Forty-Four

Three months later – October

'Granny, sit down please and I'll fix you a cup of coffee.' Taran snatched the yellow duster from Beth's hand and steered her towards the sofa.

'But my knickknacks on the sideboard are filthy.'

'No they aren't. You cleaned them yesterday.' He could add – and the day before and the day before that – but held his tongue. In half an hour they'd leave for the airport to pick up his parents. He wished that Sandy and Chip were coming too but Sandy insisted that his grandmother didn't need them all around for what was bound to be an emotional reunion. 'The house looks beautiful.'

'Naomi used to call it old-fashioned and it's only got more so since she was here last.' Her face wrinkled with worry.

'It's your home and she's ... changed herself. In a good way.' Beth didn't look convinced. 'I'll get our coffees.' He didn't admit that he was nervous too at the prospect of seeing his parents on what had become his home turf.

A couple of hours later he glanced around the room and smiled. Beth and Naomi hadn't stopped talking and there'd only been one awkward moment when his mother commented on the 'new' front porch that was built five years ago.

'Do you want another beer, Jakub?'

'No, he doesn't,' his mother answered. 'There are rules he needs to stick with from now on to decrease the likelihood of having another stroke and cutting back on alcohol is one of them.'

'Enjoying life is another.'

No one took his father's grumbling seriously and they all knew he was lucky to be alive. Back in the spring, Taran couldn't have imagined them all being together this way and he felt sure he wasn't the only one.

'I hope you aren't going to make us wait until tomorrow to meet Sandy and Chip?' Naomi asked out of the blue.

'Well yes … I thought you'd be too tired tonight.' The withering glance she gave him uncannily resembled his grandmother's.

'If the little boy's asleep we could walk over and at least meet Sandy.'

'Let me check first to see what she's doing.' Taran pulled out his phone and sent a quick text, making it clear that it wasn't a problem if she said no.

I'm not getting on the wrong side of your mom this soon! Chip's just gone to bed but I'll bring him back down for a little while. Give me five minutes then bring them over. Beth too of course.

There was a nervous flutter in his stomach. At Taran's age it wasn't as if he *needed* his parents' approval but a part of him *wanted* it anyway.

Sandy would love to read Naomi and Jakub's minds, at least she thought so. On the surface they'd admired her house and made a fuss of Chip before he went back to bed but she couldn't be sure how they really felt. Out of the corner of her eye she caught Naomi playing with one of the red bobbles around the edge of the cushion and realised Taran's mother was chattering a little too fast about their home in Cornwall. Sandy wasn't the only apprehensive one.

'If you aren't too tired tomorrow Naomi I'd love you to come with me into Nashville for the final fitting of my wedding dress. Lashonda will be there too – she's my best friend. We've worked together for several years and she's like the sister I never had.'

'I'd love to. I'm sure jet lag will have me awake far too early anyway trying to fool me into thinking it's the middle of the day.' A huge smile blossomed on Naomi's face. 'You're lucky to have your friend and I'm sure she feels the same way about you. Until we moved to St Lanow we'd never become part of a community. When it's always in the back of your head that you'll be moving on soon, it stops you … giving too much of yourself.' Her face crumpled as she glanced at Beth. 'I've neglected some of the people I love most in the world and I'm praying it's not too late to put things right.'

'Oh my love come here.' Beth opened her arms to her daughter.

'Things are going to change from now on Mom.' Naomi's breath hitched. 'I don't expect you to make the long journey to Cornwall but I promise we'll come to see you several times a year and stay for good long visits.' Her gaze rested on Sandy and Taran. 'I'm certain this pair will take care of you when we're not around.'

'We sure will.' Taran's voice cracked. In a minute they'd all be in tears.

'You didn't tell me you were having cookies.'

Chip's indignant challenge swept a welcome gust of normality through the room.

'You're supposed to be asleep.' Sandy tried to sound stern as he bounced down the stairs.

'I smelled them.'

'One.' She held out the plate. 'You'll have to brush your teeth again.'

Chip grabbed a cookie then jumped onto Taran's lap.

Jakub stifled a yawn. 'Sorry.'

'We should go.' Naomi sprang up off the sofa.

'I'm just tired honey. It was a long journey and with the six-hour time difference my body's reminding me it's almost two a.m. now in Cornwall.'

Beth stood up too. 'We'll get on home.'

'Can we read one more story Mr T? The new castle book,' Chip begged.

'Of course we can.'

Sandy blinked away a rush of tears. The seamless way Taran had settled into family life with them could still catch her by surprise.

'What time are we going shopping tomorrow?' Naomi asked.

'I thought we'd leave here around ten o'clock and after we're through at the shop we'll have lunch out together if we can trust these men here on their own. Lashonda's husband Harry is coming over to join them and bringing ribs to cook on the grill.'

'That sounds perfect although that's Jakub's diet shot for another day.' She smiled and linked arms with her husband. 'Come on, let's get to bed before we drop.'

A few minutes later Sandy stood in the quiet kitchen and listened to Taran's rumbling voice and her son's high-pitched laughter drifting down the stairs. She idly fiddled with her engagement ring but her fingers were swollen so it didn't turn as easily these days. Taran clearly paid attention when she expressed her love of Art Deco styling. With its glittering diamonds, white gold setting and delicate filigree openwork she couldn't have chosen something better herself. After the wedding next week she planned to put it away safely until after L'il Pea arrived, rather than risk it having to be cut off.

She turned on the dishwasher and wiped down the counter, smiling all the time. Upstairs her boys were waiting for her. Sandy stroked her growing belly. Would she have a female ally or would the male contingent expand with a new member? Who cared? She certainly didn't and neither did Taran. As for Chip that was another story …

Taran loved to watch Chip's intense concentration as he diced a jalapeno pepper. The little boy was getting a kick out of practising with the bright green safety knives and had already asked for a cookbook for Christmas. They'd set up a table in the garden and were making a spicy pineapple salsa to snack on with tortilla chips.

'Are we leaving the seeds in?'

'Not today.' He watched Chip's face fall. The kid forgot nothing. Most of the heat was in the seeds. 'My dad isn't a big fan of spicy food.' Jakub was standing by the grill and chatting to Harry, looking much more rested today. 'He's like your mom.'

'You mean boring.'

'No, just—'

'Excuse me, I am looking for Sandy Warner ... oh ... *Taran?*' The tall, gangly young man hovering by the gate flicked a lock of thick black curly hair away from his dark eyes.

'Alexei?' Taran's stomach plummeted. Alexei Novak couldn't have materialised out of thin air but that's how it felt.

'Mr T come on. I'm hungry. We haven't finished making the salsa.' Chip tugged on his leg.

He tried his best to answer the little boy but nothing came out, all he seemed capable of doing was standing like a block of wood and staring at Alexei. In the middle of all the turmoil going on in his head Taran was aware of his father's unabashed curiosity. When he was in Cornwall he told his parents everything about his time in Prague and Jakub was no doubt putting two and two together.

'I've got a couple of hot dogs cooked over here.' Harry came to the rescue. 'You can have one while we wait.'

'Awesome!' Chip set the knife down and ran off.

Taran finally forced himself to move. It only took a few short steps to come face to face with this grown-up version of the little boy whose fate had haunted him for years.

'I am sorry for turning up this way.' Alexei lifted his

shoulders in an expressive shrug. 'I am here because Sandy found me on Instagram and sent me a message.' A smile – Ingrid's smile – pulled at his mouth. 'Social media has a lot to answer for.'

'I didn't know she'd been in touch with you.' Frustration bubbled up inside him. Why hadn't Sandy listened? If she loved him how could she let him be ambushed this way?

'That is what I thought.' Alexei sounded sad.

'But I'm pleased she did.' Maybe not the complete truth but the young man didn't need to realise that he was struggling with a whole range of emotions right now. 'I only found out about your mother a few months ago.' Taran choked up.

'She gave her life for me. That is hard to live with. My father wasn't a good man. You knew that.' The simple words sliced through his heart. 'My grandparents took me to live with them and they did their best but it was not the same.'

'You came all this way to—'

'See you?' Alexei twitched a smile. 'No. I have started my studies to be a doctor at Vanderbilt University here in Nashville. I was fortunate to get a scholarship to such a well-renowned medical school. Sandy saw a picture of me with my acceptance letter on Instagram. It is quite a coincidence, no?'

'It certainly is and a great opportunity for you.' It humbled him to see what a success Alexei was making of his life despite all the obstacles that'd been thrown his way. Taran certainly couldn't take any of the credit.

'Do you know for many years I thought I had done something wrong and that was why you left.' His thin shoulders sagged.

'Oh my God nothing could be further from the truth! You must *never* think that.' Taran's voice cracked and he struggled to speak again. 'I loved you very much but I was young, selfish and a coward. I let you and your mother down and I couldn't be sorrier. I don't suppose you can ever forgive me but—'

'There is nothing to forgive. Please do not be so hard on yourself. I did not come to upset you or your life. I hope maybe we can … be friends again.'

'I would like that. I really would.' He worked to get a grip on himself. Taran nodded towards his father who was hovering nearby and across at Harry and Chip. 'Come in and meet everyone. Have a beer. Eat some ribs. You might as well get used to American ways.' Seeing the smart, strong young man Ingrid's son had grown into freed him from a burden he hadn't even realised he was carrying around. Sandy had been right even if from his point of view her methods left a lot to be desired.

'Oh Lord that man will drop to his knees when he sees you.' Lashonda's wicked laugh filled the bridal shop.

'I expect Sandy would prefer he stayed upright to say his vows,' Naomi chipped in.

'It might be better.' Her future mother-in-law and her best friend had clicked immediately and the three of them were having the best time together.

She twirled in front of the three-way mirror. Her worries over how she'd look had faded to nothing when she slipped on the pale ivory silk dress again. It'd been two months since she first tried it on and she'd been concerned that it would be too tight now but if anything her added curves helped. The dress reminded her of something an old Hollywood siren would wear with its off the shoulder sleek styling and she'd chosen to add an Art Deco style diamante sash at the front to break up the simplicity of the design.

A wave of pure joy swept through her. It seemed vaguely disloyal to Andy to be so happy that her first walk down the aisle would be to marry Taran but she refused to let anything spoil this special moment. 'I'll get changed and then it must be lunchtime. I'm starving.'

'You're always hungry now you're not being sick every five minutes,' Lashonda teased.

'Goodness knows what kind of mess our men are making by now in your kitchen.'

'We could go straight home now?' Sandy's suggestion made both women snort.

'No way.' Lashonda's best no-nonsense tone emerged. 'This is our time and we're gonna make the most of it.'

Sandy remained on an amazing high until they arrived back at her house after a delicious lunch and headed out into the garden. As soon as she saw Taran sitting and talking to a dark-haired young man a wave of panic swept through her. She was in trouble now.

'Mommy, you're home.' Chip raced over beaming widely. 'Come and taste the salsa I made. Mr T let me chop the pepper and I didn't cut my fingers.' He thrust both hands in her face. 'See.'

'That's wonderful.' She absently patted his head.

'Sandy come here honey I want you to meet someone.' Taran beckoned to her so she'd no choice but to plaster on a smile and walk over. After a flurry of introductions Alexei jumped up and kissed her on both cheeks.

'I am so happy to meet you and I am glad you contacted me.' A wry smile crept over his lean, tanned face. 'I gave someone quite a shock but I think he is okay now.'

A wave of guilt swept over her. It'd been an impulsive move on her part and she wished she'd thought it all the way through. This could all have gone terribly wrong.

'I'm more than okay,' Taran's glittering golden eyes fixed on her, 'but we might have a chat later about keeping secrets.'

'Do not be too cross with your lovely bride to be,' Alexei pleaded. 'She did a very good thing. For both of us.'

'Yeah, she certainly did and don't worry she has me

wrapped around her little finger and knows it.' He slipped an arm around her waist and rested his other hand on her belly.

'I'm sorry,' she whispered and pressed a kiss on his mouth. Sandy owed Taran a proper apology later but at the end of the day she couldn't regret getting in touch with Alexei. The reunion was clearly going well and if the two were able to re-establish a relationship that once meant so much to them both surely that was a good thing? She smiled and stepped back. 'You seem to have quite a party going on. A little boy wants me to sample the salsa you made.'

Taran's smile broadened. 'Did he mention the jalapeno we put in it? We took out the seeds but it still might be a bit much for you.'

'I'm a fan of living dangerously these days.' Sandy linked arms with Alexei. 'I'm going to sit down and get to know this young man while you fetch me some fiery salsa and a glass of ice water.' She'd look on this as her penance.

Chapter Forty-Five

'How are you enjoying the day so far Mrs Rossi?' Taran pulled Sandy into his arms. 'Better than the last week I hope?' They'd hardly seen each other for days because of all the seemingly endless wedding preparations. Today everything came together perfectly and the brief ceremony took place in his grandmother's beautiful garden under a cloudless blue sky.

'Much. It's been incredible.' Sandy's beguiling smile unravelled him.

'It certainly has and Chip did an awesome job. We'll have to hire him out as a professional ring bearer at this rate.' His smile faded a little. 'I know this isn't really the time or place to bring it up again but it's on my mind. Are you still absolutely sure Andy would be okay with my plan to adopt Chip now we're married?'

They'd had a lot of discussions on the subject and when they asked the little boy what he thought of the idea he was over the moon.

'He'd see what a good man you are who loves his son very much. He would trust you to love and protect Chip the same as you will do your own baby and me.'

'You'll spoil your make-up.' Taran brushed away a tear that was trickling down her cheek. 'I didn't mean to make you cry. You know I'll do all of those things for the rest of my life. Nothing else will be more important to me.' Their eyes locked. From where he was standing the formal vows they'd made earlier were no more meaningful than this.

'Did I tell you that I had a card from Andy's parents this morning congratulating us and wishing us well?'

They both knew she hadn't said anything in case it put a dent in his happiness.

'That was kind of them.'

'They're thrilled we're going to visit them soon.'

They'd decided to forego taking a proper honeymoon straight away and would wait until next spring before they ventured across the Atlantic on a family trip to England. They would spend a good amount of time in Cornwall with his parents but also planned to carve out time to visit Louise and Gerald who lived close to Reading. Andy's parents deserved the chance to get to know Chip properly not simply through photographs and video calls.

He drew her into the long lingering kiss he'd been craving all day. They'd retreated over by her back gate to watch their guests enjoying the reception as the evening started to wind down. The park with its handsome new sign was hosting its first Rendezvous Lane event and looking pretty stylish while it did so. Coloured fairy lights were strung up around the perimeter and tables and chairs decked out in Sandy's favourite turquoise and bright yellow were scattered around the grass. The Hattie B's food truck was still in business, scenting the air with fragrant hickory wood smoke, and had been a massive hit. Taran had asked Harry and Lashonda to keep an eye on Alexei as he didn't know many of their other guests. No doubt they'd introduced him to Nashville hot chicken by now and he hoped Lashonda hadn't tried to blow the young man's head off with "Shut the Cluck Up!!!". His parents were in full-on grandparent mode taking care of Chip and they'd all be sleeping in Beth's house tonight while Taran whisked Sandy off to the swanky Hermitage Hotel in Nashville.

'In case I was too dumbstruck to tell you earlier, you're looking incredibly beautiful today.'

'You did remember actually but I'm happy to hear it again.'

He sensed her beguiling shyness through the soft dusky light. Taran's hands drifted down to caress her blossoming curves and cradled the bump that would be their new son or daughter in a few short months. 'How's L'il Pea doing?' It'd been in the back of his mind ever since they set the wedding date that the stress of all the preparations might send Sandy into early labour.

'Fine.' She rested her head against his chest. 'I was concerned too.'

'I know.' They were too in tune for him to have been the only one worrying. 'We can kick back and decompress next week.' After a lot of time spent talking it over he'd made the momentous decision to sell his blog. Apart from anything else the pressure from his sponsors and gruelling, continuous travel had sucked most of the joy out of it. When they travelled as a family he could pick up guest posts on other people's blogs in those locations if he chose to. He already had the first destination picked out – New Orleans. If Sandy felt up to the journey they would go over the Thanksgiving holidays. Taran couldn't wait to expose Chip to a totally new food culture he felt sure the little boy would absolutely lap up. Sandy had the bright idea for him to put together a course to show other people the ins and outs of making a living from food writing and the first online classes had been a huge success. He was already planning to adapt the course and offer it at places like blogger conferences and travel shows. The latest concept they'd come up with was for him to write a series of digital books on street foods in different countries.

Because his new business efforts and her art sales were doing well he'd persuaded her to take an extended leave from Williamson Homes. Secretly he hoped her gruelling days at Williamson Homes were behind them.

'Is it time for bubbles?' she asked.

They'd encouraged Chip to help with the wedding plans so now all of their guests would be given a vial of bubbles to blow as he and Sandy left the party. Her son's other biggest input had been in the selection of Taran's groom's cake. Taran had been more than happy to go along with the American tradition of having two cakes at a wedding – the traditional multi-tiered one chosen primarily by the bride to fit in with the overall decorating theme and the other focused on the groom's personal likes or dislikes. The result had been Chip's favourite plain white cake, decorated with white icing and gaudy plastic Paw Patrol figures.

'I think it must be. After that I finally get you to myself.'

'We're on our own now.'

'Not somewhere I can truly make you mine. If you need me to be more specific I can be.' Taran tugged her closer.

'When we get to the hotel you can be as specific as you want.'

Her breathy voice and sultry scent threatened to drive him crazy and he forced himself to pull away. 'Bubbles first … then us … just us.'

After her third night-time trip to the bathroom Sandy relished watching him sleep as the sun rose.

'Are you drawing me again, Ms Warner?' Taran rolled over.

'Nope, just looking.' She hoped her flushed face was hidden. When she showed him her private stash of pictures his reactions were a mixture of surprise, embarrassment and amazement. No one else would ever see them. Sandy's mental pictures from last night would make it onto paper when they got home. The sight of him slowly abandoning the tuxedo jacket and the contrast of his pure white shirt against his dark olive skin was mesmerising enough but once that was discarded too his dramatic tattoos added another edge of decadence. Maybe it was shallow to soak up how handsome he was but she didn't care because he stared at her the same way.

'Come and take a closer look.' His teasing challenge made her laugh.

'And you had the nerve to call me shameless last night.'

Taran pulled her down to him. 'In case I haven't said it enough recently, I love you.'

'It's never possible to say it too much.' Sandy stroked his face, exploring the strong bones under the surface of his warm skin. 'I love you too but don't even think of cheating me out of a decadent breakfast in the Capitol Grille by ordering room service so you can have your wicked way with me again.' She waved a finger at Taran.

'I'm simply making the most of it before you turn into a whale.'

'Charming!'

'You said it first not me.' He chuckled. 'Your words when I peeled off that sexy wedding dress were "Enjoy it while you can, buddy. Another month and I'll resemble Shamu. It'll take a winch to get me out of bed and I won't be able to see my feet. You'll be fresh out of luck as far as anything more athletic than forcing shoes onto my swollen feet goes".'

'I was being honest.'

'And I love every beautiful, honest, stubborn, smart, funny inch of you.' Taran spooned her with his warm body and stroked her in places he knew would make her melt. 'Breakfast first? Or …'

A groan slipped out of her as he touched a particularly sensitive spot. 'Or.'

'My choice too.' His husky voice set her skin on fire.

Sandy succumbed; the hotel didn't stop serving breakfast until eleven o'clock.

These days she could fall asleep anywhere or at any time, only waking when her pea-sized bladder made itself known. It didn't surprise her to wake up and find her new husband showered and dressed and staring down at her with clear amusement.

'Just checking to make sure you're still breathing although the snores should've given it away.'

She caught him on the side of the head with a pillow. 'That's for being cheeky. I'm going to shower then I'll need feeding.'

'Do you need a hand up?' Taran extended his arm to her.

'I don't strictly need one but I'll take it anyway.' After he gently lifted her off the bed, Sandy waddled towards the bathroom where she luxuriated in a perfumed bath and wrapped a fluffy white towel around herself before joining him again.

'I've checked the menu and everything's safe for cautious eaters.'

'How boring for you.' Before she could find her clothes to get dressed Taran whipped off her towel with a wicked chuckle.

'You could never be boring Mrs Rossi.' He stroked her swollen belly and smiled when L'il Pea kicked. 'When we get back from breakfast you can prove it to me again. No one's expecting us back at Rendezvous Lane anytime soon.'

'Good.'

Chapter Forty-Six

Six months later – April in Cornwall

'What a difference a year makes, eh son?'

Taran smiled over at his father and nodded. They were sitting on the patio and enjoying the tail end of the mild spring evening. From inside the house they could hear Chip protesting that he wasn't tired. 'All for the better.' Little snuffles drifted up from the warm bundle in his arms and he jiggled his almost three-month-old daughter. His job was to keep Kerensa Elizabeth Rossi quiet until her mum was free to feed her again. 'You're looking great.'

'That's down to your mother. She's got me eating healthy, I dig the garden and we grow all our own vegetables and go for long walks every day.' Jakub gave a wry smile. 'I miss my strong coffee and Polish vodka but it's a small price to pay.'

He could say the same about himself. He missed elements of his old roaming existence but life was full of other new firsts now. The morning before they set off on this trip he went into Kerensa's nursery when she woke up and was the awed recipient of her first proper smile.

'How's young Alexei doing by the way?'

'Really great. Pre-med is a tough course but he works hard.'

'Your grandmother isn't driving him crazy yet?' Jakub rolled his eyes.

'Not as far as I know. It's amazing how well they get on.'

'That was one of your better ideas.'

'Yeah it was.' After Taran visited Alexei in the cramped apartment he shared with three other students near the campus he'd had a brainwave. He suggested to his grandmother that she took the young man in as a lodger – rent free in return for him cutting her grass and doing anything she needed around the house. 'Alexei took a little convincing at first – not because he didn't care for the idea but he was afraid I was offering out of some misguided effort to put things right with him.' Taran shrugged. 'I guess that came into it but it wasn't my primary reason.'

'I know your mother rests easier.' Jakub sounded thoughtful. 'We can't be there all the time and neither can you and Sandy. It gives us peace of mind to know someone is around to keep an eye on Beth.'

'Exactly. It struck me as something that could work out well for everyone. He's got himself a driving license and I've fixed him up with a used car so he can hop on the interstate and be at Vanderbilt in about fifteen minutes.'

'Ingrid would be very happy with where he's at now.'

'I hope so.' He fell silent.

'Someone wants another story and it's got to be his daddy.' Sandy strolled out to join them. 'I warn you it's that extremely long book on Cornish legends.' Her smile broadened. 'But as you're the mug who bought it for him it's absolutely your own fault.'

Taran playfully dumped a grizzling Kerensa in his wife's outstretched arms. 'We'll swap.' He popped a kiss on Sandy's forehead. 'I'll claim more than that later.' An adorable blush blossomed in her cheeks.

Outside Chip's bedroom he heard his mother's low voice and held back for a moment.

'Do you think when you're a bit bigger you'd like to come here to stay with us on your own? We could go crabbing at the beach and you could help Grandad in the garden.'

'Wow! That would be awesome, Granny.'

The woman who hated him calling her Mom was relishing every minute of being a grandmother. Once he might've resented that but he'd matured too. 'Is someone ready to read about all of those wicked ogres and giants?' He wandered in.

'Yes please, Daddy.'

Right after they married he did the parenting course that was mandatory in Tennessee and the day Chip stood with him and Sandy in front of a judge to legalise his adoption was one of the best in Taran's life.

'If he has nightmares after all those grisly tales it's all down to you.' His mom shook her head and laughed. 'I'll leave you boys to it.' On the way out she touched his arm. 'You know that being around your children makes me realise how much I missed when you were growing up.'

Taran hugged her. 'You're not the only one making up for lost time.'

'Come on Daddy or we won't get to read the whole book before Mommy spoils it and makes me go to sleep. She promised to come back and kiss me goodnight after she's fed Kerensa. My sister will want to say goodnight too.'

He couldn't help smiling. Far from being disappointed when Kerensa was born Chip worshipped his little sister. Later on when she was older and messed up his toys things might be different but right now he couldn't do enough to help take care of her. Taran settled down on the bed and picked up the book. 'Guess what I sneaked in?' He pulled a bag of chocolates from his pocket. 'They're spicy chili and sea salt.' Chip snuggled into him and they munched away happily together.

Sandy's anxiousness increased as they climbed into the black taxi at Reading station and gave the driver Andy's parents' address.

Now she was regretting her promise to stay for the three days leading up to their flight back to Nashville. She remembered Louise being extremely house-proud and Gerald had a low tolerance for small children. Those factors hadn't helped their historically tense relationship but Sandy hoped their new closeness over the last few months would help to put that firmly in the past.

'Here you are love.'

The taxi stopped outside the imposing red brick house and she spotted the Suttons hovering on the doorstep. They were probably nervous too.

'Let's get out Chip.' Taran opened the car door. 'I reckon we need to stretch our legs.'

Sandy gathered up Kerensa and clambered out after him. 'Louise. Gerald. It's lovely to see you again. Say hello to Grandma and Pops, Chip.' He was clinging onto Taran's legs and her sweet husband crouched down and whispered something in his ear.

'Can we see your garden, Pops? I had to sit for ages in the train and my legs need to run.'

'Of course we can.' Gerald smiled. 'I've got a new football. Someone told me you like playing.'

'I do and my daddy's good. Can he play too?'

Sandy caught a shaft of pain zip across the older man's face and his wife's quick intake of breath. She'd been too wrapped up in her own emotions to consider how hard this must be for them. In their eyes it should be affable fair-haired Andy standing there not Taran, the stranger who'd taken their precious son's place.

'The more the merrier. Why don't you ladies go inside and get settled in? I know someone can't wait to get her hands on a baby again.' Gerald struggled to sound jovial.

She followed Louise into the house and they stuck to inconsequential chatter until they walked into the huge guest room, complete with a cot and a single bed for Chip.

'You've got your own bathroom next door,' Louise said. 'I didn't put you in Andy's old room this time.'

A heavy silence swamped them and Sandy held Kerensa

tighter and inhaled her intoxicating baby scent. 'I'm truly sorry for what happened to Andy and I'll always feel guilty for sending him out that night.' She shushed Louise's attempt to speak. 'You don't know him yet but Taran is a good man. He adopted Chip out of love not because either of us wants him to forget Andy. We'll make sure that never happens and with Taran's parents living over here as well I promise we'll be eating up the air miles across the Atlantic.'

'You've nothing to apologise for my dear.' Louise's voice shook. 'If we made you feel to blame at the time that was our grief talking. You didn't *send* Andy anywhere, you *asked* him. He loved you very much and would've adored Chip.' She looked wistful. 'I can see what a kind man Taran is. He's a good husband to you and he'll be an excellent father … to both of your children. Now let's put the kettle on and then I want a cuddle with this sweet baby.'

Sandy passed Kerensa over. It would be cruel to correct Louise's assumptions about her and Andy's relationship, some things were too hurtful and best left unsaid. 'I'll make the tea and you can work your grandma magic to rock this little one off to sleep.'

'Not like travelling solo is it?' Sandy poked Taran's ribs. He'd finally sat down after stowing all their carry-on bags and settling his parents next to Chip across the aisle from them. Jakub and Naomi were coming back to Nashville for a month to visit Beth and spend more time with their beloved grandchildren. Kerensa was wailing in her airline cot, bitterly resenting being strapped in until the plane took off.

'Hardly.' His wry smile made her laugh. When they were weaving their way through the airport like a nomadic convoy he joked about being an overburdened camel but no one took him seriously. 'You know I wouldn't change it for the world don't you? Whoever said you can't have it all was an idiot. I forecast a lot more adventures in store for the Rossi family and plan to enjoy every single one.'

'Absolutely.'

The plane roared down the runway and as soon as they were in the air Kerensa fell asleep with a contented smile on her face.

'She's clearly your daughter and is going to be a good traveller,' Sandy joked. With her shock of black hair, olive skin and golden eyes, Kerensa had inherited more than her father's love of adventure.

'Yep, but I also think she's ready to go home.' He sneaked a quick kiss and Sandy snuggled into him. 'I am too.'

Thank You

I'm so grateful to the lovely members of the Tasting Panel who fell in love with the wonderful East Nashville community of Rendezvous Lane where two very different people find a place to call home. As always I want to say a big thank you to everyone who chooses to read my books. If you enjoy Sandy and Taran's story and have a minute to leave a review on Goodreads or the retail site where you bought the book that would be amazing.

Angela

x

About the Author

Angela was born in St. Stephen, Cornwall, England. After completing her A-Levels she worked as a Naval Secretary. She met her husband, a US Naval Flight Officer while being based at a small NATO Headquarters on the Jutland Peninsula in Denmark. They lived together in Denmark, Sicily, California, southern Maryland and London before settling in Franklin, Tennessee.

Angela took a creative writing course in 2000 and loved it so much that she has barely put her pen down since. She has had short stories and novels published in the US. Her debut novel, *Sugar & Spice*, won Choc Lit's Search for an American Star competition and is her UK debut.

Follow Angela:
Blog: www.angelabritnellromance.com
Twitter: www.twitter.com/AngelaBritnell
Facebook: www.facebook.com/angelabritnell

More Choc Lit

From Angela Britnell

Sugar and Spice

The Way to a Hero's Heart …

Fiery, workaholic Lily Redman wants more than anything to make a success of her new American TV show, Celebrity Chef Swap – without the help of her cheating ex-fiancé and producer, Patrick O'Brien. So when she arrives in Cornwall, she's determined to do just that.

What Happens in Nashville

'What happens in Nashville, stays in Nashville!'

Claire Buchan is hardly over the moon about the prospect of her sister's hen party; travelling from the UK to Nashville, Tennessee, for a week of honky-tonks, karaoke and cowboys. Certainly not Claire's idea of a good time, what with her lawyer job and sensible boyfriend, Philip.

But then she doesn't bank on meeting Rafe Castello. As he and Claire get to know each other, she realises there is far more to him than meets the eye.

Celtic Love Knot

Can two tangled lives make a love knot?

Lanyon Tremayne is the outcast of his small Cornish village of St. Agnes. Nobody knows the painful secret he hides.

But when Olivia meets the ruggedly handsome Lanyon, her trip to Cornwall looks set to become even more interesting.

The Wedding Reject Table

Once on the reject table, always on the reject table?

When Maggie Taylor, a cake decorator, and Chad Robertson, a lawyer from Nashville Tennessee, meet at a wedding in Cornwall it's not under the best circumstances.

They have both been assigned to 'the reject table', alongside a toxic collection of grumpy great aunts, bitter divorcees and stuffy organists.

Here Comes the Best Man

Being the best man is a lot to live up to …

When troubled army veteran and musician Josh Robertson returns home to Nashville to be the best man at his younger brother Chad's wedding he's just sure that he's going to mess it all up somehow.

But when it becomes clear that the wedding might not be going to plan, it's up to Josh and fellow guest Louise Giles to make sure that Chad and his wife-to-be Maggie get their perfect day.

Love Me for a Reason

Love doesn't always have to make sense …

When Daisy Penvean meets Nathaniel Dalton whilst visiting a friend in Nashville, it seems there are a million and one reasons for them not to be together. Nathaniel's job as a mergers and acquisitions manager means sharp suits and immaculate hair, whereas Daisy's work as a children's book illustrator lends itself to a more carefree, laid-back style. And, as Daisy lives in England, there's also the small matter of the Atlantic Ocean between them.

You're The One That I Want

What if you didn't want to fake it any more?
When Sarah, a teacher from Cornwall, and Matt, a businessman from Nashville, meet on a European coach tour, they soon find themselves in a relationship …

Except it's a fake relationship. Because Matt is too busy for romance, and Sarah is only trying to make her cheating ex-husband jealous … isn't she?

Christmas at Black Cherry Retreat

What if you had nowhere to call home for Christmas?
When Fee Winter books a winter break at the remote Black Cherry Retreat in the small town of Pine Ridge, Tennessee, it's with the idea that the peace and quiet will help her recuperate from her hectic life as a photographer.

But what she didn't bank on was meeting Tom Chambers and his huge, interfering yet lovable family. With them, could Fee finally experience the warmth and support that's been missing from her own life?

One Summer in Little Penhaven

Could one summer change your life?
When high-flying American lawyer Samantha Muir finds out she's lost her partnership whilst on an assignment in London, she has a dramatic reaction.

Rather than returning home, she resigns, leaves her business suits behind and jumps on the first train to Cornwall at the encouragement of a friendly stranger.

Could the Cornish village and Cadan play a part in Samantha's summer of self-discovery?

Christmas in Little Penhaven

Have yourself a little Cornish Christmas …
Wannabe author Jane Solomon is expecting an
uneventful Christmas in her Cornish village of
Little Penhaven.

But then super fit American gym owner Hal
Muir comes to town, and suddenly the holiday
season looks set to be far more interesting. Hal
is keen on embracing every British tradition on
offer, from mince pies to Christmas pub quizzes
– and perhaps some festive romance too …

New Year, New Guy

Out with the old life, in with the new …
When Laura's bride-to-be sister, Polly, organises
a surprise reunion for her fiancé and his long
lost American friend, Laura grudgingly agrees to
help keep the secret. And when the plain-spoken,
larger-than-life Hunter McQueen steps off the
bus in her rainy Devon town and only just
squeezes into her tiny car, it confirms that Laura
has made a big mistake in going along with her
sister's crazy plan.

A Summer to Remember in Herring Bay

**Essy Havers is good at finding things. But
now Essy has something more important to find:
herself**
Essy has always been curious about her mother's
secret past and her Cornish roots. So, when
the opportunity arises, she hops on a plane
in Tennessee and ends up in Herring Bay in
Cornwall; the village where her mother grew up.

But once there, she's mystified by the reactions
of the villagers when they realise who she is.
Was Essy's decision to visit Cornwall a mistake,
or will it lead to a summer she'll never forget?

Christmas at Moonsh...

Mistletoe and moonshine: a Christmas m... made in heaven?

Moonshine Hollow's famous 'Lightning Flash' might be an acquired taste, although the same could be said for moonshine distillery owner Cole Landon, what with his workaholic habits and 'Scrooge' tendencies when it comes to all things Christmassy.

But when Jenna Pendean from Cornwall pays a visit to Cole's family-run distillery in Tennessee during the holiday season, will Cole's cynicism about the existence of Christmas miracles be put to the test?

A Cornish Summer at Pear Tree Farm

Cornish charm and a Tennessee twist – the perfect pair?

Nessa Vivian is determined to keep her parents' business afloat, but Pear Tree Farm near the backwater Cornish village of Polgarth didn't do well as a farm, and it's not faring much better as a camp site.

Ex-musician Ward Spencer from Tennessee is certainly intriguing – does his arrival signal a second lease of life, and not just for Nessa's business?

A Cornish Christmas at Pear Tree Farm

Pairing up at Pear Tree Farm in time for Christmas …

Pear Tree Farm in Cornwall, owned by the kind-hearted Nessa Vivian, is known for taking in lost souls, and ex-soldier Crispin Davies is certainly one of those. Crispin soon finds himself roped into helping out with a short-notice Christmas festival, organised by Nessa's force-of-nature sister, Lowena.

Introducing Choc Lit

We're an independent publisher creating
a delicious selection of fiction.
Where heroes are like chocolate – irresistible!
Quality stories with a romance at the heart.

See our selection here:
www.choc-lit.com

We'd love to hear how you enjoyed *Spring on Rendezvous
Lane*. Please visit **www.choc-lit.com** and give your feedback
or leave a review where you purchased this novel.

Choc Lit novels are selected by genuine readers like yourself.
We only publish stories our Choc Lit Tasting Panel want to
see in print. Our reviews and awards speak for themselves.

Could you be a Star Selector and join our Tasting Panel?
Would you like to play a role in choosing which novels
we decide to publish? Do you enjoy reading women's
fiction? Then you could be perfect for our Tasting Panel.

Visit here for more details…
www.choc-lit.com/join-the-choc-lit-tasting-panel

Keep in touch:
Sign up for our monthly newsletter Spread for all the latest
news and offers: www.spread.choc-lit.com. Follow us
on Twitter: @ChocLituk and Facebook: Choc Lit.

Where heroes are like chocolate – irresistible!